Growing Acclaim

for

Going Green

"Ransom's appealing futuristic parable dives deep into issues of class privilege, inequality, and genetic modification. Sounds heavy, but she lightens the mood with clever tech and a sweet, star-crossed teen romance."

-Karen Eisenbrey,
author of *The Gospel According to St. Rage*

"*Going Green* is a confident, richly conceived and immensely readable debut where unlikely hope grows like grass punching through the cracks of an oppressive system. ...Ransom is a welcome new voice, one that rings true and clear with impressive scope and unexpected emotion."

-Dale E. Basye,
author of the *Circles of Heck* series

"...written in such a fun style that it makes you never want to put it down."

-Jake French,
author of *Life Happens. Live It!*

"In *Going Green*, Heather S. Ransom has created an enchanting & thrilling world! If high school is the time when we realize our own beliefs & self-image, this book challenges the Dreamer in all of us to confront who we really are, right alongside 'Lyssa's own tense & fascinating adventures. ...*Going Green* confronts the idea of 'otherness' at a time when we need it most. Brilliant work!"
  -Seth Maxwell,
  Founder & CEO, The Thirst Project

"Ransom has created a wonderfully imperfect world with characters striving for perfection in their own way. She combines high school crushes with real world concerns. ...I'm dying for the next instalment."
  -Micayla Lally,
  author of *A Work Of Art*

"Heather S. Ransom creates an eerily poignant futuristic world with her intelligent writing. The suspenseful storyline propels the reader on. How relevant is this quote from her novel? 'How do you stop something when you don't feel you have any power?' Bravo!"
  -Barbara Herkert,
  author of *A Boy, a Mouse, and a Spider: The Story of E.B. White*

Isaiah —
Enjoy the journey…!
Keep it Green!
Heather S. Ransom
3-25-17

Going Green

Heather S. Ransom

Dedication

For each of my students
who passionately scrutinized every single word
. . .your brutal honesty was beautiful.

Going Green

Chapter 1

Pull it together, Calyssa, I thought. *This is not the time to lose it. Not when you're this close.* Still, I felt traces of panic, like tendrils, silently descending into my body through the crazy number of tubes inserted in me, leaving a feeling of dread rooted somewhere in the back of my brain.

I tried to lie still. A relentless chill seeped up into my body. Not freezing, but close. I adjusted my legs, just a little.

"Please, Miss Brentwood, you must be completely still." A gruff voice. My eyes fluttered open, but I couldn't focus. A white coat. Disconnected movements. Blurs of motion from across the room. I closed my eyes to stop the spinning.

Soft mechanical whispers slipped through the air. And sometimes voices. Nothing I could understand. Just murmurs.

My eyes opened again, and immediately, another wave of nausea. I quickly squeezed them shut. *Why can't I remember to keep them shut?*

I must have made a sound because a soft voice whispered in my ear, "Don't try to talk. Relax. We're almost finished." A gloved hand brushed against my face. "Think about something you enjoy. Visualize yourself. And, picture yourself a beautiful green while you're doing it." One more touch, and the hand with the voice was gone.

The voice was right. In a few weeks, I'd be Green. I had to finish the Enhancement procedure.

"You must stay still, Miss Brentwood." The gruff voice was back. I hadn't even realized I'd moved again. I had to focus. I couldn't afford to mess this up.

Chapter 2

It had been three weeks since my Enhancement, and every morning I had raced to the mirror to check my eyes, holding my breath, heart racing, feeling both terrified and excited. After the procedure, people had to wait for their eyes to turn green before they went back to the facility for a check-up. Doctors had to make sure that the person's cells were accepting the new chloroplasts completely. Organelle rejection meant the Enhancement would be incomplete, and life would be, well ...unimaginable for me.

I stared in the brightly lit mirror in the school restroom. Long, straight, dark hair. Fair complexion. And, as of this morning, the most incredible green eyes.

Amazing, truly amazing. I closed my eyes for a moment and then looked at my reflection once more. I couldn't get over the change. These were my eyes I was staring into. My eyes. Beautiful. Incredible. I had waited eighteen years to see these eyes.

And, the vibrant green was a good sign. Once organelle acceptance was confirmed, I would be fully Green in another three to four weeks.

Running my hands through my hair, I realized I still needed to decide what to do with it. My hair already grew fast, and now that it looked like the organelle acceptance was a sure thing, it would start growing even faster. Lots of people dyed theirs as soon as the new green color started growing in, trying to match it so it would look like they had been Green for a while. Others cut theirs short in some current style, just chopping off the majority of the old color. I'd have to decide soon. It was more expensive, but I was leaning toward a dye job, maybe with a few streaks or highlights. Something fun. Something new for the new me.

Choosing to avoid class for a few more minutes, I focused on the tiny iBud in my ear. In earlier models, I would've had to touch the iBud in order to activate it, but now, everything was based on brain wave transmission. *Play Zimmer*, I thought.

An intricate, beautiful melody filled my head. Not only the cello part that I had learned as a child, but the full orchestra, crystal clear. This was the way to experience music. Everyone's ears heard music a little differently, but when the waves traveled from the iBud through the tympanic membrane directly into the cochlear nerve, it was incredible to experience the true vibrations of the music. I closed my eyes and began to lose myself.

I jumped when a hand clamped down on my shoulder.

"Seriously, Lyssa. You've got to lighten up a bit. You're all sorts of jumpy today." Divya ran her fingers through her ultra-light green hair. Her eyes glanced over at my reflection. She froze.

"Are you kidding me? Are you kidding me! Look at me!" Divya commanded, yanking my chin toward her. She was practically shrieking, dancing around me. "I cannot believe you didn't message me first thing this morning when you woke up! And, to wait until fourth period? Of all days for Mom's driver to drop me off late at school." She kept twisting my chin in different directions. I smiled. I loved surprising Divya. She was usually the one that did all of the surprising.

"They're gorgeous! Absolutely gorgeous! Look at her, Jessalyn," she demanded, "I told you she'd go vibrant emerald. I knew it! You are going to be stunning when you're completely Green! I love it! I absolutely love it!"

Jessalyn silently stepped into my view, her knowing smile telling me she'd slipped in with Divya and witnessed the whole conversation. She closely inspected my eyes, then enveloped me in a warm hug. "You are beautiful. Those eyes make you pop," she said softly.

"You are so lucky that you messaged us to meet you in the bathroom. Jess would have been totally ticked off if I had seen you first. Right, Jess? So much better that we're all together," Divya said.

Jessalyn just smiled and stepped in beside me, her coloring a rich, forest green that contrasted with Div's soft, spring green skin. Hopefully soon, my fair complexion and brown hair would be a striking shade of green somewhere between the two of them.

I put my arms around both of them. "It wasn't easy, not messaging both of you as soon as I woke up this morning and saw my eyes. But it was totally worth it. That look on your face was priceless, Div."

"Really, Lyssa, I was not that surprised. We knew you'd be turning any day now. Jess was way more surprised than me. Did you see her reaction?"

That made me laugh. Jess raised one eyebrow, and then rolled her eyes.

"Whatever. Come on, Jess. We need to take Lyssa out to strut her stuff. Everybody needs to be checking out her new eyes." Divya linked her arm with one of mine.

"We have to go back to class, remember? School? The place we come to learn? Class doesn't get out for another fifteen minutes, and I need to get back to make sure I don't miss any last minute assignments from Ms. Steiner in Advanced Enhanced Human Anatomy." Jessalyn's brows furrowed, and she stepped toward the bathroom door. She paused as she stepped out. "See you at lunch, Calyssa?"

"Absolutely."

The door closed behind her. Divya was in no rush to get back to class. While Jessalyn hustled from advanced math to advanced science classes, Divya had made it a priority to skate through as much of this year as possible, sauntering through the halls to theater, fashion, and vocal performance classes. She reminded everyone who would listen that she was going to be a famous digital star, and that she had already scored a part in a digital thriller this summer.

One more hand through her hair, then she turned and gave me another big hug. "Seriously, Lyssa. I am so excited for you. So is Jess. She's just all caught up in finishing with honors in her classes because of her scholarship. The whole Enhancement thing is still new to her, with her parents being non-Greens and all. We'll get her straightened out. We Greens know how to party."

"Jess is fine, Div. Some people actually like school, you know."

"Sorry, I refuse to wrap my mind around that. I prefer freedom, fun, and fashion!" She let out a little hoot, then snapped her fingers and wiggled her hips. Stopping abruptly, her hand flew to ear. "Uh-oh. Just got the word. Hoffleman is looking for me. Gotta jet. See you at lunch, Lyssa." She blew me a kiss as she flew out the door.

Glancing one last time in the mirror, I smiled at my reflection – a mini-skirt in the exact shade of the green in my new eyes, and a scoop-neck shirt that shimmered with a beautiful, digitally enhanced, holographic, hexagonal pattern in a variety of gorgeous greens. Large silver earrings, bracelets, rings, necklace, and knee-high boots. I looked good.

As I turned to walk out, an emergency news broadcast replaced the soft music in my ear. I paused at the door. I hated when they did that – blurting right into my brain. Dramatic voices discussed a recent rebel attack on security enforcers at the outskirts of SciCity. Fields burned. Some of them were advancement fields connected to Father's work. *Oh, boy. That's not gonna make him happy. He'll be in a great mood tonight.*

The interruption dragged on – security enforcers engaged with full force, exchanging fire with rebels, but the terrorist assaults still showed significant increases. Requests had been made to government officials to "step in and liberate the area from these radicals." Due to substantial injuries and loss of property, the government was calling in additional security enforcers to put a stop to the "unnecessary violence."

As if there wasn't enough to deal with at school. Now more of this. It seemed that as the rebel attacks increased, tension at the school surged right along with it. Greens versus Drones. Another high drama day.

Back at my classroom, I sighed, slipping into my seat, wishing that Div or Jess were in this period with me. We had been friends as long as I could remember, but with this being our senior year, we all had very different schedules.

Unlike Divya, I had a father who felt I needed to "keep a rigorous academic schedule that matched my ability level," which meant I hustled from Advanced Contemporary Lit, to New American Government, then Current Digital Trends, and finally to the class where I sat now, Math Prep for Universities, all before lunch.

I felt like I had a pretty good handle on operations with radicals, so I mostly just swiped past the practice questions. Today was a "review day," which meant everyone in the room sat silently with their noses pressed to their table tablets, preparing for the big test tomorrow. I had other things on my mind. Like Ashton Bordeaux.

Chapter 3

An old-fashioned school intercom interrupted my thoughts, blasting a voice into the classrooms and down the halls because not everyone had current tech, like iBuds.

An administrator announced in a very official voice, "Please excuse the interruption. Due to recent additional rebel attacks, there have been some road closures in our area. We are confident that our SciCity Security Enforcers will have everything under control by the end of the school day, but we have been asked to close campus for lunch, which means that all of you will be remaining on the premises until the end of the school day."

Groans rose from every part of the room, followed by various levels of grumbling. Then the bell rang.

I scanned the crowd as I walked along the edge of the mass bobbing toward the cafeteria. At that moment, Divya whipped around the corner and ran smack into me. "Whoa! Who you scoping the crowd for? Wait a minute. Let me guess. You're looking for Ashton, aren't you? You've got it bad for a girl who's only been on a couple dates with the guy."

"No," I replied, a bit too adamantly. "Where's Jess? I was just looking for you two drones." Divya punched me in the arm. I feigned pain as I scanned the area some more.

Was I that obvious when it came to Ashton? Just thinking about him made me drool a little. His luscious shade of hunter green and those super sexy eyes – my heart started beating a little faster.

On the Friday before I went in for my Enhancement, Ashton had found me after school and hugged me. He had whispered in my ear, "I can't wait for my girl to come back Green and hot." He winked at me, and then his lacrosse teammates showed up so he had to take off. *My girl. Hot.* I smiled to myself. *That's me.*

"Oh, Divya, lighten up on her," Jessalyn said. I hadn't noticed that she had walked up behind me. "He's totally into her. He just had to play it cool until she went Green because his dad is a big time politician."

"Yeah, I guess Ashton can't 'play with just anybody' until he gets his daddy's approval so they could really go out. Like officially." Divya's eyebrows bobbed up and down. "And seriously, Lyssa, take a look. We're Green and we're hot ...we can't be drones." Then she tossed her hair dramatically over her shoulder for emphasis.

"Whatever," I said as I laughed.

"Oooo, Jess, let's scoot." Divya grabbed Jessalyn's arm and gave me a mischievous grin. Then, they melted into the crowd. I turned around to see where they had disappeared and instead saw Ashton walking toward me. I felt red creeping up my neck – thank God he couldn't hear my thoughts because he looked absolutely exceptional today. He was visiting with a bunch of guys. He winked at me and kept right on walking.

Seriously? Had he actually just done that? Walked right on by? Not even a "Hey," or "Hi, Lyssa." Nothing but a wink. I turned and watched as they continued moving along with the surge of students. My mouth dropped open.

"Really?" I said to no one in particular. Then, I clenched my teeth. I didn't know if I wanted to scream or cry. *He was supposed to come over and tell me how beautiful I am now, how I'm everything he thought I would be, how he wants to go out with me now, how he wants me to meet his family,* I thought. *Then he should have grabbed my hand, so we could walk down the hall, hand-in-hand, showing everyone that we are now officially "together."*

Forget it, I thought. *What a jerk.* Sometimes I didn't know what I saw in him ...well, until I looked at him again. I sighed. *He was probably in a hurry,* I thought. *Somewhere important he needed to be. I'm sure he'll make it up to me next time I see him.*

Walking into the cafeteria, I searched for my friends. I figured they'd be over near the windows since Green citizens didn't need to eat. Many Green students reclined in lounge-type chairs set near large windows that promoted "efficient photosynthesis." A few lined up to purchase nutrient drinks. Most Green students simply hung out in the area, visiting, and letting their chloroplasts "fill them up" for the day. I headed in that direction.

With the campus closed so no one could leave for lunch, it was wall-to-wall students. I glanced over at the opposite side of room, known as the "Drones" area. Those students were never going Green. For many of them, their refusal was a "statement." I just couldn't wrap my mind around why a person wouldn't want to go Green. I thought that most of them either didn't have the test scores to be scholarshipped or the family money to pay for the Enhancement. I dropped my eyes and looked away. I knew we needed the common community workers for SciCity to function, but I was relieved that I was finally a real part of the "Green side" of the room.

Until a couple of weeks ago, I sat in the center of the cafeteria with the other "Pledges," students who knew that when they turned eighteen, they would be going through with the Enhancement. Some students, like me, came from Green families and sat in this area as soon as we began school here.

Mixed in with the Pledges were the "Dreamers." The kids who wanted to go Green but had no realistic way to get there. They probably should have joined the Drones, but they held out hope that someday, somehow, they would make it to the Greens' section before they got out of high school.

Many of the Dreamers were friends with the Pledges, but once Pledges were enhanced, they really didn't associate with non-Greens outside of class time. It had always been that way. We all knew we would be doing what was best for our community, but we just didn't have much in common once we knew what our future held.

As I neared the Greens' area, I heard a commotion behind me. I turned around and saw a blond girl who looked about my age picking up a bag she had obviously dropped. Her stuff had spilled out everywhere. A tube of lip-gloss rolled by my feet. I leaned over, grabbed it, and walked it back to its owner.

"Thanks." She bent over, retrieving more items. A beautiful golden star hung from her neck.

"Cool star," I said as I picked up a few more things and handed them to her. She turned to take them from me, and got a puzzled look on her face. "I'm okay," she said. "Really. I can get the rest myself."

I squatted down next to her. "Oh, it's okay. I don't mind. I hate it when I dump my bag. Such a pain to get everything back in there – you don't want to miss something that you'll wish you had later."

As she reached out to grab a hair clip, a couple of Green guys walked by, and one of them kicked it, sending it sailing across the room. The other two laughed. She scowled up at them.

One guy leaned down and whispered something in the girl's ear. She jumped up and got right in his face.

"You're such a Gimp! It's too bad that genetically modified people don't get any smarter when they get enhanced." She glared at him. Then, slowly, a smirk slid across her face, like she knew something that he didn't, and she said, "Poor boy. You're just stuck stupid forever," and she tipped her head back and laughed.

It all happened so fast that I found myself still squatting down on the floor. As I began to stand up, the guy stepped in closer to the girl, and I recognized him from my New American Government class. Rykker. He had been Green for almost our whole senior year.

He said something and her hand whipped up to slap him, but he caught it in midair, and laughed again, along with the other two guys.

"Hey guys, knock it off!" I snapped, more loudly than I intended, noticing that the whole cafeteria had gone quiet as my voice echoed across the room. The air suddenly felt heavy and tense. Everyone was watching us. I felt a knot forming in my stomach.

Rykker shot a glare at me. "Mind your own business, Newbie. We can't have 'the help' being mouthy," he said to me, and then to her, "Important to know your place, Drone."

Before I could respond, some guy stepped up next to the girl and grabbed Rykker's wrist, shaking it roughly enough to make him let go of the girl's hand. The new guy leaned in and said something that I couldn't quite make out.

Anger flashed across Rykker's face as he slowly turned all of his attention toward this guy. I took the moment and bent back over to quickly help the girl finish picking up her stuff. Rykker may have been a Green, but he didn't need to be a total jerk about it.

As we stood up, the other guy leaned over, saying something to the girl under his breath and tipping his head toward the Drones' side of the room. She nodded, threw me a quick "thanks," and briskly walked away.

The other guy started to walk away, too. But Rykker grabbed his shoulder. I didn't like the look on Rykker's face. He was smiling, but his eyes narrowed and his jaw clenched.

"Hey," Rykker said mockingly, "I get it. You've got a sorry excuse for a life. I don't blame you for standing up for a girl to try to impress her. I mean, it's gotta be hard for a guy like you to get a girl. I can't imagine what it would be like to be stuck a Drone for life. I guess you gotta get what you can, Bro."

I started to tell Rykker to leave the guy alone, but the whole Green section began to snicker. A couple guys let out hoots. I sucked in my breath and stepped back. I knew I should say something, but the girl was safe, out of the picture, and the other guy was walking away. I didn't want to piss Rykker off. Not a good choice on my first day as a Green.

Then Rykker smacked his hand down hard on the other guy's shoulder, gruffly pulling him to a stop. The guy slowly turned back toward Rykker.

Oh, no! I thought. *Just walk away.*

His face darkened as his jaw tightened, and his lips pressed firmly together. He shrugged Rykker's hand off his shoulder, and again, turned to walk away.

Good choice. It's over. I turned to walk away, too.

"Hey, wait a minute. I know who you are. Don't you have a little sister who's a Dreamer? Maybe I could help her out and make sure she gets a special scholarship to go Green – I'm sure she and I could be great friends." Rykker turned to one of his friends and gave him a high five as he laughed.

The other guy whipped back around and stepped so close to Rykker that their noses touched. "Are you trying to start something? Say yes and we can step outside."

Rykker didn't answer him. He just stood there, glaring back at the guy. The knot in my stomach grew, and before I knew what I doing, I stepped right up to them. My heart was racing, but I couldn't stop myself. This was so ridiculous.

"Guys, walk away. It's not worth it." I looked back and forth between the two but neither broke eye contact.

"Gentlemen, is there an issue here? Something we need to discuss?" Out of nowhere, a teacher had appeared. She looked back and forth between the two guys. Ten full seconds ticked by in complete silence. Everyone waited.

Then the other guy stepped back and shook his head. "No, Ms. Chambers," he said, his face now neutral. "Sorry. I was just leaving."

"Thank you," said Rykker. "I accept your apology." He turned toward the teacher and began talking in a syrupy sweet voice that dripped with a haughtiness that made me sick. "I was explaining to him that I thought my family might be interested in scholarshipping another member of his family. I think he misunderstood what I was saying." Then Rykker turned back to the other guy, holding out his hand. "No hard feelings, right?"

"I'm happy to hear you're working this out. Very mature and responsible of you." Ms. Chambers smiled at both guys and Rykker smiled sweetly back at her. The other guy's face didn't change.

But he took Rykker' hand to shake it. Rykker pulled him forward just a bit and said, "The offer still stands for your sister. Let her know for me, will you?" Rykker winked. The other guy ripped his hand away abruptly, scowled, then turned and left.

Rykker turned back to the teacher and continued to visit with her. The cafeteria returned to its low roar as hundreds of simultaneous conversations picked back up, and the tense energy that only moments before had filled the room was gone. I realized I had been holding my breath.

I jumped when Divya tapped me on the shoulder. "Whoa, that was intense. And a little insane. What were you doing with that girl?"

I shook my head and looked at her. "What do you mean? She dropped her stuff and I was helping her pick it up."

"You're a Green now. You've got to remember that. People are watching. Just try to stay out of the drama." Divya looked around cautiously.

"Are you kidding me? I just stopped to help another girl pick up her stuff. You would've done the same."

Divya just looked at me.

Chapter 4

I started to say something, but my iBud chimed, followed by a message that Father had sent a driver to take me to my organelle check. He was waiting outside to take me to AHGA. Not surprising that Father didn't come himself. Father was always "busy."

"Sorry, Divya." I smiled at her, shaking off the incident that had just taken place. "My ride to 'Green Confirmation' has pulled up outside the school. That's not a ride that I want to keep waiting."

Thirty minutes later, I arrived at Advanced Human Genetic Assessments. The sun shone brightly, bouncing off an immense amount of metal and glass. AHGA was one of the most prominent human genome research and advancement facilities in New America. Located next to an enormous dam, it also monitored and managed the power for SciCity and most of the surrounding areas.

The dam, more than 200 years old, consisted of concrete as far down as the eye could see. The power plant was housed inside, connected to huge metal girders that supported power lines, crisscrossing the mountain, suspended over the valley deep below. My sister, Livvy, hated coming here as a child, but I had always been mesmerized, gazing out over the valley at the patterns, both synthetic and natural, that interwove around the complex.

The front of the AHGA complex was simple. It didn't expose the secrets that hid behind its walls. Originally constructed as a visitor center for the dam, now the building tunneled much further back into the mountain behind it, and down deep – over thirty stories. The deepest levels were highly classified areas, allowing only those with top security clearance.

Carved out over the years as more space was needed, the whole inside of the mountain now encased the complex. Some levels were devoted to research and development. Others housed the enhancement centers for citizens who were going Green. Offices, tech rooms, labs, clinics, kitchen facilities, x-ray units, chemical analysis and storage, you name it, it was probably here – a little of everything. Father said that if anything ever happened we could live here, so I assumed there must even be living quarters, too. Kind of creepy to think about, because there were cameras everywhere. I didn't even like to go to the bathroom in the complex.

Father, standing there with one hand on his ear, was holding the door open for me. I picked up my pace. He had obviously been waiting for me, and Father didn't like to wait.

I could tell he was in a deep conversation on his iBud by the look on his face. As I walked past him into the lobby, a man in a lab coat and a frown rushed up and spoke rapidly in hushed tones, pulling Father toward the elevators. Father nodded his head as he turned toward the elevator door being held open for him.

"I'll only be a minute, Calyssa," he said as the elevator door slid shut.

That's how it was when I came here. Someone always needed Father, it was always important, and it was always urgent. Now, it was my turn to wait. Livvy would have been bored. But I didn't mind.

I walked across the waiting area to the floor-to-ceiling glass windows that flooded the room with sunlight. There wasn't much vegetation outside. Just dirt, concrete, and metal as far as the eye could see. Lots of buildings in the valley below. New tech replaced old every day. I wondered what it would have been like to be here before.

On the other side of the room, the lighting was softer, focused on large photographs hanging on the walls, displaying the events that had led to the birth and development of AHGA. I had viewed these pictures hundreds of times, but each time I saw them, they still drew me in, like a magnetic force.

As I approached the pictures, my iBud softly chimed, and an official-sounding male voice said in my mind, *To play the accompanying audio for the Advanced Human Genetics Assessment Gallery, please direct your iBud to "connect to AHGA Gallery." Thank you for your visit to AHGA today.*

As directed, I connected.

At the first set of pictures, a female voice filled my head explaining that a little over one hundred years ago, scientists around the world had been developing numerous kinds of genetically modified organisms known as GMOs. About this same time, researchers had also discovered that viruses could be altered to carry genetic modifications into hosts. Extensive projects had been carried out in both fields. While some countries were strict in their research and development, others were more reckless.

The female voice never stated who was at fault, or exactly how it had happened, but she said that not long after scientists learned that modifications to GMOs could leap species, the unthinkable occurred. An altered virus containing a new GMO mutated and began infecting plants around the globe. It had a long name that no one could pronounce, so it became simply known as "PK," or the "plant killing" virus.

When PK hit an area, all plant life there died. It traveled fast and seemed unstoppable. There had been no way to kill it – since viruses weren't living, they couldn't be killed. They simply had to "run their course." Pictures showed withered plants, barren fields, and desolate forests. A feeling of despair emanated from the entire grouping.

Next, a male voice talked about how entire populations of people around the world were scared and angry. This set of pictures showed ransacked buildings. People breaking through windows to get to stockpiled food. Viciousness in the streets. Picture after picture with faces full of fear or rage. Young to old, no one seemed to escape the violence.

As time passed, panic intensified. Everyone knew that all living things depended on plants for survival. Basic biology. Plants turned the energy from the sun into energy that all other organisms used to live. Within a month, landscapes changed dramatically. Now the pictures showed areas with no plant life anywhere.

The female voice continued explaining that within a couple of months, large numbers of people were dying from starvation. Every continent on the planet had been infected. Underdeveloped countries were hit the hardest. With no plants to eat, the herbivores died first. Followed closely by the carnivores. There was water, but water wasn't enough to support life. The pictures in this grouping were the hardest to look at. They showed people dying from starvation ...families ...children ...babies. The images were disturbing, her voice was haunting, and it made me shudder as I walked past.

As I approached the next set of pictures, I searched for my great-great-grandfather, Kassius Brentwood, Sr. A new male voice began talking about the creation of a scientific "think tank." People from all over the world converged to try to stop the extinction of life on Earth. Sixty-seven people stood together in the first think tank picture. They included different kinds of scientists and botanists, farmers, military specialists, even a philosopher. Their names and occupations were noted below one of the pictures.

The voice continued, explaining that this group had met here, at the current location of the AHGA complex, because the power plant at the dam had still been functional. And, that after a few intense weeks, they developed a two-part plan.

The next picture showed the think tank participants divided into two separate groups. The first group developed "Project Noah's ARC," focusing on creating a stasis chamber for plants and seeds. The "ARC" (or Arbor Restoration Collection) would hold plants and seeds that were free from contamination until the virus was gone. The second group developed "Project Double Helix," concentrating on genetically engineering modified chloroplasts that could be utilized by human cells, which would bypass human need for plants and allow the human body to change the sun's energy into a usable food source. Both groups had one goal, the same goal: to work together to do whatever it would take to save humanity from extinction.

A female voice mentioned that Dr. Kassius Bentwood had been on a previous genetic research team known for successfully reprogramming the HIV virus to fight leukemia and other diseases. He brought this knowledge to the Double Helix group. They used a "hollowed out" form of the HIV virus that had been modified with plant DNA, and found a way to "trick" human cells into reproducing modified chloroplasts in the human body. The first trials were filled with errors, mutations, sickness, even deaths. But the group persisted.

As did their counterparts with Noah's ARC, collecting and cataloging plants from every plot of soil that still had life. The ARC grew, protected in secret, because now hundreds of thousands of people were dying daily. It became a dangerous job to take plants and seeds away from areas, but what good would the plants and seeds be if they were left to die from the virus?

Back to the male voice who introduced one large picture that hung alone. It was the photograph of a twenty-three-year-old woman who had survived the first successful "Green treatment." Rowan Johanssen. A huge single picture of her beautiful green eyes. Eyes that represented hope for the future.

I moved on to pictures of masses of people. Torn clothes, unnaturally thin bodies, gaunt faces, exhausted eyes. A female voice explained that this new process was expensive and time consuming, and supplies and funds were limited. All think tank participants and their families were treated first. People from around the world converged on this site, the origins of SciCity, known then as Science City. But not enough could be produced for everyone. More people died every day.

During this time, the Noah's ARC group diligently planted seeds, trying unique measures, different techniques, anything they could come up with to try to get plants to grow again. And then, one day, a miracle happened. Plants began to sprout and grow in a field north of SciCity.

Then more. And more. No one knew why. The voice simply said that the virus came to the end of its "lifespan," had run its course, and that with so few plants still growing naturally, the virus had stopped spreading, and that was the end. But the damage was done, less than a million people left on the planet. Countries devastated. Some land was so barren that scientists weren't sure it would ever be able to support plant life again.

Back to the male voice, who stated that humans were a remarkable species, and through new technology, genetic enhancements, and sheer human innovation, life returned to our planet. And it was AHGA, founded by the Double

Helix group, which led the way. Right here where we were today.

Once scientists had "gone Green" (or had the Chloroplast Advancement Enhancement as it was now known), they no longer had to eat or worry about food, so they could focus solely on their work. "Going Green" allowed them to spend all of their time and energy on bettering their community and our world.

And here I am, today, ready to join those ranks, I thought. The last, large picture in the series had four Green citizens on it, two women, two men, all four beautiful, intelligent-looking, dressed-for-success types. They stared straight at me.

Both voices continued, taking turns to emphasize the last remark of the audio presentation, *Are you ready to make the commitment to do your part in making our community, our world, a better place? If your answer is yes, your journey begins here. AHGA - Helping Citizens Help Our World.*

Was I ready? Yes, but could I? I mean, what was I going to do to make the world a better place? Sure, I was smart, but not like "cure-the-crazy-diseases" smart. I played the cello, made beautiful music, but did that really make the world a better place? Many people never had the opportunity to go Green. *Why should I get to? What made me so special?*

I knew the answer, but I didn't like to think about it. My family was wealthy, connected, in the right business. I'd heard it a million times in whispers around me. All the Brentwoods had gone Green since the beginning, since

Kassius Sr. Livvy said we were entitled. But Father insisted that going Green was a commitment to a choice, that we must do something every day to prove we were worthy of our "Green status" in the community.

My iBud beeped and I jumped, startled back to my surroundings. *Answer*, I thought.

Chapter 5

Immediately, Livvy's voice filled my head. *Seriously, Lyssa. If I'm going to get you the best and newest tech out on the market, use it. Not just anybody can have the new iBud 24 Plus yet, you know.*

I sighed. *Connect,* I thought, then with as much positive enthusiasm as I could muster, *I know, Sis, you rock. Being able to talk to you by thinking is incredible. I'm so glad they got the brain wave recognition software worked out in this new model. It was totally weird when that old guy down the street starting butting into our conversations.* Creepy. I gave an involuntary little shudder.

And then, in rapid-fire succession, Livvy's voice continued, *You ready for the big day? Sorry I missed you this morning, I am so excited for us, Little Sis! Big day in the Brentwood family! You're the last one to finish enhancement so we'll be completely Green. I can't wait. You'll be gorgeous. Of course, it'll take another month, and we'll need to get you under some express lights. We better talk to Dad about buying you your own set because it would be inconvenient to share, right? But anyways, by your graduation, no one will ever know that you haven't been Green all your life.* Livvy sounded absolutely giddy.

Nobody's Green their whole life, Livvy, I thought back at her. How, in only a few seconds had my sister got so under my skin? Nobody annoyed me faster than Livvy.

Seriously, Baby Sister. No kidding. It's just an expression. Lighten up. I hope your mood improves with your looks. Even in thought, her disapproval and sarcasm dripped through.

Oh, oops, gotta run. Dahnte is beeping in. He's such a doll. I'm sure he wants to see what I'm doing tonight. I've been crazy busy between my studies at the U and my work at AHGA. Feels like I'm constantly on the run. I think we're going to try to hit the G Cubed concert tonight. You know, Global Green Garrison? It's got those three crazy hot guys, Hunter, Forest, and Kelly.

Shaking my head and rolling my eyes, I thought back at her, *Of course I know who they are, Livvy.* Even though I didn't.

Well, you're not always up on things, Lyssa, and it's only for Green citizens. Anyway, everybody knows I have the hook-up for backstage passes. See you this afternoon. Hugs and kisses. And then, silence. I closed my eyes. Just blessed silence.

I looked at the last picture up on the wall again and willed thoughts of Livvy out of my mind. This wasn't about her. Or Father. It was about me. All my life, I'd been referred to as "that nice girl — you know, the younger daughter of Kassius Brentwood IV, CEO of Advanced Human Genetics Assessments." Or as "that quiet little sister of the totally awesome Naleeva Sophia Brentwood," known (to those who mattered) as Livvy, and who at only twenty years old was already considered "a super socialite" in SciCity.

Or just as that girl in music class who played the cello. Or as the girl whose mom died when she was little. I was tired of being defined by what surrounded me. I was ready to be me, to be recognized for who "I" was.

Calyssa Grace Brentwood. Eighteen years old, and finally a member of the Green Commonwealth of SciCity. And I was ready. I would find my place in the world, out of their shadows. I would be a part of something great, of something bigger than just me. I lifted my chin and took a deep breath. *Today is my day.*

The ping from the elevator caused me to turn in time to see Father motioning for me to join him. As soon as I was on the elevator, it began to descend.

"We've had some complications with the rebel damage at the advancement fields west of the city. Hopefully, things will be cleaned up soon. Only minor damage this time, but it makes more paperwork for me. I'm growing tired of these ridiculous rebel attacks. I've requested the security enforcers step up our field rotations. It is beyond me how they keep allowing 'those people' to escape." He shook his head as he continued to mumble under his breath.

He had forgotten I was in the elevator with him. He was like that. One of the most intelligent people in SciCity, but when he was focused on something, he was completely engrossed, and nothing outside of his focus existed for him. It made him an incredible businessman and scientist, but it wasn't the greatest attribute for a father. I loved him, but his work had always come first at our house.

When the elevator door slid open, Father snapped back to the present. "Here we are. This way." He walked down a softly lit, short hall and bypassed the front desk with a nod to the stunning receptionist sitting there. A couple of years ago I'd realized that all of the people I'd ever seen working at AHGA were truly beautiful people. I asked Father about it and he said it was one of the benefits of going Green, that the modified chloroplasts produced the exact amount of nutrients that the human body needed for optimal performance and maintenance. And, Livvy reminded me that you never saw a fat, gross, or ugly, out-of-shape plant.

We continued through a maze of soothing earth-toned hallways — creamy tans, warm browns, rich chocolates, vivid emeralds, soft mints, forest greens. Thick carpets hid the sound of footsteps. Incredible landscapes, with focused lighting, hung on the walls. Some, I assumed, were pre-PK years because I had never seen places like them. Fields of colorful flowers that seemed to go on forever. Gigantic trees around crisp blue lakes. Close-ups of leaves with delicate vein patterns. Other pictures showed familiar landscapes and plants, ones that had been genetically modified to survive more easily on our planet today.

My favorite featured a miniature razzlemelon berry bush, full of ripe razzlemelon berries, hot pink and neon orange, ready to be snatched off the branches and popped into your mouth with a light squeeze between your fingers. Lena, our domicile attendant (and nanny after Mom was gone), had taken Livvy and me to pick razzlemelon berries once when I was about ten or eleven. The pink ones were sweet while the orange ones were tart, and together, they made the most wonderful, zany explosion inside your mouth.

We'd stayed at the berry farm for several hours. I was in heaven, but Livvy got bored, and before too long, Lena gave into her pleas to "get us back to civilization." Soon after that, those particular fields were blown up by rebels, and Father refused to let Lena drive us out of the city anymore. He said it wasn't safe for the children of Green Citizens, that we could be "taken."

Rounding a corner, Father nearly ran over a man in a lab coat. "Dr. Cayson. Just the man we were looking for. I have Calyssa here for organelle acceptance testing. I am assuming that everything is in order and that you are ready for her." It was a statement, not a question.

"Definitely, Dr. Brentwood. Calyssa, we're ready for you in room six. Right this way." He stopped in front of an unmarked door, typed in a code on the keypad and the door silently slid open.

"I won't be staying. Please let my office know when Calyssa is finished and I'll be back to pick her up. With the craziness in the fields this morning, my attention is sorely needed elsewhere." Then, turning toward me, Father asked, "You'll be fine with that, Calyssa?"

"Of course," I said, trying hard not to look nervous. But I actually felt sick. And afraid. I knew that I didn't have a thing to worry about, that everything would be fine, but I had assumed that at least for this, the final testing, that Father would take the time to be here with me.

He looked into my eyes, and I saw his impatience growing. *Buck up*, I thought to myself.

"Don't worry about me. I'm fine." I pulled my shoulders back, standing up a little straighter.

Relief flashed through his eyes. "Excellent." Then his hand flew to his ear, a universal signal that someone was engaging in an iBud conversation, and his face was lost in concentration again. Obviously talking to someone important.

He looked up, paused, and said, "Dr. Cayson, please let one of my assistants know when you're finished with Calyssa." And with that, he left.

"Well then, are you ready?" Dr. Cayson smiled at me. I nodded, holding my breath as I stepped into the room.

Chapter 6

After I had changed into an exam gown, Dr. Cayson and two techs returned to the room. "Did you have any more questions or concerns that have come up in the past few weeks?"

"No. I think we covered all of it already. Thank you, Doctor." I smiled. I took another deep breath, then slowly exhaled. *Well, this is it. No more wondering. Soon, I'll know for sure if I'm truly a Green,* I told myself.

As Dr. Cayson began to hook me up to the monitors, I thought about the last couple of months. I'd seen him quite a few times. First had been the physical, right after my eighteenth birthday. He had gone over all of the paperwork with me. It would only take one procedure to introduce the chloroplasts into my body, but I would still need to eat until my skin was completely green and the chloroplasts in my cells were fully functioning. That usually took about six to eight weeks from the time of the Enhancement procedure.

Several more techs entered the room. Machines began making noises. I tried not to think about the last time I was in here. The entire process was incredibly nerve-wracking.

There were three requirements for being enhanced. First, a person had to be "scholarshipped" for the very expensive procedure, either by a family member or a community supporter. Being Green would allow the person to focus all their time and energy on working for the betterment of our society. That was why we went Green. And, why not everyone needed to go Green.

Second, to be enhanced, a person had to be at least eighteen years old. This was for two reasons. One was that the human body and brain had to be mostly finished with the hormonal and physical changes from adolescence to adulthood, usually between the ages of sixteen to twenty. Completing the battery of physical and mental challenges, blood work, x-rays, and brain scans was a physically and mentally exhausting process. And scientists had found that the process wouldn't work in children. It didn't "stick." If the body wasn't physically ready, it wouldn't work, and then the process had to be started all over again. A huge waste of time and money.

But the other reason for waiting until a person was at least eighteen, even if they were physically ready sooner, was because the enhancement was permanent. At eighteen, people were considered legal adults, and no one could sign for another person to have this process done. If a person couldn't sign for herself, she couldn't be enhanced. And, once enhanced, there was no going back. It was an adult decision – one that was irreversible. One that would affect the rest of a person's life. Once the Green Enhancement was complete, it meant the person would be Green for life.

Dr. Cayson had reiterated several times that a person had to be old enough to truly understand the liability and risks associated with the procedure. And the permanence. When people first started going Green, it did have some side effects, and some people even died, but over the years he assured me, the process had been perfected.

The final requirement, if the first two had been met, was to go through the Green Commonwealth Screening Committee. Because of the expenses and the risks, there was a pretty serious application to complete. Father had said to read everything and fill it out carefully. Livvy had said it didn't matter for us because, hey, our father owned the company that does the Enhancement, like they wouldn't recommend me. And then she laughed. "And you've got some talent," she had said. Still, when the official memo came saying my approval for Green citizenship had been recommended by the committee, I knew we all had breathed a sigh of relief.

So here I was. Paperwork signed. Enhancement procedure done. Eyes now green. And me, one more time, on the table. I looked at the equipment all around me.

What if I was that one in a thousand that had an adverse reaction? What if something happened and the modification didn't "take," or there was something wrong with me and I couldn't finish going Green, or ....

Stop it, Calyssa. Quit making this a big deal, I told myself. I was pretty sure that Livvy hadn't been nervous when she was here. She said it was the first day of her "real" life, and that she loved how it felt. Bigger, better, faster, stronger — like when you were a kid and you got new shoes, and then you ran down the aisle at the store and you knew that you were so much faster than you ever were before those new shoes. I blew out a long, slow breath.

A tech injected something into one of the tubes attached to my arm, and I began feeling sleepy. Comfortable. Relaxed.

I'm ready. Bring on those new shoes.

I didn't remember leaving AHGA. Dr. Cayson had told me that if all the tests came back positive, he would send me home but I would probably sleep until the next morning. I vaguely recalled Father coming to get me from the testing room, and the next thing I remembered was being in my own bed at home. Then, just a few blurs – Livvy talking to me, Lena walking in and out of the room, taking a sip of water ...everything seemed so ...disconnected.

And then I woke up.

I felt revived, refreshed, cheerful, healthy – ready. I knew I should get up, but my bed felt awesome. And then I remembered. I jumped out of bed and raced to my mirror.

Still that stunning green. Since I was at home with green eyes, it meant only one thing – the testing was done and I was going to be completely Green in a few more weeks!

I spoke to the digital enhancer beside my mirror. "Mom at Eighteen," I said, and instantly, my mom appeared in the mirror beside me, standing right next to my reflection, and we both stared back at me. She smiled, laughed a little. She tipped her head to the side and casually ran her fingers through her hair, flipping the long, chocolate brown tresses over her shoulder. She pursed her lips, blew a kiss, and smiled again. It lasted about twenty seconds. Then the loop replayed.

This was one of my favorite loops of her. She looked so young – so full of energy, enthusiasm, and hope. It was taken on the morning before she started her Green Enhancement. She had told both Livvy and me that we would record ourselves on the morning before our enhancement, too, so we could always look back at the way we were.

Two years ago, when Livvy had been ready to start, I reminded her of what Mom had said. She told me to quit being stupid. She said she didn't care if she ever saw her ugly blue eyes again, so why in the world would she record a loop to remind her? For her, to be Green meant being more, so why would she want to be reminded of a time when she was less?

"Play combo loop, 'Mom at Eighteen with Calyssa at Eighteen,'" I said. Now there were three of us there in the mirror. The recording of my mom when she was eighteen continued to play, but there were two of me there now - one image I had recorded a few weeks ago, and the reflection of me today. The two images of me were virtually identical except for one small, yet incredibly important, difference: my deep brown eyes from a couple of weeks ago were now vibrant green.

I just stood there and looked at my mom and the two of me. If someone else viewed it, they probably would have thought that we were sisters, not a mother and daughter, our images recorded twenty-nine years apart. Mom would have been forty-seven this year. I wondered what she would have looked like now.

"Stop loop. 'Mom and Calyssa, Fifth Birthday.' Play loop," I said, more softly this time.

Two people once again appeared next to me in the mirror, but this time it was my mom and me at five years old. Mom looked so different from the girl she replaced. It was definitely her, but the brown hair, fair skin and brown eyes were gone. Instead, her hair was a rich, beautiful, dark green, and her skin a soft green that accentuated her vibrant emerald green eyes. Her wavy hair almost reached to her shoulders, and at five years old, I had mine cut just like hers. From the depths of the mirror, she smiled as she picked up a brush and began to gently work it through my hair.

"Happy birthday, Sweetie. I can't believe how big you're getting. Smile for the loop." The image of Mom leaned down and kissed the top of my head.

"I wish I looked like you," my five-year-old self said, and sighed as she gazed in the mirror in front of her. "You're so beautiful." The little me sighed again, such a big, heavy, sad sigh for such a little person.

"One of the boys in class told me yesterday that I'm ugly. He said I looked like a drone, and that the Council would never let me go Green, no matter how rich my daddy is." Tears glistened in the corners of those little girl eyes.

"Calyssa Grace, you listen to me," my mom said, her voice soft but stern as she stopped brushing and lifted me onto her lap.

"You are the most beautiful person I know, and not just on the outside," she said as she wrapped an arm around me and placed her hand on my chest, "but on the inside, too, where it really counts." I could still remember how it felt as she stared intently into my five-year-old eyes and enfolded my tiny body into her arms.

"There are many people who others believe are beautiful, but their beauty is only on the outside. People who are cruel or thoughtless are not truly beautiful people."

"Like the Drones?" the little version of me asked, my voice quivering.

She frowned. "Calyssa, you know I don't like that word. People who don't go Green, for whatever reason, are people like you and me." Then she smiled softly again.

"They work hard, they care for others, and they play with their children, just like your father and me. Being Green is not better or worse. It's simply another color. It allows some people to focus their talents and abilities in ways to help our whole community. But those who don't go Green are still very important people. I want you to remember that. They work in our community, and they grow the food you and your sister eat every day."

"But how can they be happy? I mean, adults should be Green. Livvy says if they're not, they're either poor or stupid," I whispered.

Mom's frown was back. "Your sister is not always right, Calyssa. Naleeva often speaks about things she doesn't understand. She repeats things she hears. She doesn't think about speaking with kindness." Mom sighed. But then she smiled and gave me a little squeeze.

"What do we know about kindness, Calyssa?"

"It's the universal remedy," my chin lifted as my five-year old self proudly replied. "It can make any situation better. It can calm storms, fight fires, and comfort those who are lost."

"Beautiful and smart." My mother smiled again. "And talented. Which reminds me that we need to finish getting you ready for your cello session with Professor Zimmer."

My tiny face brightened with a smile. "Today, the professor is going to teach me one of his great-great-grandfather's pieces from an old, old movie. You know, like back in the really old days." My little eyebrows rose as the excitement spread across my face.

"But even though it's super old, it's beautiful, Mom. I can't wait until I know the whole thing and can play it for you. Professor Zimmer says he thinks I'll have it in a couple weeks but I'm going to try to learn it all this week, then I'll play it for you." My eyes were wide, full of anticipation.

This time it was my mom's turn for glistening eyes. "I once read," she told me, "that 'what you do, the way you think, makes you beautiful.' You remember that, Calyssa. You are a truly beautiful person. I can't wait to see the woman you become." She squeezed me again. "I love you."

"I love you, too, Mom," I said in unison with my five-year-old self.

"Stop loop," I said. I appeared alone in the mirror again. "I love you, too."

That had been the last loop I'd taken with her. Two days later, she had begun to feel weak. Within days, her beautiful green color had diminished to a sallow yellow. Father took her to AHGA since he had the best doctors and researchers in all New America working there. Livvy and I never got to visit her, and a couple of days later Father told us she was gone.

I looked in the mirror once more. I had been without Mom now for more years than I had been with her, but I still ached inside when I let myself think about her.

"Ummmm ...really, Little Sis? Biggest week of your life and you're standing in front of the mirror looking like you're gonna cry?" Livvy stood at my door staring disapprovingly.

Chapter 7

I felt my cheeks flush. I always felt so inadequate when Livvy was around. Sometimes it still amazed me that Livvy and I were actually sisters. That we had the same parents.

But when your family owned the most advanced human genetics lab in the world, then you could literally "pick a kid," as Livvy liked to call it. Livvy was born blond haired, blue-eyed, and golden skinned before she went Green, and grew up tall and slender with a cute nose and high cheek bones. She was athletic, muscular (but in a feminine way), witty, quick-thinking, and analytical.

She really was the feminine version of Father. Don't get me wrong, he was as handsome as she was beautiful, and although no one would ever mistake one for the other, they were definitely father and daughter. Livvy loved it. She was, in all respects, Daddy's little girl.

And I was ...practically her opposite. Just as Livvy's conception was planned, enhanced, and modified, so was mine. But I took after Mom, and when I was born, everyone said I was a perfect re-creation. I mean, I wasn't her clone, that sort of tech was still illegal, although I'd heard it was available on the black market, but I was definitely her daughter, right down to my love for music.

It had been a beautiful blend in our house until Mom died. I mean, I knew Father and Livvy always wanted what was best for me, we just didn't always agree on what "best" was. And Father and Livvy always were on the same wavelength. Two to one. I shook my head and sighed. I just didn't feel up to fighting with Livvy today.

"Excuse me, ladies." Lena placed her hand on Livvy's shoulder, and looked around her at me. "Lyssa, you need to leave for school in about an hour. You don't want to be falling behind with your graduation around the corner. And Naleeva, aren't you supposed to be at the U this morning?"

Lena cocked her head to one side and raised an eyebrow the way she always did when she asked a question that she already knew the answer to. Livvy, still facing me with her back to Lena, rolled her eyes.

I headed toward my closet, relieved that Livvy would be leaving.

Livvy instead walked over to my mirror, running her hands through her perfect green hair. "Yes, Lena. I'm off to god-awful boring Business Strategy and Planning with Professor Whittaker this morning. He is truly the most monotonous, dry human I've ever had to listen to. Dad should teach the class. He and I have far more relevant discussions on advancements for AHGA, a real company. Not like all the ridiculous simulations Whittaker makes us take part in."

She frowned and continued, "I'd like to know how he got to go Green. Must have family money or something." Livvy breathed out hard, like she had to deal with a small child who was being unreasonable.

She turned back to me. "Do have fun today, though, Little Sis. Make the Brentwood name proud." She switched her designer bag to her other shoulder and gave her skirt a little tug. "And keep that iBud in. You'll be getting lots of congrats today from important people. I put the word out there that you're on your way to great things with your new scholarship, your acceptance to the U, and now your official Green citizenship since the testing is complete." Then she turned and left. Lena and I both just stared after her.

"I say relax and enjoy yourself today, Lyssa," Lena said as she turned back to me. "Your school days won't go on forever. Friends will move away, people change and grow apart. Enjoy today for what it is – today."

"Thanks, Lena." I wasn't going to let Livvy bring me down.

Multiple times in the next hour, news broadcasts continued to interrupt the music on my iBud. In the background was gunfire and lots of screaming and yelling, as correspondents updated citizens about rebel assaults. It sounded like more of a mess than yesterday, so one of Father's drivers was delegated to ensuring my safe arrival at school. But once I was at the school, things seemed surprisingly normal.

After lots of congratulations from my friends and classmates on my Green confirmation, the morning continued much the same as the day before. A few minutes before lunch, another announcement was made that campus was once again closed. Identical groans to the day before. This administrator often ended her announcements with a quote, and today she said, "And remember, 'Never doubt that a small group of thoughtful, committed citizens can change the world. Indeed, it is the only thing that ever has.' Margaret Mead, cultural anthropologist."

The bell rang and everyone exited the room. I walked down the hall, falling into step with another girl. I noticed she looked like her Green Enhancement had been recent — light, but definitely green skin, and short green hair, tipped with a reddish blonde that was probably her hair color before she enhanced. I thought I'd seen her before. *She must have a late birthday, too*, I thought.

"Interesting quote Ms. Halloway chose. Isn't that exactly what the rebels are and what they're trying to do ...change the world?" I raised my eyebrows as I said it.

She shrugged her shoulders, "Hmm. I don't think I've ever thought of the rebels as thoughtful, or even citizens at all. I mean, they're always causing trouble. You know, stirring things up, and then running away and hiding. I don't think there's a whole lot of meaning behind that kind of crap. My father's a security enforcer, and he says that's what a limited education does to you. Those people don't have anything to contribute to our society, so they get all wrapped up in trashing other people's stuff. Personally, I get tired of hearing about it."

She shook her head, then saw some friends waving at her. "And hey, congrats on the green eyes by the way." She tossed her hair over her shoulder and readjusted the bag she was carrying, which caused it to bump into a girl with lots of dark, curly hair, walking in the opposite direction.

"Watch where you're walking, Drone," she said as her green eyes hardened into a mocking glare.

The girl whipped around, her hair spinning to follow her, "I'm not the one having trouble walking down the hall, Gimp." She sneered at me, then leaned over to whisper, although not too quietly, to one of her friends. "Another wasted human, compliments of genetic modification." Then back at me, "What's next? How about something useful, like eyes in the back of your head so you can see when someone's coming after you?" They all cackled.

Wait a minute. How did this become about me? I hadn't even said anything to her. Then I noticed the Green girl I had been talking to seconds ago was gone. The girl with the curls must have thought that I was the one who made the comment. Seriously. I did not want to deal with this kind of drama today.

Chapter 8

I found Divya and Jessalyn in the cafeteria, lounging in the chairs and sharing a nutrient shake. I wasn't hungry. It made me smile to think that soon I would never have to eat lunch again. Just lots of sunshine and a few shakes when I felt like it.

Jess needed to check with one of her teachers about an upcoming test before the end of the lunch period, so we each headed off a little early to our afternoon classes. For me, it was Human Biological Studies, not my favorite. I was sure that Dr. DeBeau would have lots of work for me to make up, even though I had only missed yesterday afternoon.

I looked at the clock; it was still about fifteen minutes before class as I walked into Dr. DeBeau's room. An older, Green woman with her long hair pulled back in a tight bun, she always wore a professional-looking shirt with a longer business-type skirt and heels. It didn't matter what we were doing in class – experiments, lectures, dissections – no matter how messy or flammable or gooey – she looked the same. Unruffled. Professional.

Dr. DeBeau was probably the most consistently organized person I knew. Livvy absolutely couldn't stand her, but I thought she was fine. A little on the tough side, but for students who were on time, got their work done, and didn't make waves, it wasn't a terrible class. I'd definitely had worse.

Dr. DeBeau was already speaking with another student, rather intensely I judged by the level of her voice and her hand gestures. The guy she was talking to had brown hair and an athletic build, but I couldn't see his face. I shrugged and thought, *Better him than me.*

Then that funky science room smell hit me. I knew I wrinkled my nose – I couldn't help it. Chemicals, cleaners, and air fresheners, with a touch of something burnt lingering in the background. I'm not sure where or what that smell came from because the room was always immaculate. Two stools at each black, granite-top lab station, with all the regular lab equipment-type stuff set on top – gas nozzles, tubing, beakers, graduated cylinders, and other pieces of equipment that forever remained nameless to me as my mind refused to sort them out.

As I stood waiting for Dr. DeBeau, another girl walked in and peered past me to see what was going on. She was already a Green Citizen, with short, spiky hair on top that came down about to her chin in the front, emphasizing her delicate facial features. I knew her from my morning Digital Trends class. We didn't talk much, but she'd always seemed nice.

"Lyssa, right?" she asked.

I nodded. "You're Giselle?"

She nodded. "Love the eyes. I was wondering when you were going to enhance. Nice that you'll be Green before graduation. It's a bummer for the ones who have late birthdays and have to wait." She wrinkled *her* nose. "I know it shouldn't matter, but I would be so embarrassed if I had to walk the stage at graduation looking like a drone." She shuddered.

Glancing back toward Dr. DeBeau, I asked Giselle, "Do you know who she's talking to?"

She looked past me. "Um, I think his name is Gabe – hmmm, I can't remember his last name." He briefly turned his head toward us, still totally engaged in his conversation with DeBeau, adamantly pointing to something on his paper. I was shocked to see that it was the guy from the cafeteria, the one who had gotten into it with Rykker. Giselle didn't mention it, so I didn't either. Maybe she hadn't seen what had happened.

"Oh, yeah," I replied. "Now that I see his face, I think I know who he is."

Giselle leaned over a little more, watching their interaction. "Yeah, he seems like a nice guy – I mean, he's never been a jerk or anything to me. But I wonder how smart he is. He looks old enough, but he's not Green." She looked down and adjusted the collection of bracelets that decorated her long, thin arm.

"He could be a late bloomer, I guess, but I wouldn't count on that. He looks pretty ...mature," she said glancing back at me. Then, with a sly little grin, she added, "Well, actually pretty hot, I mean for a non-Green guy. I'd guess he's not going Green. Bummer."

I looked back at him, too. "Yeah. But at least he's sticking it out and finishing school. A lot of kids who haven't gone Green by now just quit school to get a job somewhere."

Right about then Dr. DeBeau looked toward the door and saw us. "Ah, Calyssa, just the student I was waiting for. Come over here. Oh, and Giselle, can you come back to see me later this afternoon? I need to talk to these two before class begins."

"Sure. I'll be back after school," Giselle said to Dr. DeBeau. Then she turned to me. "Cool talking to you."

"You, too," I said. I walked over to the table where Dr. DeBeau and Gabe were standing.

"Calyssa, Gabe is moving into this period starting today in order to attend a science tutoring class that he and I have been discussing. Since you were the only student from this period absent yesterday when we started our new project, I'm putting you two together as lab partners. You can work together the rest of the week. Project's due on Friday. Here's the handout and expectations," she said as she handed me some old-fashioned papers.

Where did she even get this stuff? DeBeau was the only teacher I knew who still used paper. I was never sure why she didn't just send assignments digitally in flash packs, but then, I wasn't going to ask her about it.

"Questions?" she asked, but I could tell by her tone she didn't want any.

"Got it," I answered as I took the sheets. *Oh great,* I thought, *already starting this project a day late, and now I have to nurse this slow guy along, bringing him up to speed as I figure this out. At least he's starting tutoring. Maybe I won't have to do all the work.*

"Gabe?" She looked at him as well.

He looked at me and back at her. "I don't mind completing the project that I've already started alone." He wasn't smiling. He was serious.

I felt my eyebrows shoot up, but before I could say anything Dr. DeBeau shook her head. "Sorry. It's a partner project for everyone." And then she simply walked across the room and began arranging equipment on a table.

Gabe looked at her, then at me, and let out a big sigh. A *huge* sigh, like Livvy did when she thought she was going to be stuck dragging me somewhere she didn't want to take me.

Well, two can play that game, I thought. I rolled my eyes, adjusted the bag I was carrying, and headed to the back of the room where I usually sat.

"I usually sit in the front," Gabe said as I walked away.

"Front's all taken up this period. Guess you'll have to make do at my table." I set my things down, pulled up a stool, and watched as he stood there, like he was trying to decide what to do.

I began to feel a little sorry for him. New class period, new partner who happens to be a hot Green girl. *Probably feeling a little insecure,* I thought. "Come on, Gabe. I don't bite and there's a seat right here for you." I flashed him a grin. It was only one period a day for the next four days. *I can do this.*

Gabe closed his eyes for a second, then grabbed his stuff and walked slowly to the table. He closed his eyes again briefly, then took another deep breath, and pulled up his stool.

Poor guy, I thought. "Hey, Gabe, I'm Calyssa Brentwood. Most of my friends call me Lyssa. Either is fine with me" I held out my hand to let him know I was ready to work with him.

"I know who you are. We've had classes together in the past." He sighed and shook my hand. Again, with that sigh. Seriously? This guy needed a little positive pick-me-up today.

"Is something funny?" he asked. He didn't look at me when he said it, but I could tell from his voice he wasn't feeling particularly amused.

"Not at all. Just trying to be friendly, since we're working together this week."

"Fine, let's keep it project-focused and get this done." He glanced through the paperwork in front of him.

"Don't worry," I told him. "I'm pretty decent in science. I can even help you outside of your tutoring class if you need it. I mean, sorry to bring up the tutoring if it makes you uncomfortable, but I heard DeBeau mention it."

A look of surprise, quickly followed by distaste, crossed his face, finally settling into some sort of mild amusement. "DeBeau didn't want me to be tutored. She wants me to be the tutor. She talked VanMilton out of keeping me as his tutor for Advanced Calc so I could help some of her students instead. That's why I had to change periods." He laughed, but it wasn't a very nice laugh, more dry and cynical.

And I felt red rapidly move up my neck to my face.

Chapter 9

I always knew when I blushed, and I hated it. I looked away and stammered something, awkwardly apologizing for the misunderstanding, and he just laughed again. But it was a nicer laugh this time, more genuine. I looked back at him, and now he was staring at me with that "I-feel-sorry-for-you" look that I had given him earlier.

I continued stammering, "I – just – I guess – I mean – I just assumed you were having trouble because you're not, well, Green, and you're obviously old enough, I mean I think you are, but ...." My voice trailed off. I definitely was not making this any better.

"Forget it," he said. "Not everybody goes Green you know. It's not that big of a deal." He looked through his papers one more time, selected a single piece, and placed it on top. "Let's get on with this. Class is going to start in a minute, and you're already a day behind everybody else. I can catch you up on what I worked on yesterday, if you want to continue the project I came up with. If not, we can start something new. It doesn't matter to me either way."

"I'm fine with your work from yesterday. I mean, I'm more than willing to do my fair share in this, so I'll let you decide." The red was easing back down my neck. *Maybe it won't be so bad working with Gabe after all,* I thought.

"My paper it is then," he said. "Let me catch you up. How much do you understand about the properties of osmosis? Because our job in this project is to design an experiment based on the principles of diffusion and osmosis that could be used to determine the molarity of flasks that each contain a different unknown solution. After we design the experiment, we need to carry it out, proving or disproving our hypothesis with accurate and reliable data collection results."

When I hadn't said anything yet, he stopped and looked at me. "Following me?"

"Um, back that up a bit. I glazed over for a minute there, but I'll focus this time." I grinned.

Another sigh. "It's going to be a long week, isn't it?" he asked. I just laughed, which actually got a grin out of him.

Gabe was a pretty good teacher, and I, probably (hopefully), wasn't as dumb as he assumed based on my initial reaction. His plan was a good one and easy to understand once I'd caught up on what I had missed.

And Gabe was smart, like scary-science smart. I don't think there was anything I asked him that he couldn't answer, and a couple of times I asked him questions just to try to stump him. After the third or fourth time, he laughed and said that he came from a long line of family with strong science backgrounds, so I should forget trying to catch him off guard on a topic and focus on our project.

In just one period this guy had me convinced that he might be the smartest person I knew in science, and that was saying something, because my father owned one of the top science research facilities in the world, and I had met some incredibly smart people. *But it's not just that he's smart,* I thought. *He knows how to explain things in different ways that don't make me feel stupid if I don't get it the first time.* And I felt on top of the project. After only one day. *Sweet. Rockin' lab partner!*

It was weird, though. Anytime I said anything about being Green or going Green, Gabe quickly changed the subject. It was obviously an "off-limits" topic, and it made me wonder why. Maybe he came from a family that didn't have any money, and was embarrassed to talk about it. I figured I wouldn't push it, at least not today. I was just stoked that we were bound to get an awesome grade on this assignment!

When the period ended, Gabe and I said good-bye and headed our separate ways, him to some sort of advanced drafting and design class, and me to Advanced Symphonic Performance – where I could be the genius.

I felt totally confident on my cello, and I savored the sensation of playing music: the vibration of the strings beneath my fingers, the rosin floating off the bow, leaving its sweet, pine impression dancing in the air. To play live before a crowd was truly an unmatched feeling. I moved their very souls, touching something deep inside them with my gift, my ability. It was a powerful thing to share, and I loved giving the gift of beautiful music to those around me.

I walked into the room, and it went silent. Everyone was looking at me. *What?* I thought, suddenly frantic. *Something on my face, hanging out of my skirt, in my hair?* Then a round of applause – for me.

As the applause died down, Mr. Hazelbrook stood up. "Congratulations, Lyssa. You are the last of our advanced music production students to be enhanced. Now, you will all be Green for your final performance at the end of this year. Take a minute to imagine yourselves there now, in the Grand Hall of the Majestic Theater. You are the most advanced group of students that I have had the privilege of working with in many years. I cannot wait to see what you'll do in the future."

The students nodded and congratulated each other, talking about the upcoming performance. Mr. Hazelbrook walked over to me. "Especially you, Lyssa," he said softly. "You truly have a unique gift. Congratulations again on your acceptance into the Green Commonwealth. It is so refreshing to see young adults joining us who actually have something to offer, besides, well, just their parents' money."

"Thank you." I felt a bit embarrassed, but it also felt good to know that Mr. Hazelbrook thought so highly of me.

I joined the other students and we played a few warm-up pieces. Then we began to play a new piece we had been working on. It was by Phillip Glass, an influential composer of the late twentieth century. I loved it when the music built in intensity, the vibrations from the strings surging through my body. Feeling totally in tune with my instrument, my body moved rhythmically, the music conveying a familiar degree of directness and warmth. My bow flew through the notes, some gently, some passionately, evoking combinations of emotions in me that allowed me to lose myself. What science was for Gabe, music was for me.

When the class ended, I stayed in the room. Finally, my one easy period for the day — being an aide in Mr. Hazelbrook's Musical Performance Appreciation class. I had taken the class a couple of years ago, and it was the one period of the day where I could just relax and help other students. As the advanced students filed out and the classroom began to fill with new, younger students, I saw one smiling face with a bouncing, dark blond ponytail headed directly toward me.

"Hi, Ana. How's it going?"

"I heard the news. Let me see – oh, they're even better than I expected. Wow! I hope you know how lucky you are." She looked so awed, it was almost embarrassing.

"Hey, with the way you play that violin, you'll be in my shoes in no time."

"Right," she said, rolling her eyes in her typical Ana-like fashion.

"Oh, Ana, you crack me up! You *know* you'll be scholarshipped to go Green. You've got it all – looks, talent, and now, a super-hot music mentor." That made her laugh, and I leaned over and gave her a half-hug. "Don't make me make you pinky swear to keep practicing." That produced another eye roll, but one that came with a partial grin. I liked this kid. She always made me laugh.

Time passed quickly. Hazelbrook lectured the whole period, so I kicked back and worked on assignments from my other classes. Ana kept rolling her eyes at Hazelbrook's corny jokes, and then glancing at me with a "save-me-from-this-awfulness" look. I barely kept from laughing aloud.

When class ended, Ana came up, shaking her head. "Really? You couldn't like make up an excuse to get me out of here? Hazelbrook set an all-time record for wackiness today. I thought I might puke." For emphasis, she fake-heaved a couple times.

I had to laugh. "It wasn't that bad." More eye rolling. "Okay, it was, but it was only one period. And he has a good heart, and he's a great music teacher. You have to give him that."

"I know." She sighed. "I'm just ready to get into more advanced classes. So much basic stuff is boring."

"It'll come. Give yourself time. And I do believe what I said," I told her. "You're a gifted musician. If your parents can't pay for the Enhancement when your time comes, let me know. I can talk to my father. He usually scholarships at least a couple kids every year, mostly science and math types, but I feel confident I could talk him into giving you one, too. I've got a pretty good eye – and ear – for identifying musical talent."

Ana suddenly looked solemn. "How about whipping out a miracle and getting me enhanced early? It's killing me. I swear I'm ready now." She shook her head and looked away from me.

"Hey, come on. You know it wouldn't work yet. Your time will be here before you know it."

She rolled her eyes one more time. "Yeah that's me, Princess of Patience." I laughed again, and gave her a quick hug, and we both headed out of the classroom.

Hmm. I wonder why Livvy hasn't called, I thought. *She was all over me about all the calls I'd get today on my iBud.* Instinctively I reached up and touched my ear, thinking, *Reconnect.* I heard a soft chime, followed by a woman's soft voice, informing me that I had fifty-six missed calls, twenty-five voice mails, and seventeen urgent call-back notifications.

Chapter 10

Crap, I thought. *I must have accidentally silenced my iBud at some point, and I was so busy today I didn't even notice it.*

My first call-back, even though I preferred not to make it at all, was to Livvy. *Hey, Sis,* I thought when she connected. *Are you – ?*

Livvy interrupted, her thought-stream smothering mine. *Seriously, didn't I tell you how important it was to stay in touch today? I mean, really Lyssa, out of all the days to space out. I had important people messaging you, and then they were coming back to me saying they never heard anything back.* She went on and on and on, how she couldn't believe me, how could I be so irresponsible, think of the family name, about all the stress and trouble I put her through. When she finally paused, I thought, *Sorry, Livvy. It was an accident. I'll get hold of everyone tonight and thank them for their wonderful wishes.* That calmed her down a bit.

BTW, Little Sis, where in God's Green society are you? Dad sent me to pick you up. I've been parked outside for the last fifteen minutes waiting. Get a move on. I've got places I need to be. She disconnected.

Really, outside the school? Couldn't that have been the *first* thing she told me? We could have been almost home by now. I hustled out front, rearranging my homework tablet in my bag, checking to make sure I wasn't forgetting any of the memory flash packs that had to be turned into various teachers tomorrow. I didn't get why teachers couldn't all connect up and find a common flash pack to use. They may have been tiny, but multiples were a pain to keep organized.

I found Livvy waiting impatiently out front in her Peugeot Angel 17, which was, of course, the newest concept car. I had to admit - I loved it. With a maglev engine system and rear wheels working on opposing magnetic fields circulation, it developed a magnetic field that levitated the car in the back once some speed was built up. Riding in it felt like floating on air.

I was supposed to get my own car for my eighteenth birthday, but Father had been so wrapped up at work lately that we hadn't had a chance to go looking. I was about ready to ask him to just get me the same car as Livvy, because it was cool, and I wanted my own transportation, instead of driving one of the family cars. But I knew Livvy would have a fit.

Livvy started talking about her day as soon as I got in the car, what she'd been doing, how her classes were, who she saw, what had happened at work that day at AHGA .... I tried to sound interested, making all the appropriate noises, nodding at the correct times, but I wasn't really listening to anything she had to say. I looked out the window and sighed. It had been a good day.

And the next couple of days were just as great. I ran through the same schedule each day: classes in the morning, lunchtime with the girls, science lab work with Gabe, and music classes in the afternoon. I felt like I had everything under control. I was caught up in all my classes.

And Div, Jess, and I were back to making plans for the upcoming summer, talking about places we wanted to go and things we wanted to see.

Time with Gabe was much more serious. Our lab plan was perfect and everything was going as we predicted. Gabe was incredibly focused. At first, I tried some small talk as we worked.

"Do you like my new tech suit?" was met with, "It's fine. Will you pass me that beaker?"

"How do you feel about security enforcers?" was answered with, "I don't talk personal politics at school."

"Where do you live?" only got me, "Outside the city."

"What's your family like?" earned me an eye roll and, "Probably pretty much like everybody else's."

And, "What do you think about the rebel attacks around the city?" was simply met with silence.

I figured he was uncomfortable telling me about himself, so I launched into my views, my answers to my own questions, what I thought, what I liked. He quietly continued to work as I talked. I smiled a lot, and thought I was making our time together a lot more comfortable.

On Thursday I told him he was brilliant; that he could work at my father's company after college in one of the science research departments. He looked at me with an odd expression on his face, like he wasn't sure of what I'd said or that he didn't believe me. Then he just went back to work.

That night, at home, I told Father about him. "Gabe isn't like any other guy I've met at school. He's brilliant. The way he talks about things and explains them in Human

Biological Studies is on a totally different level. Sometimes even Dr. DeBeau will ask him how he would explain something in front of the whole class, and he jumps right into an explanation that is usually better than the one she gave. It's amazing."

Livvy smirked. "Sounds like Lyssa has a new crush."

I glared at her. "It's not like that at all, Livvy. We don't talk about anything but science." As always, she was making things into something they weren't.

I turned back to Father. "I think his family might not have any money. He's super-reluctant to talk about anything connected with college."

"Oh, that's what this is," Livvy interjected. "Lyssa's got a new project. Is this little poor boy going to be your newest rescue?" I turned and glared at Livvy. I couldn't believe how much I wanted to slap her across the face! She just continued to smirk.

I paused for a second, staring at Father until he looked back at me. I took a breath and continued. "I think you should look at scholarshipping him. I know it's late in the year, but the teachers at school would write him stellar recs. I think he's Dr. DeBeau's favorite student." I knew that would get Father's attention.

"As in the Dr. DeBeau that consults with my research department?" he asked. I nodded. "Well, that is interesting. I can't understand why she continues to work at a high school when she's been offered a staff position multiple times at AHGA."

I waited. Father was silent.

"Well, what do you think?" I asked after a few more seconds had passed. "About a scholarship for him, I mean?"

He rubbed his eyes and then the back of his neck, glancing toward the digital news monitor. It noted that rebel updates were coming up next, and when those came on, I knew I'd lose his attention for sure.

I continued to stare at him. It was all or nothing. I had to get him to say yes now while he was even possibly considering it. "Please, Father. Agree to meet him. Maybe over spring break or something. I know you'll be impressed." More silence. More staring. "Please."

More seconds ticked by.

Finally, he answered, "All right, Calyssa. If Dr. DeBeau will recommend him, I'll set up an interview with this young man. If he has the science aptitude you seem to think he has, I'll consider scholarshipping him."

I rushed over and gave him a hug. "Thank you. You won't be disappointed. I know you won't." The hug was awkward and over quickly, and then he turned back to the news again.

One of his favorite newscasters, Saxony McClefe, had just appeared on the screen. She was one of the darkest Green citizens I'd ever seen. Her super-dark green skin and hair contrasted dramatically with her flashing white teeth. She had a glamorous yet untamed feel about her, like behind that silky voice was a coiled intelligence ready to spring on an unsuspecting target. She captivated her audience, and she knew it.

I wasn't sure I wanted to hear more about the rebel drama. I preferred to think about Gabe and telling him about his new scholarship.

"Seriously, Lyssa. You've got it bad for this guy." Livvy was still on my case.

"Butt out, Livvy," I said, then clenched my teeth to stop myself from saying anything more. I didn't want to let her push me into a fight in front of Father; but when I turned to look at him, I saw it didn't matter. He had been pulled in by Saxony and was now fully engrossed in her news story.

I glared at Livvy, then turned back to the digital monitor, pretending to be as completely tuned in as Father. Livvy's hand flew to her iBud, and she got up quickly and left the room. With Livvy gone, I started to leave the room as well. But the seriousness in the newscaster's voice caused me to pause and turn back once more to the broadcast.

Behind Saxony, on a huge screen, a rebel attack was currently unfolding, this incident further out in the farm lands. It showed huge government vehicles blocking the roads. Two hovercopters flew onto the scene, one setting down near a large group of security enforcers. The other continued hovering over the area, swooping back and forth, vigilantly watching for more rebel outbursts. Occasional gunfire ripped through the background.

Saxony informed SciCity residents that several more of its security enforcers had been injured in this attack. One had died, several others were in serious condition. The situation was obviously tense, and the grim faces on the screen made me realize that this was worse than I'd realized. She reminded all of us that our security enforcers were placing their lives on the line every day to protect everyone in SciCity, Green and non-Green alike. We needed to "rally as one group to support the end of this violence, of these aggressive, unwarranted attacks on our city and its outlying areas."

She closed the piece by saying that SciCity government officials were meeting with the head of the security enforcers to determine further actions to stop what they now were referring to as "terrorist acts against the city." Terrorist acts. That made me shudder. I hoped the government and the security enforcers would get rid of the rebels soon. SciCity should have been a safe place for everyone to live. It felt chilling to think that there might be unquestionably bad people out there hiding, waiting to steal from the people of our city, even hurting or killing them for rebel profit.

I headed back to my bedroom and closed the door. I was glad I lived here, in the middle of the city, in a high security zone house with "executive surveillance." I now understood why Father had stressed the importance of home security, and I felt relieved remembering that AHGA had a whole army of monitoring professionals watching over us.

As I started to get ready for bed, my thoughts returned to my conversation tonight with Father. I couldn't wait to tell Gabe the incredibly good news. Maybe he could start his Enhancement right after spring break and finish the process before graduation.

"Lights off," I commanded, and my room immediately dimmed, leaving only a soft glow coming from a small light in the corner. It felt good to be helping someone who had helped me.

Tomorrow, I'll find Gabe. Tomorrow, I'll change his life forever.

Chapter 11

The next day I rushed through the morning. I kept looking for Gabe, but I didn't see him. Everybody at school seemed a little more excited than usual, voices louder, more laughter, high fives, and talk of spring break plans everywhere. Lots of happy faces. At lunch, an intercom announcement came on reminding us "not to forget that there was no school the following week." Divya, Jessalyn, and I looked at each other, and then, simultaneously, groaned.

"Really, they think they need to remind us about that?" Divya rolled her eyes. "I am so ready to be out of here for a week."

My iBud chimed softly. *Answer,* I thought. I was always amazed that the brain recognition software in my iBud knew when I was thinking for it, like to answer a call or send my thoughts, versus when I was just thinking in general. New tech was crazy, but I loved it.

Calyssa? It was a female voice.

Connect, I thought, then, *Yes?*

Oh, good, she continued. *This is Shaylara Striker, one of your father's personal assistants. He wanted me to let you know he's being called out of the country on urgent business. He'll be traveling to Eurasia to a new branch of AHGA. They're having some technical issues that he needs to personally oversee. He'll be gone for about a week, but he wanted me to let you know not to worry, that he's already talked with Naleeva, and she'll be staying home with you this next week. He said you can call him later today if you're concerned.*

Okay, I thought back, *tell him not to worry about us. And to be careful. Thank you for calling.*

Of course, then she disconnected.

"Hello, SciCity to Lyssa. You in there?" Divya was waggling her head back and forth at me. Jessalyn just raised her eyebrows.

"Sorry. I was on my iBud. It was a call from my father's assistant. He's been called out of town unexpectedly." I wrinkled my nose. "It's just going to be Livvy and me this next week."

"Oh, man, I wish I was going to be in town," Divya said. "Party at the Brentwoods'!"

"No way." I shook my head. "Father would kill us. Not worth it."

Divya laughed. "You've got to take a few risks in your life, Lyssa. Right, Jess? I mean, loosen up a little. Less school, more fun."

Jessalyn smirked. "Maybe you can meet up with Ashton," she said. "Have you talked to him any more yet?"

"No, I've been so busy getting caught up the last couple days. And now that I think about it, it's kinda weird that I haven't run into him." I turned my head to the side, thinking about that. Actually, it was kinda weird that I hadn't even thought about him at all until now.

My iBud chimed again. "Hold on. Another call." I turned away from my friends, thinking, *Answer.*

Hey, Lyssa. Did you get the message from Dad? He's leaving for business. Livvy, more eye rolling, probably on both ends of the connection.

I sighed. *Connect,* I thought, then, *Yeah. I talked with his assistant.*

Good. So here's the deal, Lyssa. I've already got big plans this next week. I'm going with a group of friends to a new resort that recently opened up. It's like six or seven hours from here and I'm already completely invested in this trip. Can't back out now. I haven't really talked with Dad about it, but I think I can make some business connects while I'm there. I want to surprise him.

That's fine, I thought back. *I don't care if you go.* I wouldn't mind having the place to myself, hanging with Lena, sleeping in, no Livvy to boss me around.

Sweet. But here's the deal, Little Sis. Dad already gave Lena the week off, but he doesn't want you to stay alone. With all the rebel trouble and whatnot lately. I told him you were old enough and all that, which you know I think you are, but he wouldn't hear of it. Said it would be good bonding time for us, that he's noticed we've been arguing more lately. Whatever.

Anyway, I told him I already had plans, and he told me that it was not negotiable. Lyssa, I cannot miss out on this trip. Cannot. It would put me completely out of the loop. This is a big chance for me to show Dad that I can bring in a new market to our business, not to mention Azra Sommersett personally asked me to go. You know, Azra Sommersett, as in Sommersett Concept Designs. His family does all the premier new home tech. I have to go to this.

Livvy finally stopped. I had to shake my head. When she rapid-thought like that, it felt like there was more of her in my head than me.

I don't care if you go, Livvy. Have fun. Hang with Azra, do some work, whatever. Don't worry about me. I'll be fine. I'd never actually stayed home alone, but I wasn't worried about it.

Lyssa, Dad will go ballistic if he finds out you stayed home and I left after he specifically said I had to stay home with you. But ...if you were to tell me that you already had plans to stay with a friend, like say Divya or Jessalyn, and that you had your heart set on it, I just wouldn't be able to say no to my little sis, Livvy thought.

Right. Livvy never had a hard time saying no to me. *I don't know Livvy. I ....*

She interrupted. *Come on, Lyssa. Do you want to spend all that time with me? I've already boarded out Lulu for a week to the Uptown Pet Spa, and Lena is going to visit relatives. That means it'll just be you and me. Alone. Wouldn't you rather spend time hanging with your friends? Seriously, Sis. Do me a huge favor. Find somebody to stay with for the week. I won't go if you don't agree. Just realize that it will screw up my personal and professional life, not to mention ....*

Fine, I interrupted her this time. *Go. I'll figure it out. No big deal.*

So you're not going to stay home, right? Please? Promise me you'll work out the details. Come on, Lyssa. Please. I mean run by and get your clothes and whatever you need, but you're telling me you've got other plans, right? That you're going to hang with friends for the week, right? That's where you'd rather be, right? Livvy was totally coaching me, making sure that I would say what Father needed to hear if he called me.

Right, Livvy. Absolutely. Plans set. All that. Whatever. Don't worry, I've got the story straight. I promise.

Thanks, Lyssa. Livvy sounded relieved. *I'm headed out of town in an hour. I'll be back next Friday evening. I think Dad's supposed to be back later sometime on Saturday. Plan on being home Saturday morning. I'm so happy that this is going to work out for both of us. Have fun, Little Sis. Gotta run and finish last minute packing. Azra will be here any time to pick me up. See you next weekend. Have fun. Hugs and kisses.* Then she disconnected.

Divya and Jessalyn were staring at me. "Let me guess," Jessalyn said. "That was Livvy. You always get that look on your face when she buzzes you." She scrunched up her face, trying to look disgusted, mimicking me. Divya laughed.

"Yeah, she's going out of town, too. Apparently it's something Father doesn't know about, and she made me promise I'd stay with friends so she can tell Father I already had plans, too."

I looked at both of them and grinned. "So ...?"

Chapter 12

Divya and Jessalyn both contacted their parents. Divya begged, pleaded, threatened, cried, yelled – did the whole theatrical bit, which was a little comical because she was on her iBud in the lunchroom, storming around like a mad woman, mumbling to herself. Total drama act played right out in front of us.

But in the end, her parents were used to her tirades and refused to give in. Divya's father was the one of the directors for SciCity's Security Enforcers, and her mother was a professor at the U. It was hard for them to schedule time off together, but spring break was always a family trip to somewhere exotic. They were headed out of town as soon as school was out. Their plans were already set.

"Sorry, Lyssa," she said. "I can't believe how stubborn they are. It's not like I ask for much."

Jess and I exchanged a glance. Divya caught it. "Okay, fine. Maybe I do ask for a lot, but come on. I'm their only child. I should get what I want. What's wrong with that?" She looked at us expectantly.

We simultaneously dropped our mouths open in mock surprise. Like we had never heard this before from Divya.

"You're spoiled," Jessalyn said. Divya pretended she was hurt, grabbing her chest, dramatically shaking her shoulders in fake sobs.

Then she stuck out her lower lip. "I can take the abuse from my parents, but not from my dearest friends."

"Right," I said. "You're so abused. Poor Div. Horrible life. Has to go on some glamourous vacation, being waited on every minute of the day, meeting hot new guys. You're right. Your life sucks." We all laughed.

"Sorry, Lyssa. I tried. I wish I would have known sooner. I think I could have broken them down over time." Divya put her arm around me.

"No worries. Jess, what do you think? Have you got ahold of your parents yet?" I asked. Jessalyn's parents were business owners in SciCity. She was the first in her family to be scholarshipped to go Green.

"Haven't heard back. I did leave messages for both of them. We have lots of family coming into town this weekend, but I don't see why one more would be a problem." She smiled at me. "I'll catch up with you as soon as I hear from them."

"Sounds good." The bell rang, and we all got up to head to our next class.

"Back to the grind," Divya said as she pressed her hand to her forehead. More eye rolling and then we each headed our separate ways.

I walked into the biology room and saw that Gabe was already at our table. Of course he was. He was reading through some papers, probably taking a last look over our final draft. He was so engrossed in his reading that he didn't even notice when I walked up and sat on the stool next to him.

"Fascinating reading you got there?" I asked. "Must be riveting when you don't even notice the cool girl sitting next to you." I punched him lightly on the shoulder.

He looked up at me. "Where?" he asked, looking around the room. He looked puzzled as he craned to see around me.

"I ...huh ...you know ...um." I stumbled through the words as I felt my face flush.

Gabe laughed. "You're too easy." Gabe didn't smile much, but when he did it was contagious. His whole face lit up.

"You're mean," I said, but I was smiling, too. "Hey, I have some awesome news for you. I mean, like 'make-your-day, make-your-year, make-your life' type of news."

He stopped reading and looked back up at me. "What?"

I reached over and grabbed Gabe's hand. "I talked with my father. He's the CEO at AHGA, you know. I told him how brilliant you are. About how impressed DeBeau is with you in science. Long story short, I talked him into giving you a Green scholarship! All you have to do is get a recommendation from Dr. DeBeau, who basically worships the ground you walk on, and you'll be in! I'm so excited for you!"

Gabe ripped his hand away from me as if it was suddenly unbearably hot. His face and neck flushed an immediate red. He clenched his teeth and looked away from me. When he looked back, there was real anger in eyes.

"Did I ever, ever tell you that I wanted to go Green? That I was even vaguely interested in all that crap? I have sat here for the past week and put up with listening to you talk all about yourself, your life, your family, your-super-awesome-powerful daddy, and how cool you think you've got it." He stood up and shook his head. I was stunned. I couldn't even say a word.

"Did I ever imply to you even once that any of that was something I wanted? You don't know anything about me, about my life, about my choices, what I want. Because you don't listen, you're just so into Calyssa. You're totally dense. Thank God this project is done. Tell your daddy to go push his Green scholarship on somebody who actually cares." He started gathering up his papers.

"Gabe, I ... I ..." I stuttered. I stood up, too, but I didn't know what to say. This was so not the reaction I had expected. "I'm sorry. I didn't mean to presume to know anything about you. I ...."

"Forget it." He cut me off. "Whatever. I'm not interested. Since we finished our paper yesterday, I proofed it last night. It's done. I'm turning it into DeBeau now." He started to walk away.

"Wait a minute," I said. The shock of his comments were starting to wear off. "You don't get to be an ass just because I tried to help out and you don't like it. Sorry, I didn't check with you first. I thought you'd be excited about this. I went to bat for you because I wanted to help you. Sorry I don't know more about you and your family. You never, ever talk about anything but science. I've tried to talk to you about other things. You may think I'm dense, but you're rude. And you've ...you've ...you've got crappy social skills." It was a stupid thing to say, but I was mad and couldn't think of anything witty. I felt my face turning red.

"Who do you think you are that you can treat me, or anybody for that matter, like this?" I stepped closer to him.

He leaned even closer to me. "I know who I am, Calyssa. I'm not out there searching for something to make me 'better' or 'more' because I feel like I'm not enough the way I am. I like me, who I am, today, here, right now. I don't need some out-of-date medical procedure to make me feel better about who I am!" His voice was getting louder. People in the room were staring at us. I didn't care.

"Wow, you're really into yourself, huh?" My voice matched his in intensity and volume. "Obviously, you don't understand why people make the decision to go Green. It's an intellectual choice. One you make so you can better, more fully serve your community." We were nose-to-nose now. "But you wouldn't understand that concept because, hey, in your mind 'I'm Gabe, wonder science boy, super smart, perfect already.' It must be tough packing all that perfection into one person."

He stepped back but continued to stare at me. Unrelenting, not flinching, not looking away. We both just stood there, staring at each other, breathing hard, hands in fists, probably looking like we were ready to duke it out.

Dr. DeBeau came back to our table. "Is there something wrong here? Gabe? Calyssa?" She looked back and forth between us. "Do we need to sit down and talk?"

Gabe broke away from the stare first. He looked down, unclenched his fists, and pressed both of his palms flat on the tabletop. He took a deep breath. "No, Dr. DeBeau. Calyssa and I obviously have a difference of opinion here." He looked at her. "But it doesn't have to do with the project. I'm sorry we let it disrupt your classroom." He looked at me. "Calyssa and I completed our paper yesterday. I've already gone through it one last time. As soon as she reads it again, it'll be ready to be turned in." He slid the papers across the table toward me.

He turned back toward the teacher. "I have several students that I'm working with in the tutoring center. I told them I'd try to get in there this period to help them if I could. Since I'm done here, is it all right if I head down there?"

Dr. DeBeau looked back and forth between us again. "Calyssa, are you fine with that? Is there anything else you need from Gabe for this project?"

"No." I looked down at the papers on the table. I pulled my stool back up behind me, sat down, and pretended to start reading. I knew I was being rude, but I didn't trust myself to say anything else with DeBeau there.

"All right then. Gabe, you may go to the tutoring center. Calyssa, when you're finished with the paper, please bring it to me." She turned and walked back toward her desk. Everyone watching slowly went back to what they had been doing before, and voices began to fill the room once again.

"Calyssa, I . . .," Gabe was the one stumbling through his words now.

"Save it." I said. "I'm not interested. Just go. I'll make sure the paper gets turned into DeBeau."

I felt him staring at me, but I refused to look up. After a few more seconds, he grabbed his stuff and walked away. Then I looked up. *He was right,* I thought. *I don't know anything about him. Except that he's a complete and total lunatic.*

Chapter 13

When I left science and went to music, I was still angry. I ran into Divya outside the door of the room. Literally ran into her.

Divya put her hands on my shoulders to steady herself, then looked at my face. "Whoa! What happened in there? You look like you're ready to knock somebody out."

"Remember my lab partner, Gabe, the one I was working on the project with?" Just saying his name made my jaw clench again.

"Yeah, he's pretty hot for a non-Green guy." Divya smiled. I didn't. Her smile faded.

"Yeah, well I think the guy you're thinking of as Mr. Hottie is actually Mr. Crazy! He totally went off on me! And you want to know why? Why he screamed at me in front of the entire class, basically saying I was stupid and self-absorbed?" I could hear my voice rising again, but I didn't care. "Because I talked my father into scholarshipping him to go Green. That's what makes me such a horrible person." I laughed, but I wasn't smiling and it wasn't a nice laugh. Divya winced.

"Did he ask you to get him a scholarship?" Jessalyn had walked up behind me while I was giving Divya the rundown.

Spinning around to look at her, I said snidely, "What difference does it make if he asked? He's obviously brilliant. He clearly has not gone Green yet. Anybody who wants to contribute to society goes Green. A plus B equals C. Right, Jess? That's basic math." Divya raised her eyebrows. Jessalyn just stared at me. A couple of seconds of silence ticked by.

I blew out a deep breath. "Sorry, Jess. I'm taking this out on you."

She reached out and put her hand on my shoulder. "This isn't math, Lyssa. It's life. Formulas are only accurate in math. Life's not so neat. Did he tell you why he didn't want to go Green?"

I thought for a couple seconds. "He said something about it being an out-of-date process. And that I didn't understand him or his family. I guess I wasn't listening to him once I got mad." I closed my eyes and felt my anger drain out. I sighed. "And, I guess I don't really know him. Maybe outside of school he's got a crazy, hard life."

Jessalyn's hand slid down my arm and grabbed hold of my hand. "Or maybe he wants to go Green, but his family won't let him. It could be a really hard thing for him if he knew the money was there but he wasn't allowed." She gave me a half-smile.

"Oh, man, what if that's it. I was a complete jerk to him, up in his face, telling him ...oh, wow. Thinking back on it, I wasn't nice. I got wrapped up in the heat of the moment." I dropped my chin and looked at the ground. And I had accused him of being the ass!

"Or maybe," said Divya, raising an eyebrow and twisting her mouth into a smirk, "he's a rebel who's secretly fallen in love with you, and now he has to make a choice on whether to stay with his rebel cause or go to the enemy's side so he can be with the woman he loves. Because now he has the opportunity, the money, to change everything. And, all that pent-up passion is what caused your 'heat of the moment.' I'm going with that version - it would make a great storyline for a movie. Think about it. I'm good."

Jessalyn and I looked at each other and just started laughing. The tension was gone.

"Only you, Div, would come up with something so absurd. You two always know what to say to make me feel better."

"Yeah, well my versions are always far more captivating than Jess's lame explanations." Divya winked at Jessalyn who just rolled her eyes and shook her head.

"Speaking of captivating, look who's checking you out." Divya nodded over my shoulder down the hall.

I flipped around. Ashton! "I haven't seen him around since Tuesday. I think he's been avoiding me."

"Don't assume the worst, Lyssa. Go talk to him. He clearly wants you to. He's standing alone at his locker and he's gawking at you." Jessalyn nudged me forward. "Do it."

"Yeah, go see what he's doing for spring break. Your dad would kill you if he found out you spent it with Ashton, but I bet it would be worth it." Divya gave me a shove that almost made me trip.

I turned around and shot her a look. "You don't think I'll do it, do you? Well, you guessed wrong today." Maybe it was all the adrenaline from the fight with Gabe, but I felt a new sense of confidence. Before I could really think about it and change my mind, I tossed my hair over my shoulder and shot a smile at Ashton. Both girls giggled and turned to watch as I walked toward him.

He was lounging against his locker. Long, lean, and muscular in all the right places. His hair was significantly lighter than his skin, giving him a kind of wild, sexy look. He had one hand in his pocket, and I walked right up to him, leaning in so our faces were less than a foot apart. I looked back at my friends. They thought I was all talk. Maybe usually, but not today. I needed to find somewhere to stay for a whole week. I wasn't sure that Ashton was the best idea, but I was running out of options.

I smiled, not a friendly how's-it-going smile, but a you-look-like-chocolate-and-I'm-hungry smile. At least, that was the smile I was trying to pull off.

I leaned to one side of his head, placing my hand on his chest, and whispered in his ear, "What's a girl gotta do to get a little attention around here?" Then I blew a small, warm breath into his ear. I heard his breath quicken, and felt his heart beneath my hand pick up the pace.

I leaned back a little to look in his eyes. His free hand came up and traced from my ear to my chin, and straight down until it ran into the top if my shirt, and I let out a small, audible gasp. He stopped at the fabric and looked down, then back up. His eyes looked smoky, and I thought that maybe I was in over my head. Okay, I knew I was in over my head.

He leaned to the side and whispered in my ear, "Babe. You've already got my attention." I swear I felt his tongue touch my ear. It made me jump a little, and I giggled nervously.

He leaned back and laughed, dropped his hand, and put it in his pocket. He stood up a bit straighter which adjusted for more space between us.

"You got plans for spring break?" I asked, feeling the moment was gone but trying to keep him interested.

"Why?" He licked his lower lip.

I tipped my head coyly to the side. "My family is going out of town. I thought maybe we could spend some time together, now that I'm almost completely Green."

"Wow." He looked me up and down. "Don't get me wrong. I am definitely interested. This is a side of you I haven't seen before. And I like it." He paused for a second, and my heart skipped another beat.

"But I've been invited to a huge party at one of the mega-hotels just outside of town. Grand opening for the super elite young adult crowd. I heard even Hunter Garrison from *G Cubed* is going to be there."

"Sounds fun." I scooted back toward him. "Surely a cool guy like you could bring somebody. I could be your 'plus one.' I mean, I don't eat a lot and I won't need to pack much, probably just a couple bikinis."

"We've definitely got to explore this side of you when I get back," he said in a low, breathy voice as his face moved closer to mine.

I moved away. "When you get back? As in 'no go' for me?"

He put his hand on my waist, and pulled me back toward him. "Whoa, girl, this is a Green-only thing. You know, I'm just thinking about you. Your eyes are beautiful, but I think it would be uncomfortable for you, you know, 'cause you're still so ...not totally Green yet. I don't want you to be embarrassed by the way you look, comparing yourself to all those gorgeous Green people. I'm trying to protect you here. I'm looking out for you." He smiled, flashing gorgeous white teeth, and leaned in toward me.

I pulled back a little so I could look into eyes. "Just looking out for my best interests, is that it?" I kept my voice syrupy sweet, but I could feel my jaw tightening up again. "Not 'cause you're on the hunt for some out-of-town Green babe, huh?" I batted my eyelashes at him.

"Well, you never can tell who you might meet at one of these things. There's always potential hook-ups. But when I get back, and you're completely Green, we will definitely party. Believe me, I'll rock your world, Babe." Then he brushed his lips against the end of my nose, moving down toward my lips, but, oops, I turned my head at the last second, and he got a mouthful of hair.

"Sorry about that, I thought I heard someone calling me." I stepped back, completely back, to where we were no longer touching. "So not now, but when I'm completely done with the Green process, then we can party together – go out together." I tried to hide the annoyance in my voice.

He smiled and winked, obviously missing my cynicism. "I knew you'd get it. Oh, sorry, Lyssa, gotta run. The guys are coming." He turned and started walking toward his friends who were coming down the hall.

I just stood there, staring after him, mouth gaping open. Again. Hadn't he left me like this before? But I didn't move.

Until my friends walked up and snapped me back to reality. "Ooooo – that totally looked promising," said Divya.

She wiggled her eyebrows and made little kissy noises with her lips.

"I'm beginning to think that all guys are jerks. Either they're crazy or they're creeps." I shook my head.

"What'd he say?" Jessalyn asked, concern in her voice.

"That we couldn't be together right now because I'm not completely Green yet so I'm not good enough, but when I finish going Green, then he'll be nice and show me a good time." I shot a dirty look down the hall. "And then he just walked away as soon as he saw his friends coming. I don't think he wants them to see him with me."

"Are you kidding me? What a jerk!" Jessalyn glared after him down the hall as well.

"Yeah, well, I guess one guy can't have it all. He's got the looks, but he's definitely missing out in the brains department if he thinks you're going to stand around waiting for him. Right?" Divya was glaring after him, too, then turned back to me. "Right?"

I sighed. "Yeah, right. Because I've got so many guys beating down my door right now." He did look good walking down the hall. Really good.

"Don't do it, Lyssa," Jessalyn said looking at me. "I can hear your resolve crumbling. Making excuses for him. Forgetting what a creep he just was because he looks so good in those jeans. You deserve more than that." Divya nodded, but she was still watching Ashton walk away, too.

Then the bell rang. "Be strong," Jessalyn said. "You deserve better." She and Divya both hugged me and then took off in opposite directions.

I do deserve more, I thought. *But maybe Divya is right. Maybe you can't have everything wrapped up in one package.*

Chapter 14

Symphony class, as usual, helped me forget everything, at least for a period. After we warmed up, Mr. Hazelbrook let us pick pieces that we wanted to play for each other. We had to tell the class a little about it, and then play a few minutes of it. When it was my turn, I chose the Zimmer piece. I simply said, "I learned this song when I was five to play for my mother. She never got to hear it." And then I picked up my bow and played.

The bow became my cello's voice and everything revolved around it. The low pitch accentuated the melancholy notes. The piece was deep and rich, vibrant in sound, producing an almost human-like voice as it floated through the room. Engulfed by the music, I dipped the bow into the strings and then drew it away from the bridge. Over and over. The notes went from light and wispy to harsh and intense. I thought about my mom as I played.

It's funny, how whenever I played this song, about eight notes in, there she was. This was when I could still feel her. Her voice, her touch, her laughter, her grace as she had played her violin. My memories of her danced on the music, swelling and dipping, celebrating and aching. And as my bow fervently pushed and pulled across the strings, each note bringing me closer to the end, I felt myself losing her all over again. When the song ended, when my bow drew that long, last note, she would be gone. And I would be alone again in silence.

It wasn't until I finished that I looked up, with tears in my eyes, and realized that I had played the whole piece rather than only a few minutes of it. Several students had tears running down their faces. The room was completely silent.

Then one girl stood up and applauded. One by one others rose to join her, until the whole class was clapping for me. I stood and bowed. I knew my cheeks were red, but it was okay. These people had seen the inner me, and they approved.

We listened to several more beautiful pieces, and when the period ended, I set my stuff out of the way, heading into the hall in search of Jessalyn. I saw her walking toward the music room, and from the look on her face – frowning mouth, wrinkled forehead, scrunched brows, and downcast eyes – I knew it wasn't good news.

"I'm so sorry, Lyssa. I can't talk them into it. We have a lot of relatives coming into town. Mom and Dad said I have to focus on helping out, both with the relatives and working in the store. I'm sorry. I tried. I did." Her shoulders sagged as she kicked at a loose wrapper on the floor. She looked like she was going to start crying.

"Don't worry about it. It's okay," I said giving her a hug, but thinking to myself, *What am I going to do?*

Divya joined us. "Oh, boy. Bad news, huh? Lyssa can't stay with you either, can she." She said it as a statement because she could read Jessalyn as easily as I could.

"What will you do, Lyssa? Livvy and your dad are both already gone, aren't they? You can't stay with Divya or me, and it didn't work out with Ashton, although that was probably for the best, so what are you going to do for the next eight days?" Jessalyn looked worried, her eyebrows even more deeply furrowed, like she was trying to figure out a mathematical problem that was harder than she expected. We all just stood there for a bit staring at each other.

Divya put her hand on my shoulder. "Don't stress about it, Lyssa. Something will work out." Divya and Jessalyn walked away, throwing out ideas of where I could go for the next eight days.

As I watched them walk away, Ana tapped me on the shoulder. "Sorry, Lyssa. Not trying to eavesdrop, but I couldn't help overhearing." She looked down at her jeans and nonchalantly brushed off something.

"If you don't have anywhere else, you could probably come stay with me. It wouldn't be as exciting as staying with your other friends. I live on a farm, so it's way different than the city. But we do have two extra bedrooms at our house, so you wouldn't be an inconvenience, and we don't have any plans because my dad is overseeing some planting and harvesting between several of our properties." She looked back up, crossed her arms, and shrugged her shoulders. "Spring's a pretty busy time for him, so we never go anywhere for spring break."

She bit the side of her lip slightly as she glanced away, then looked back at me. "I mean, only if you're interested – and I totally get it if you're not." She turned and started to walk away. "It was a stupid idea anyway. Never mind."

"Hey, Ana, that's super nice of you, but I don't want to get you in trouble with your family or put you guys out." She turned her head back toward me, tilting it to one side.

"It wouldn't be trouble but it won't be fun and exciting either. But, if you don't have anything else, at least it's an option for you." She casually adjusted her bag on her shoulder, and shifted her weight. She looked anxious even though I could tell she was trying hard to appear cool and I thought she was holding her breath.

"Okay. You check and let me know."

She exhaled. Her shoulders relaxed, and the bag slipped down her arm. She grabbed the strap and tossed it back over her shoulder. "All right, but only because you're practically begging me. Admit it, without me, you'd be left out in the cold all by yourself."

"Oh, so that's how it is. Don't put yourself out." I tried to sound serious, but I wasn't doing a very good job of it. My lips wiggled, but I was determined not to be the first to crack a smile.

"Fine." She broke into a grin. "I'll go talk to Hazelbrook to see if I can call home. My brother has an iBud, but I don't yet, so I'll have to go to the office." She dropped her stuff on a chair.

"I'd let you use mine," I said, "but I've got the new one with the built-in security feature for one owner in the brain recognition software. So it only works for me. Sorry."

"No worries. I'll let you know what I find out." And then she was off to talk to Mr. Hazelbrook.

When I checked after the bell rang, Ana wasn't back yet. Hazelbrook sent me to run some errands around the school for him, and by the time I got back, there were only a few minutes left of class. The students were all packing up, excited to be leaving for spring break. The classroom was crazy loud, and Hazelbrook must have been mentally done, too, because he wasn't even trying to quiet them down. He was just sitting at his desk with his feet up, hands interlaced behind his head, watching the chaos.

I walked over to his desk. "Everything's done," I said.

"As I expected it would be with you on the job, Lyssa." He looked around the classroom. "Too much energy to control. I figured I'd let it go." Then he looked back at me. "Do you have something fun planned for spring break?" he asked.

Just then Ana walked over to me. "It's all good, Lyssa. I talked to my grandma, she lives with us, and she said it would be 'great to have a friend out for spring break.' Can you believe that?" She rolled her eyes. "I'm sure it will be just 'great.' Remember, I'm not promising anything cool." She shrugged her shoulders and raised her eyebrows. "I mean, if you want to."

At that moment I realized I couldn't tell her no because, who was I kidding, where else was I going to go? Neither Divya nor Jessalyn had messaged me to tell that they had come up with anything, and if I went home and stayed alone, Livvy would have a fit. She'd get in big trouble with Father, and our house would be a war zone for who knows how long with Livvy's anger targeting me since I had promised I'd take care of things.

"I'm in," I said quickly, before she could talk herself out of having me over. "Can we run by my house and grab a few things before we go?"

"No problem. Let me go find my brother and tell him. He'll drive us to your house and then home. I'll meet you back here in a few minutes. Is that okay, Mr. Hazelbrook?" She waited until he nodded, then she grabbed her bag off a nearby desk and headed out the classroom door.

I looked back at Hazelbrook, noting an odd expression on his face.

"Does your father know that you're going home with Ana?" he asked.

That's a funny question for him to ask me, I thought. "No, he had to go out of town unexpectedly. My older sister did, too, and things got a little mixed up. But I like Ana. She's kind of like the little sister I never had, so I think it'll be fun to hang out on spring break together."

"Hmmm. So you're going to Ana's family's farm, and staying for a week, but your father doesn't know. You may want to talk with him about that. Up to you. You are eighteen now. And it will definitely be an experience for you." He brought his hand up and rubbed his chin. "I'll be interested to hear all about it when you get back."

"Okay," I said slowly. I felt a little uncomfortable, like he knew more than he was saying. "Mr. Hazelbrook, is there something wrong with going to that farm? Like is it dangerous or something?" I thought of all the recent media coverage. Rebel trouble outside of the city. *What have I gotten myself into?*

"Oh, no, I didn't mean it that way. Ana's family, they're good people. Very well-known in the business community, and in the science world, I believe." He looked thoughtful. "I just meant that farm life is very different from what you know here in SciCity."

I still felt as if he wasn't telling me everything, but right then the bell rang and I saw Ana trying to push through the gush of students flooding out of the door.

"Ready?" she asked as she made it past the last student. "My brother's coming right now. I told him I was bringing a friend home for spring break. He said it was fine as long as Nana Jane said it was okay. So we'll run to your house, and then head to the farm."

"Okay," I said to Ana. "Wish me luck," I whispered as I turned back to Mr. Hazelbrook. He just stretched as he stood up. "Bye, Ladies. Have fun."

Ana hooked her arm in mine and scooted us away from his desk. We waved as we headed out the door, turning the corner and almost taking someone out.

"Oh, sorry," I said as I bent over to grab the bag I had dropped.

I stood up and froze.

"Lyssa, this is my brother, Gabe Stayton. Gabe, this is Calyssa Brentwood, my friend coming home with us for spring break." Ana was all smiles. Gabe and I were not.

"We already know each other," Gabe said. Then, without another word, he turned around and headed for the main exit.

Chapter 15

Ana watched Gabe walk away, her mouth open. "You two know each other? I mean, I figured you might, but I've never heard either of you talk about the other one. And I've never seen Gabe act like that. He must have had a really bad day." She shook her head and looked toward the direction where Gabe had gone. "So, how do you know my brother?"

We began to walk toward the exit door. "We're in Human Biological Studies together. He just started coming to my class this week since he changed his tutoring schedule."

"Oh, yeah, he mentioned something about that. He's usually a pretty good guy. You know, for an older brother. We get along for the most part." Ana turned toward me as she walked. "Sorry, he was kinda rude. Usually he's a lot more talkative after school."

I stopped just before going outside. "Maybe this isn't such a good idea, Ana. I hate to disrupt your family. I can always go stay somewhere else," I said, but Ana quickly cut me off with a wave of her hand.

"No way. Nana Jane is expecting you now. If you don't show up because Gabe was a jerk, he'll be in loads of trouble. By going, you're actually doing him a favor. He's gonna owe you and he doesn't even realize it yet." Her eyebrows lifted. "But don't worry, I'll make sure he knows."

We laughed. Her laugh sounded happy, mine – not so much.

Oh, right. Going to the farm was a real favor to Gabe. He gets to spend the next week with a girl he can't stand, who tried to bite his head off in class – who he thinks is stupid. Well, I'll show him. Maybe it'll be good for him to be a little uncomfortable for a while.

Gabe rumbled up in a car I had never seen before. Actually, I wasn't even sure it was a car. It was huge and super loud, not at all sleek and silent like Livvy's Angel. "Open," I said as I walked up to the door. Nothing happened. Ana laughed at me. She took my school bag and gently tossed both of our bags over the side into the back of the vehicle. I hoped they'd be safe back there.

"Sorry, Lyssa. You've got to do everything by hand with this old truck." She grabbed a silver piece of metal on the door, lifted it, and the door opened. *Hmmmm, so this is a truck. Well, this will be – interesting.*

Gabe sat inside. Silent. Looking straight ahead. Awesome.

"Jump up in there," she said to me.

I looked up at the seat, and back at Ana. My eyes darted around. *Too late to run,* I thought.

"Maybe you should go first." I didn't want to sit next to Gabe, and as far as I could tell, there was only one seat, with barely enough room for three people to sit right next to each other.

"Nah, you go ahead. You won't know how to work the door or the window or anything. Besides, if you sit by Gabe, you can see the gauges and he can tell you all about how it runs. This truck's his baby. He brought it back to life out of an old junkyard. Even makes his own fuel for it. Bio – bio – what's the fuel called, Gabe?" Ana angled her head sideways, peering around me to see him.

"Biodiesel." Flat. Monotonous. Still staring straight forward out the window.

Yep, this is a huge mistake, I thought.

Ana stood with her hand on the door. "Just waiting for you." She smiled, motioning toward the door. "Jump on up there."

I took a deep breath. I was sure I was going to be doing that a lot in the next eight days. Then I hoisted myself up into this monster vehicle. There was no delicate way to do it. I half-jumped, half-pulled, and then added a wiggle and a twist to get myself up onto the seat. I could have sworn that I saw Gabe smirk, but when I looked back again, he was still just sitting there staring out the front window.

We started to pull out and Ana yelped for Gabe to stop. He slammed on the brakes and my head came about an inch from smacking the dash in front of me.

"What?" He didn't sound happy.

"I almost forgot my violin. I have to go back and get it. If I don't bring it home to practice over break, Nana Jane will be absolutely unbearable. She threatened me with a list of chores that no human could finish in a whole week." Rolling her eyes, she shoved her shoulder into the door to swing it back open. Then she paused, door wide open. "This is ridiculous. I'm going to have company. I should leave it here and tell her I forgot it." She started to close the huge door again.

Gabe shot a look at Ana. "Forgot it? Are you kidding? No way. Get in there and go get it. I heard you promise Nana Jane last night. Don't be a flake."

Ouch. I think Gabe might be misdirecting some of his anger at me toward Ana. I looked at Gabe. "You know what? I'll go grab my cello, too. I shouldn't be taking a week off practicing either." I looked at Ana. "We can practice together."

"Uggggh! Don't side with Gabe." She crossed her arms. But the truck didn't move. "Fine. Whatever. We can if you really want to." I didn't even have to look to know that there was more eye rolling from Ana. "Stay here, Lyssa. I can grab them both. It'll be quicker if I just run back in."

Ana slid out and dropped to the ground. "I'll be just a couple of minutes." Then, turning back one more time, "Be nice while I'm gone, Gabe." She shot him a look, slammed the truck door and took off for the school.

Silence. I couldn't take it anymore. I turned my whole body toward him in the seat.

"Listen, Gabe. When Ana asked me to come stay with her this week, I had no idea you were her brother. This has nothing to do with you. I like your sister. I've been an aide in her class this whole year, and she has talent. Real potential. Just because you hate me, for whatever reasons you have in your crazy mind, don't take it out on her. She doesn't deserve it." *I don't think I deserve it either, but that's probably more than I should hope for right now.*

Gabe finally looked at me. "You're sure this is not some sort of stunt – using my sister to try to get close to me? To convert me to going Green or something?" He was dead serious.

I couldn't help myself. I burst out laughing. That made him look angry and that just made me laugh harder. I was laughing so hard that there were tears in my eyes. In reality, it probably wasn't that funny, but it struck me as so bizarre that I couldn't stop. That, and the fact that I was nervous about being back with Gabe again after our argument earlier today.

"Knock it off." Gabe was scowling. "I mean it. This isn't funny."

"Well – really – it is – I – can't believe – that you – think – I would go – through – all – of – this – just to – be – with you." I could hardly talk I was laughing so hard.

"It's not that crazy of an assumption. Your dad is the CEO of AHGA. I'm probably one of the smartest students at school. How do I know you're not trying something for him?"

"Like – what?" I was starting to get it under control. Little spurts of laughter were coming out now. "How could I make you do anything – you don't want to do? I mean – look at you and then – look at me. I don't think I'll be wrestling you to the ground – taking you hostage any time soon. I'll leave that kind of stuff to the rebels." One more snicker as I thought about that scenario.

Gabe stared at me. "Okay, when I say it out loud like that, it doesn't sound quite as sinister as it did in my mind."

I wiped my eyes. "Can we start over? We have a whole week to get to know each other now. The real you and real me. No pressure about going Green. I promise. I'll stay out of your way if that's what you want, but I really do like Ana. You're lucky to have such a cool little sister. My older sister is not so – nice."

"All right, I guess I can give you another shot. Not that you deserve it." He grinned. It wasn't a full out smile, but it was a start.

Ana opened the door. "Hey, I grabbed both of our instruments. Gabe, wanna help me put them in the back? I don't think I should toss Lyssa's cello over the side." She looked from me to Gabe then back to me. "Did I miss something? Never mind. I don't even want to know. I'm just happy that you're done giving each other dirty looks."

Gabe went around the truck to help Ana put our instruments in the back. They both loaded back up and slammed their doors. "Where to? Ana said you have to grab a few things. Just a few, right?"

"Yeah, don't worry. I'll be quick." I gave him directions. "Seat belt," I automatically commanded. "Oops. Keep forgetting that won't work." Gabe shot another look at Ana, and then she showed me how to "buckle myself in."

The ride in the truck was a little scary at first. I mean, I never realized there were so many bumps in the road. I felt every single one, bouncing around like a ping-pong ball. I white-knuckled the seat around the corners, and held my breath every time we needed to stop. This thing was huge. We could have plowed over most other vehicles on the road. About fifteen minutes later, we pulled up in front of my house.

"Wow. This is cool. I bet you have all the most current tech." Ana jumped out and I followed her.

"You can come in if you want. You, too, Gabe." I looked back in at him.

"No thanks. Go ahead, Ana. I know you want to. But hurry up. We still have a long drive home. And Ana, just because Calyssa's coming with you doesn't mean that Dad is going to let you out of your chores. We have a lot to do when we get home." Ana ignored him and closed the truck door, following me up to the house.

I stopped at the eye scanner at the door, leaned in, waited for the scan, then the door slid open. Ana followed me in and the door slid closed behind us. "Whoa. Super cool house."

"Feel free to look around. I'm gonna run to my room and throw a few things in a bag. It's just down there." I pointed down the hall and then took off toward my bedroom. *What would I need on a farm? How would I know? I've only seen "a farm" in pictures.*

I grabbed a few of everything out of my closet, some shoes and jewelry, and my make-up. Looking back around the room, I saw my old memory bracelet. Livvy had recently given me a newer model, the one I was wearing now, after she got tired of it. But my old one still worked great as well, so I grabbed it and threw it in my bag. Just in case I wanted to take more pictures.

Ana walked in as I finished. "I love your house. Ooo, and your room." She walked over and sat on my bed. Bounced a little.

"Thanks." I scanned the room one more time. "We better get going. I don't want Gabe ticked off that we took too long. I'd hate to see what driving angry would be like in that truck."

Ana lay back on the bed. "Can I come back and visit you sometime?"

"Absolutely." I grabbed her hand and pulled her back to her feet. "Wait a minute. Come over here." I dropped my bag on the floor and walked over to my mirror. "Come here. Stand right next to me."

"Oh, wow! Don't tell me you have a digital enhancer? I've wanted one of these forever." Ana smiled at herself in the mirror, running her hand through straight, dark blond hair, batting her lashes over big, soft brown eyes.

"Ready? I want to record us together. Just look straight ahead."

"Record loop, Ana and Lyssa, Spring Break," I spoke toward the enhancer. We both gave our best smiles, then turned to look at each other, and then back to our reflections in the mirror. After about twenty seconds, I said, "Stop loop." I turned to Ana. "Now I'll have that forever. I'll make you a copy and send it to you when I get back home."

"Sweet!" Ana picked my bag up. "I got this. Let's go."

At the door, I stopped in front of a panel. "Record message," I said. A green light went on at the top of the panel.

"Hey, Livvy or Father, whoever gets this first. I thought I was going to be staying with Divya or Jessalyn, but I have a super cool opportunity to go home with another friend for spring break. Her name is Ana Stayton. We're in music class together at school. We're heading out to the farm where she lives. I hope you both had a great trip. See you at the end of the week. Love you." I touched the panel and the light went off.

"Just in case they get back before I do," I said to Ana.

Then I tapped in a code on the panel, the door slid open, and a voice came on that said, "Security will be set in thirty seconds. Please stand clear of the door." We walked through and back to the truck.

Gabe sat tapping his fingers on the steering wheel. "I was beginning to wonder if you two had decided to stay here for spring break instead." With a thunderous roar, the truck started back up.

"Maybe next year." I winked at Ana as she threw my bag in back and then followed me up on the seat. With a heave, she hauled the door shut.

"Whatever." Gabe pulled out and started down the road. "On to the farm. Hope you know what you're in for, Calyssa. No more city." He glanced at me.

"I'm ready," I said. *I mean, really, how different can it be?*

Chapter 16

It took about twenty minutes for us to get out of SciCity. Gabe messed with a knob and some buttons in front of him on the panel. I jumped when the news came on. Obviously, I needed to relax. Top story of the hour was, of course, about more rebel activity, new issues at the outskirts of the city.

"We don't have anything to worry about at your farm, do we?" I asked.

Gabe and Ana glanced at each other. "You mean with the rebels?" he asked. I nodded.

He shook his head. "No, we don't have any rebel trouble." Then he pressed a couple more buttons, and the news changed to music. Ana immediately started singing along, bouncing in her seat and bumping into me. I joined in. Dance party in the truck. Gabe just shook his head.

After about five more minutes, I settled back and enjoyed the ride as we drove for about another twenty minutes or so to get to their farm. I had read somewhere that "life is not measured by the number of breaths you take, but by the moments that take your breath away."

I hadn't realized how true that was until today. "Breath-taking" was the only way to describe the view. I tried to stay involved in Gabe and Ana's conversations, but I kept getting sidetracked by the scenery around me.

It was like looking at a digital story display. Craggy mountains in the distance that pressed toward the sky. Trees so tall I had to crane my head back to try to see the tops. Fields with grasses that billowed softly in the wind. Flowers grew at the sides of the road in gentle pinks and bright yellows. A stream meandered its way along the valley floor.

No hustle, no bustle, no tech. Completely peaceful. *How odd,* I thought, *that we buy all types of tech in the city to help us feel relaxed in our own homes, and yet here, with none of that, peace seems to radiate from everything.*

"We're only a few miles from the farm now." I realized that Ana was talking to me.

"Sorry. I zoned out again. I just can't get over how beautiful it is out here." I smiled and turned to look back out the window. I didn't know if I would ever get used to all this beauty in one place.

I shook my head and tried to focus on the road in front of us. "Who's going to be at your farm this week?" I asked.

"Well," Ana said, "Nana Jane is our grandma. She's always around. And, of course our dad. His name is Andrew. He'll probably still be working when we get there. Oh, and our little brother, Ben. He's ten."

"There may be some farm hands around throughout the week, too," Gabe added, "but they usually don't come to the main house."

"You have more than one house?"

"Well, yeah. But we only have one that we live in." Gabe pointed out toward the left. "Stayton Farms actually consists of six separate locations. One smaller location is just over that knoll there. All our farms are in the GMO free zone. Each location has a main house, and then a couple other smaller houses where the people who are working there can stay.

"Our farm is the 'main farm.' We have some livestock, most of the grain fields and bee colonies, and a good sized garden. The other locations specialize in different things, like producing legume crops, breeding cattle, cultivating potatoes, and raising feed for all of our animals. We even have a farm that specializes in developing and utilizing natural energy sources, like solar and wind power. We're pretty much self-sustaining here."

"Wait a minute, you don't get your energy or your food from SciCity?" I was having a hard time wrapping my mind around this as well as about half of the words Gabe had just used.

"Nope, we produce what we need and we sell the extra to others. That's how a farm works, Calyssa. Have you never been on a farm before?"

"Seriously, Gabe. Why would Lyssa have been on a farm? You should have seen her house. She had everything she needed inside her house." Ana nudged me with her elbow. "Right, Lyssa?"

"Maybe, but not like this." *Not even close*, I thought.

Gabe turned off the main road, following a smaller, curvy road up a slight hill. As we crested the top, I got my first look at the main Stayton farm. There was a massive, pale yellow house directly in front of us. To the right were several large red buildings, and to the left were fields as far as I could see. "What's in the red buildings?"

"Livestock mostly: one houses our horses, one is for the cattle that we keep here, and another has hogs. The furthest one back usually has pieces of farm equipment in it, and that's where Dad and I work on anything that breaks down. I make my biodiesel out there for my truck, too." Gabe eased the truck to a stop in front of the house.

An older woman with soft silver hair and a young boy in a baseball cap came out on the porch. She put one hand over her eyes, shading them from the sun, and used the other to tuck strands of wispy waves that escaped from her ponytail behind her ear. Her face looked worn and weathered, but her eyes twinkled. The little guy just stood there, staring at us, dark eyes with long, dark lashes.

We got out of the truck and went around the back. Gabe somehow lowered the back wall of the truck. I grabbed my bags, and Gabe and Ana grabbed the instruments.

"Well, you must be Calyssa Brentwood. I'm Jane Rutherforse, but everyone around here calls me Nana Jane. Please feel free to do the same. And this is Ben. Ben, say hello to Calyssa."

"Hello." His voice was soft and very serious. *Probably a little scared of strangers,* I thought.

"Hello, Ben. And Nana Jane. Thank you for letting me spend spring break at your farm."

"Absolutely. Any friend of Ana and Gabe is welcome at our house. Ana said this is your first visit to a farm. That right?"

"Yeah, I haven't been outside of SciCity much."

"Well then, this is going to be a real treat for you." Nana Jane squinted out toward the other buildings, then held out her hand to Ben. "Ana, Gabe, why don't you take Calyssa on a quick tour of the farm. Your dad's still out in the fields. Gabe, while you're out, your dad wanted you to check on the hives and then join him over at the far west pen. They've been having some trouble with the gate functioning correctly over there."

"Yes, Nana." Gabe started up the stairs to the porch.

"Lyssa, do you want to go look around?" Ana asked. "We definitely don't have to if you don't want to."

"I'd love to see more. There's so much out here. It's amazing."

"Well, you three go on then. Ana, bring Calyssa back to the house when you're done and she can get set up in one of the spare bedrooms upstairs. Why don't you just set your things on the front porch for now, and you can bring them in after you look around a bit."

After we'd set everything on the porch, Gabe recommended that we walk out to the hives first, then he could head out to help his dad, and Ana and I could visit some of the livestock barns. I was excited to see the animals. Ana said the cows and the horses were her favorites.

"Oh, I adore cows, too. I have one at home. Lulu. She's a real doll. I would have showed her to you, but Livvy boarded her out at a pet spa for the week since we're all gone. If she would have been home, she would have been at the door to meet us. Lulu loves company."

"You have a cow that lives in your house?" Ana and Gabe looked shocked.

"Well, where does your cow live?" I asked.

"First of all," Gabe said, "we have about fifty cows at this farm. More at the others. And they stay in the fields during the day and usually in one of the barns at night."

"Fifty? Whoa! How do you have time to take care of all of them? And doesn't it get too cold for them at night out here? I mean, I know Lulu may be spoiled, but she loves to sleep with me every night."

Now, it was Gabe and Ana's turn to look confused. "You sleep with a cow, too?" Ana shook her head. I laughed at Ana's continued surprise.

"Of course, she loves to cuddle. Hold on, let me find a good picture of her on my memory bracelet so you can see her." I scanned through some photos until I found one that I liked. "Here she is. Isn't she adorable? It was taken last year. That's Lulu sitting on my lap."

Lulu had been a present for Livvy and me from Father a couple of months after Mom died. Someone told him that a pet would be good therapy for us while we were learning to deal with our loss. He brought Lulu home from work with him one night.

Livvy and I had immediately fallen in love with her. I mean, what little girl wouldn't absolutely love a little knee-high cow with long, bright pink hair that grew from the top of her head and down her neck. The soft hair seemed almost human, and Livvy and I used to curl it, or crimp it, or straighten it, depending on what new look we wanted to try out. Lulu just stood there and let us play with her hair for hours. Just seeing those long eyelashes made me want to kiss her nose.

Ana and Gabe looked at the picture, looked at each other, and then back at the picture again. When they both looked back at me, they had huge smiles on their faces.

"What?"

"Cute cow," Gabe said. "Just wait until you see ours."

Chapter 17

Gabe led the way across a field. The plants were about waist high, and I walked with my hands out, feeling their tops brush gently against my palms. It tickled a little. The sun was warm on my face, lower in the sky, but still shining intensely. Wind blew softly around us, causing the plants to dance slowly, gently, bending ever so slightly one way, then the other.

I snapped several pictures with my memory bracelet, trying to capture the beauty that filled every inch that I could see. Grabbing that second bracelet had been an excellent idea. Just telling my friends about this would never do it justice. I'd have to show them.

Gabe and Ana were talking again, but I wasn't listening to them. Instead, I listened to all the sounds around me. The swish of the plants as we walked through them, the whisper of the wind as it occasionally lifted my hair, the songs of birds that I couldn't identify as they darted past with grace and speed, and very softly, as if somewhere in the distance, a creek bubbled as it raced over rocks that I couldn't see.

Everything smelled fresh and clean. A natural clean, not like cleaners or air fresheners, or the laundry after it had been cleaned with an "outdoor fresh scent." That was a lie. It didn't smell anything like this. I stopped for a minute, closed my eyes, and tipped my head back. Felt, listened, and smelled.

"Calyssa, you coming?" I opened my eyes. Gabe was staring at me. I jogged a bit to catch up with them.

"Sorry. Just soaking it all up."

We slowed down as we approached several small, white buildings. I jumped back and swatted the air as I felt something whiz by my face.

Gabe grabbed my arm. "Stand still. Don't flail around and you'll be fine."

As I looked more closely, I could see insects flying everywhere. "Are those all bees?" I asked. My eyes darted from building to building as I noticed, hundreds, no, thousands of insects, moving through the air. The area was literally abuzz with activity.

"Yep. Our farm maintains the latest tech in electronic hives to monitor our colonies. We use entrance counters to monitor the coming and going of every bee. Pressure transducers track changes in hive weight, and automatic traps empty into time-sensitive trays that document the bees' pollen gathering.

"We also have sensors that follow the bees' efforts to stabilize the temperature and humidity once inside, and other sensors that measure sound. We can even track airflow with digital indicators that measure fanning activity as the bees attempt to cool the hive and drive off excess moisture from newly harvested nectar. All of it helps us keep our bee populations healthy, which naturally increases our crop production."

"Gabe, seriously, we're not in science class here. Give us a break. We're on vacation, remember?" Ana then turned to me. "We don't have to stay. We can head out whenever you want. The bees are Gabe's and Dad's thing. Personally, I don't like to get too close." She scrunched her nose. "I don't know how they can stand to let the bees walk all over them." She shuddered.

I looked at Gabe, astonished. "You let them land on you? And walk on you? Like on purpose?" I couldn't believe it.

Gabe shrugged his shoulders. "It's not a big deal. I've grown up with the bees all my life."

He turned back toward the buildings that I realized must have housed the hives. "In fact," he said, "when my dad was young, he was the one who developed the electronic bee robots that helped re-stabilize the bee colonies today."

"I thought your dad's a farmer."

"He is, but his college background is in research and design in electrical nano-engineering. It comes in useful on the farms."

I must have looked lost because then he said, "You know, he can program really small computers. It's how he made the robobees. Mechanical worker bees programmed to live and work with other bees in a specific colony. They can communicate with the other worker bees, providing support for a weak colony and actually training them to work the areas where we want them to stay. Almost everyone uses robobees in their hives now."

"You train bees?" Where was I? I had never heard of this tech. And we always knew about the latest tech at my house.

Gabe laughed again. I'm not sure I liked how much he laughed at me out here. "We program and manage the microcomputer that runs each robobee so it can communicate with the real bees at the hive. It tells them where they need to go to find food for survival, and it keeps them pollinating the areas where we want them focused. It's important to us to keep our bees in the GMO free zone, otherwise they might cross-pollinate with fields experimenting with genetic modifications. We don't do that kind of stuff out here."

Ana rolled her eyes and looked bored. "Yeah, Gabe's a real bee whisperer. Don't ask any more questions or we'll never escape. I swear, he'll keep you here forever if he thinks you're listening, captive audience and all that."

Okay, I thought. *So much for non-Green people only being poor, uneducated workers that don't make any real contributions to better our society. The Staytons have blown that idea out of the water.* Livvy would never believe this. I wondered about what other totally off-base assumptions I had grown up with. As Ana grabbed my hand and led me away from the bees, I was pretty sure that I was well on my way to finding out.

Chapter 18

We left Gabe there, taking digital notes on a tech pad that he had pulled from his pocket. "How long will it take him to finish up with the bees?" I asked as we moved back across the field toward one of the big red buildings.

"Oh, not too long with the bees, but then he has to go find Dad to help with a pen gate they've been messing with for the past few days."

"A pen? Out in the field? What?" Confusion. Again. Seriously.

"Oh, Lyssa, you crack me up. You know, a pen, like a big caged-in area where they can round up the livestock. The gate keeps sticking open, then everything gets out, and that kinda defeats the purpose. It's a tech issue, I think. You know how crazy new tech can be."

"That I do know about," I said as I nodded my head. *Maybe the only thing I understood out here.*

As we headed toward the closest red building, I noticed a different smell. I covered my nose and mouth with my hand. "What is that?"

Ana looked at me as we walked. "Oh, you mean the smell. That's our cows."

Wow, the Stayons really need to put their cows through an autocleaning cycle in the shower a little more often. "I've got some super awesome, neutralizing, deodorant powder that I use on Lulu at home. I'll give you the name of it. It'll help with that smell."

"Okay." Ana just smiled. I didn't think that stinky pets were a joke. It was totally preventable and much more enjoyable when they smelled nice. I couldn't imagine lying in bed with Lulu if she smelled like that.

"I'll show you my favorite cow. Her name is Bella. We've raised her since she was a calf." Ana heaved open a huge door. *There must be a lot of cows out here. Way more than fifty. Maybe Gabe meant a hundred and fifty.*

As I followed Ana, my eyes adjusted to the light. There were wood partitions along the walls that made partial little rooms. The first few were empty except for what looked like old, dried-out grass spread around in the bottom of them.

"Oh, here she is." Ana disappeared around one of the partitions ahead of me.

I stepped around the partition, then immediately twisted backward as my heart tried to jump out of my chest.

"What the ...!" My feet were moving faster than my brain, and although I couldn't take my eyes off the most gigantic, colossal monster of a cow-shaped creature that I had ever seen, the bottom half of me was trying to go backward while my top half wouldn't turn away from the mass in front of me.

In my contorted attempt to scramble away, I tripped over something long and metal, sending it clattering across the room into a couple other metal items, knocking them over as well. The clanging of all the metal made me jump again, banging into the partition, causing a bunch of rope to fall. Attempting to move away, my foot got tangled in the rope, sending me sprawling backward across the floor. Still staring at the gigantic creature, I triple kicked the rope off my foot, then scooted backward on my hands and feet, my butt dragging on the ground, until I hit a wall behind me, which made me jump and yelp one more time.

"Lyssa! Lyssa! It's okay!" Ana yelled at me. She ran toward me, reaching me about the time I hit the wall.

My heart was racing. My hands, knees, and butt were stinging. And, my eyes stayed glued to the enormous creature in front me.

"That is not a cow!" I yelled. "Seriously – I have a cow! I know what a cow is! And that's not it!"

Ana kneeled down beside me. "I'm so sorry, Lyssa. I didn't mean to startle you. It's okay. It's just Bella. And, she really is a cow. She's a dairy cow. She produces milk for our farm."

I looked around Ana. Actually, now that my heart was finally slowing down, I noticed it did kind of look like Lulu. On steroids. Tons of steroids. And lots of genetic engineering.

Ana put out her hand and helped me up. I looked down. I was filthy. I brushed myself off some and followed Ana tentatively back over toward the beast.

The whole time, it never moved. It had just been looking at me. Chewing on something. Watching me with its big brown eyes. Batting its long eyelashes. *Huh, like Lulu's.* I looked more closely. It did look like Lulu, minus the size and without the beautiful, long, pink hair. "What happened to its hair?" I asked.

"What do you mean?" Ana stood right next to it, petting it, stroking the immense body. She turned to look at me. "Oh, you mean like your little cow's pink hair?"

I nodded.

"Real cows don't have hair like that. Yours must be some kind of GMO cow. This is how cows are found in nature, like, how they've always been. We basically have cows for two reasons. Some give us milk. Others are butchered for meat. I don't think your type of cow would be very good for either." I shook my head. I definitely was not milking or eating Lulu.

"Lulu must be something one of your dad's scientists came up with." She picked up a brush and started to stroke Bella's side. The cow mooed softly, nuzzling Ana's arm with its nose. "Bella, that tickles." She giggled.

"Yeah, I guess Lulu is a GMO. She must have been engineered to be a house pet. I never really thought about where she actually came from. This is incredible." I took a couple of hesitant steps closer.

"Come here. You can pet her, even brush her if you want to. She's super nice. My favorite. Not all the cows are so gentle and friendly, but Bella is special. Don't be afraid."

I took in a deep breath, then blew it out. *I can do this.* I walked over next to Ana, and slowly, carefully, gently, reached out and touched Bella's giant side. It was warm – soft, but still a little scratchy – and it made my hand look like it should have belonged on a baby. She turned her nose toward me and blew out a huge breath. "Whoa!" I jumped back again. Ana laughed.

"It's okay. She's just smelling you, checking to see if you brought her any treats. She'll eat right out of your hand if you let her. Wanna try it?"

"No thanks," I said quickly. "I like my hands the way they are."

Ana laughed more. "She won't bite you. Bella doesn't eat people, do you, Girl?" she said as she continued to brush her.

"No, thanks anyway. I'm good." *That's one risk I'm not ready to take yet. Maybe Bella only likes the taste of city people.* A little quiver ran down my spine.

I did finally brush Bella for a bit. She seemed gentle. She just stood there the whole time, seeming to listen to Ana and me talk about what other "animals" were on this farm. I told her I didn't know if my heart could take any more gigantic surprises.

We left the first building and went to the next one. It was full of horses. I had seen these before on quick flicks and digital motion stories, but not in real life. It was cool when I saw a couple of the farm hands ride in. We stayed and watched, and I took more pictures, as they hopped down, took off the mounted seats (or saddles as Ana called them), then brushed the horses down before putting them into their "stalls" for the evening. The farm hands, two men and a woman, were nice and answered all the questions that I asked them about their jobs and riding the horses.

I also saw the hogs, which smelled even worse than the cows, and the chickens, which I didn't trust because, seriously, they just had a weird, wild look in their eyes, like they might chase after you at any given minute. The cows did seem the nicest. And maybe the horses.

Ana asked if I wanted to go riding at some point over the break. It didn't look too hard, but, well, I told her that I would have to think about it more before I'd make that commitment. She laughed. I was a regular comedian here on the farm.

We left the barns and walked toward the house. "Does your mom not live with you guys?"

Ana kept looking straight ahead. "She died when I was little."

"Oh, I'm sorry," I said, but she interrupted me before I could say anything else.

"It's okay. Nana Jane is great. And Dad is pretty cool most of the time, too. I don't get to see him so much right now because of how busy he is. It's better later in the year." I could tell she was changing the subject, but I was okay with that. I knew how hard it was to lose a parent and then have other people want to talk about it. If she didn't want to talk about it, we wouldn't talk about it.

"Your little brother is cute. Ben, right?" Ana nodded. "He doesn't go into the city with you and Gabe to go to school?"

"No, Ben has some trouble learning. He's super smart in math. He can do all that kind of stuff in his head. But he doesn't talk much, so Dad and Nana Jane decided to homeschool him." She glanced back toward the fields.

"Nana works with him during the day when Gabe and I are at school. They do writing, and reading, and history, that kind of stuff. Then he usually works with Dad some in the afternoons, on science stuff, and the tech that needs to be checked on around the farm. He's good at looking at how things work and then noticing if something is out of place so it can't do its job right." We had reached the porch and Ana stopped.

"Nana says that's what makes him so special, his gift to focus so intently on something in order to figure out the answer. He's a pretty serious little kid. I love him to pieces," she said.

"I bet you're an amazing big sister." *How cool would it be to have a big sister that loves you like Ana loves Ben? I thought.*

"Let's grab your stuff and put it in your room." She grabbed our instruments and I picked up the bags. I followed Ana through the front door.

The house was beautiful. Everything was done in cherry woods, smoky blacks and marbled grays. High ceilings made it feel spacious and airy. Big windows were on every wall, allowing sunlight to cascade into the living spaces. We crossed a small foyer that had a bench by the door and headed up the stairway.

"Wow. It's amazing in here." I stopped to look around and take it all in.

"It's not super cool like your house, but it's okay." Ana continued up the steps.

At the top, we turned right and went to the end of the hall. Ana stood in a doorway on one side. "This is my room. Yours is right there, across from mine. We already passed Ben's and Gabe's." She nodded back at the rooms we had walked by as we came down the hall. "Nana Jane's room was the first one at the top of the stairs, and you turn the other way to get to Dad's bedroom, as well as the other guest bedroom."

She took her bag from me and set it down in her room along with her instrument, then she walked with me into the guest bedroom and set my cello down. "My bathroom is right next to my room. I suggest you use it. There's another between Gabe's and Ben's rooms, but I won't guarantee what you'll find in there."

"Sweet. This room is great. I love all the blues, and what an awesome bed." I sat down on it. "And super comfortable, too. Thanks again for rescuing me and asking me to stay with you this week. I love it here." I looked around. Even in the house, everything felt calm and peaceful.

"Let's head downstairs. Maybe we can get a quick snack from Nana in the kitchen, then we can figure out what you want to do next." Ana walked to the door. "And Lyssa, thanks for coming."

I followed her back down the hall, noting that both Gabe's and Ben's rooms looked pretty tidy to me. I couldn't have imagined that their bathroom would have been a mess, but who knew, they were guys after all.

We reached the top of the stairs. I hadn't noticed before that above the front door were more huge windows that went all the way to the ceiling and looked out over the farm. *That's what made it so light in here, even upstairs,* I thought. *Standing here you can look out and see for miles.*

I wonder what Gabe's doing right now? Huh? Why am I even thinking about Gabe? And why did I wonder if he had been thinking about me?

My thoughts were interrupted by Nana Jane's voice.

"Ana, downstairs, on the double." She sounded like she meant business.

Chapter 19

Nana Jane and Ben met us at the bottom of the stairs. Nana Jane had a towel in one hand and the other hand on her hip. Ben stood silently next her, but no cap now. His hair was about the same color as Gabe's, and he wore that same serious look that Gabe often had as well.

"Ana, friends over or not, rules are rules. I need the dishes dried and put away. It'll only take a few minutes if you get on it right now." Then looking at me she added, "When you're done, would you girls like to make some cookies with me?'

"Oh, Nana. Lyssa doesn't want to be stuck in the kitchen for the next hour." Ana had a disgusted look on her face as she took the towel.

I turned to Ana. I wasn't sure why Nana Jane wanted my help to unload an automate, but I thought we could spare a few minutes. "Oh, it's okay, Ana. Would you like me to help take the cookies out of your automate?"

"Um, Lyssa, we don't have an automate. Nana insists on cooking like back in the ancient days. Dad said he would get the new tech installed, but Nana won't hear of it. Not in *her* kitchen." Ana wrinkled her nose.

"What do you mean?" Why was it that I felt totally out of touch here? It seemed like I didn't know anything about anything. *Seriously.*

"You don't *have* to do this, Lyssa. Nana is always trying to get Ben and me in there with her. And Gabe, too, when he's home. It's just a chore – it's not that cool. Really. I'm sure you would much rather do just about anything else." Ana shot a look at Nana Jane, pleading silently with her.

"Ummmm – Nana, Ana – I really don't know what you're talking about."

"Of course not, Lyssa. You shouldn't have to do all of that old-time stuff. It's totally outdated. Just let me dry up a few dishes and we'll go hang out in my room." Ana turned to walk toward the kitchen.

"Wait a minute, Ana. Nana Jane, what do you do? I mean, to actually make cookies?"

Nana Jane's head tipped to the side, both hands on her hips.

"You've really never made home-baked cookies?" She shook her head. "Well, let me tell you, we do it the right way here on the Stayton farm. With real milk and butter from our cows. And real flour from grain grown in our fields. The cookies are all natural, all GMO free.

"And the smell that fills the house – that smell of homemade cookies baking, like the laughter of small children, is indescribable in the way it fills your soul with happiness. It's the way the sweet smell fills your nose, the way the warm, rich flavor melts on your tongue and fills your mouth with a gooey, soft sensation. When you swallow, it simply makes your whole body feel satisfied. There's no doctor, no exercise, no meditation, medication or treatment that will wipe away all that troubles you better than indulging yourself in baking cookies."

I stared back at Nana Jane. "Let's do it," I said turning toward the kitchen.

Nana Jane turned toward Ben. "Okay, then. Get on into the kitchen and wash up. I think this is going to be an adventure."

I could have sworn I glimpsed a small smile slide across Ben's face before he darted past us through the kitchen door. I looked at Ana. She simply shrugged her shoulders and sighed with resignation, joining Ben and Nana in the kitchen.

Just as I was about to follow, Gabe came in the front door, a smear of dirt on his face and several more on his shirt. He moved slowly to the bench just inside the door and stiffly began pulling off his dusty, worn boots, sighing. When he looked up, he saw me standing there watching him. I glanced away quickly, but I knew that he knew I was watching him. I felt my neck and face turning red. He laughed. At me. Again.

I stared back defiantly at him, chin up. Red-faced or not, I looked him in the eye. "Did you get the cage fixed?" I asked.

He looked smug. "Cage? Oh, you mean the pen? Yeah, it'll hold for now until I can help Dad design something better. I think I can come up with a new trigger to change up the gate – never mind – you're glazing over already." He leaned over to finish with his boots.

Me? Blushing again. *Seriously*. I was a confident woman with skills that he couldn't even dream of and he made me feel like a silly little girl. "No. Go ahead. I'm interested in learning more about your gate trigger." I stared intently at him. And we sat there like that for an uncomfortable ten seconds. Then fifteen. Then twenty. I felt the heat moving up my neck one more time. Well, maybe just another shade of red because I'm sure I had never stopped blushing since Gabe had walked in the door.

Ana walked back in. "Whoa! Wait a minute – what did I miss here? Gabe, are you hitting on Lyssa?" Her eyes were huge as she pursed her lips and crossed her arms across her chest, foot tapping on the floor.

Now it was Gabe's turn. I believe an immediate and intense scarlet would be the best description for the color that rapidly overtook Gabe's face.

I broke into laughter. Gabe glared at me and that just made me laugh harder. Then Gabe smiled reluctantly, and we all laughed together, even Ana. That good kind of laughter. I doubled over and grabbed my stomach. Tears were streaming out of my eyes. This was the kind of laughter that hurt so bad it felt good. The kind that was best because it was shared with friends.

Nana Jane poked her head back around the corner, followed by Ben. She took one look at the three of us all doubled over, and simply shook her head, returning to the kitchen. That just made us laugh harder, if that was possible. Ben stared at us for a few more seconds, then actually cracked a real smile as he said, "Everybody is happy." Then he turned and followed Nana into the kitchen.

I felt good. This home was so different from mine, and for the first time, I felt deep inside my heart that maybe I'd missed something growing up. To experience a family that

not only laughed at each other, but also with each other —
and with love. A new kind of contentment filled me.

I must have stopped laughing because Ana and Gabe
were both staring at me with concerned expressions. So
many thoughts rolled through my mind. *They really care
about me. I don't have to do anything special. I don't have to
prove my importance, my value, my worth. They like me for
me, right here, right now, just me, Calyssa, here today. No
Green, no sparkles, no music, no connections. Just me.*

All those thoughts flickered through my mind in simply
a matter of seconds. Gabe stood up and stepped toward
me. The look on his face made me start giggling again,
which made them start laughing again as well.

At that moment, there was a loud knock on the front
door. Ben stepped back into the room and looked at Gabe.
"Gunner," was all he said, and then he went back into the
kitchen.

Chapter 20

For a split second, I saw a worried look pass between Gabe and Ana. Nana Jane calmly stepped out of the kitchen. "Take Calyssa upstairs right now, Ana. Put her in my room. Ben, you come on back in the kitchen with me. Gabe, you stay to answer the door." And then, she simply turned around and left.

A second knock. Ana flew into action. She grabbed my wrist and pulled me toward the stairs. Gabe had already moved to the door.

"What's wrong?" I asked in a hushed voice. I didn't know for sure what was happening, but from the lightning fast change in the atmosphere, I could tell that whatever this was, it was serious.

"Rebels," was all I heard Gabe say as we topped the stairs. Ana held a finger to her lips and then gently pushed me through the first doorway into a bedroom.

"Stay here," she whispered, and with that, she turned and was gone.

I could hear new male voices downstairs, but I couldn't make out what they were saying. *Rebels?* I thought. *In Gabe's house? Had they found out I was here? Were they here to take me? Kidnap me?* All the stories of rebel radicals taking family members of powerful Green citizens came flooding back to me. *What was I doing here? Was I crazy?*

What if I never saw my family again? How could I have trusted the Staytons?

Then I heard laughter. What was going on?

I slipped out the bedroom door and positioned myself at the top of the stairs so I could partially see the front door area, but where I was still mostly in the hallway, in the shadows.

Gabe, Ana, Ben, Nana Jane – they were all standing there with two other men. *Men with guns. Rebels! What are they doing?* I wanted to scream for them to run! They should have been running, screaming, fighting for their lives! Why were they just standing there? *What should I do?*

I stiffened as I saw one of the men put his hand on Nana Jane's arm. As I was about to step onto the stairs and, well, I didn't know what I was going to do, I watched in astonishment as Nana Jane leaned forward and kissed the guy on the cheek, ruffling his blond, curly hair. Ok, I was totally confused, again. Might as well slip back into that state of normalcy here for me – confusion. *What in the world is going on?*

Maybe I didn't know Gabe and his family like I thought I did. Maybe this was some sort of a set up – keep the girl here and entertained until the rebels could send someone to pick her up. And of course, I had been stupid enough to fall for it. My heart raced. My head pounded. I thought this family liked me, cared about me, but who was I kidding? *Livvy was right. Drones. They're just all drones, can't be trusted, always waiting to find a way to take us down – serious stupidity on my part, so stupid ....*

The Green Commonwealth was right - they knew what was best for us. They had been governing for years, keeping order, keeping everyone happy and healthy. How could I have been so stupid to believe that I could just waltz in and "be at home" with a non-Green family? A family that obviously didn't understand the importance of the Enhancement in our society. Of the commitment and strength it took to go Green. I felt like I was going to be sick. *How could I have been so trusting, so naive, so dumb, so ... so ....*

As Nana Jane turned and walked back toward the kitchen, she glanced over her shoulder to the top of the stairs, and gave a quick, little wink with a smile. I jumped back further into the hallway. *What?* Did she know I was there? And what did that mean?

I slouched to a seated position, hugging my knees into me. I knew I was breathing too hard, too fast. If I wasn't careful, I'd pass out. I focused on my breathing. It slowed. And as it slowed, I listened to the conversation below.

Ana was saying something about school almost being out, and the blond guy Nana had kissed was saying something about her studying hard so she could pick up some of the slack for Gabe. Ana punched him in the shoulder.

I focused on him as he spoke. He was tall, but younger than I had originally assumed, probably around Gabe's and my age, and his skin was deeply tanned, like he spent a lot of time outside. *He would turn a beautiful green color in the transition*, I thought. *Oh, right, what transition? With that* huge gun hanging over his shoulder, he'd probably shoot anything that even looked vaguely Green!

Ana and Ben went into the kitchen, and the blond guy came over and stood with his foot on the bottom stair. That caused me to inch back a little more. I was going to crawl back to the bedroom, when I heard him say, "Gabe, I miss having you around. You know, the way it was before, when we were kids." There was something in his voice that made me stop and turn back.

This guy cares about Gabe. In those couple of sentences, without seeing his face, I knew. I felt the warmth in those words, the sincerity, the wistfulness. Again, I wondered, *What is going on?*

Gabe looked a little uncomfortable as he glanced at the other guy, the one who hadn't spoken yet. I guess he wasn't much older than them but he was much bigger with lots of muscles and a constant frown that made him look a lot scarier. He just stood there and kept looking nervously back at the door, keeping his hand on his gun. He gave me the creeps. *Yeah, that guy is a rebel for sure. Big, bad, and mean.*

Gabe dropped his head and sighed. "You know I care about you, Gunner. We've been friends for as long as I can remember. You know I'd do just about anything for you."

"That's why I'm here, Gabe. We need you. I need you. You and me again. Just like the old days." He smiled.

Wow, what a great smile, his whole face lights up. I could totally introduce him to Divya or Jessalyn – well, if he wasn't a REBEL. What am I thinking? I'm losing it. These rebels might be here to take me away and I'm playing matchmaker for friends that I may never see again with a guy that would most likely shoot them dead rather than take them out dancing.

"I'm not coming with you, Gunner. You should take Kye and head out," Gabe said, nodding toward the other guy who seemed more than ready to leave. "My answer hasn't changed and my reasons haven't either. My family needs me here. I'm not going to leave them to try to run this place on their own." He looked Gunner in the eyes. "Some of the rebels are going too far. There're doing things that I'm not willing to support, to defend. Things are getting out of hand."

Gunner backed off the stair and took a step closer to Gabe. They were about the same height. Neither broke the intense stare. "We're taking a stand for what's right, Gabe. We're out there protecting our families – your family – from people who would take it all away from us given half a chance." Gunner's face had turned red and his voice had risen with each word.

"Gimps would take your land, your equipment, your inventions right now without any hesitation if they thought they could get away with it. You're only still here, untouched, because of who your dad is, because of your family name. I didn't have that luxury. Neither did my family, and now they're all gone.

"You're all I have left. Don't you realize you're a brother to me? I love Nana Jane, and Ana, and your dad – and Ben. You better be thinking about Ben. Because if something were to happen to you and your dad, Ben would be gone. Shoved away in one of those horrible hospitals or worse, because he's not perfect, not complete, not ...."

"Enough!" A voice boomed through the house, and then it was completely silent.

Chapter 21

No one had noticed the older man with the rugged, weathered face who had quietly opened the front door during the heated discussion. He stepped toward Gunner. Gunner stepped away from Gabe. Kye tightened his grip on his gun. The tension was so thick that it felt like time had literally stopped.

"Ben, you go help Nana Jane. Run on now." The man took off his hat, exposing dark hair peppered with silver. He dusted it off and hung it on the wall beside the door. Gabe and the other two guys turned to see Ben slip back through the kitchen doorway.

"I didn't see him there, Andrew. I didn't know. You know I love Ben like he's my own little brother. I'd never say or do anything to hurt him intentionally. I didn't know he was there."

"Gunner, you are always welcome in my house. Seems like you've been in and out of here as you've pleased since you were four years old, but those guns are not welcome in here. We've had this discussion before. I've had a long day, and I don't believe that we'll be discussing anything political again tonight. I think it's best if you and your friend went on your way." He reached out his hand to Gunner.

Gunner stepped forward and shook Andrew's hand. "I really am sorry. Have a good evening with your family."

Gunner nodded at Kye, and they both stepped toward the door.

Gabe, who had remained silent throughout their exchange, slid on his boots, and said, "I'll walk you out."

Andrew nodded at the three of them and walked into the kitchen. Gabe followed Gunner and Kye out the door, and I released the breath that I had been holding.

I slipped out of the hall and back into the bedroom. I crossed the room in the semi-dark. *When had the sun set?* I walked to an open window, heard voices, and dropped to my knees.

Gabe, Gunner, and Kye were standing below. I eased up slowly so I could watch them, trying not to make any noise. I was pretty sure that without the bedroom light on, they couldn't see me in the darkness of the room behind me.

"Come on, Gunner, it's getting late. We need to get back soon." Kye fidgeted with the gun again, looking across the field. "I don't like being in the open after dark, especially not lately."

"Give me a minute with Gabe."

"Fine. You've got five. Then I'm leaving. I don't think you'll want to walk back alone."

"Great guy," Gabe said under his breath as they watched Kye walk away. "You sure he's got your back? It is starting to get dark out here. Won't be long 'til it's black."

"Kye's fine. He seems a little rough around the edges until you get to know him. He and I, we have a lot in common. Both lost our mom and dad. He lost a younger sister, too. It tore him up. He felt responsible. Happened in that blast a couple months ago around Free Fields, north of SciCity. Remember that one?"

Gabe nodded his head. "Some sort of equipment malfunction or something, wasn't it?"

Gunner looked at Gabe, narrowed his eyes, then shook his head. "No. It wasn't an equipment malfunction. It was a bomb, planted by the security enforcers, trying to push the GMO free zone back. Open your eyes, Bro. Things are getting bad out there."

Gabe scowled. "How do you know that's what it was? How do you know that's not just rebel propaganda to try to incite more people to follow the Fitting brothers? The Fittings are always saying, 'Got to take back what's ours.' Isn't that right? Something like, 'It's our responsibility to rid the world of all GMOs, to take it back to the way it was before the PK Years.' Take out everything that's been genetically modified because then everything will be perfect again. Right?" Gabe was in Gunner's face now, and the tension was back.

He poked Gunner in the chest. "You in on killing people now, too? Taking out the Gimps? Being the big, bad drone avenger?" he said mockingly. He poked Gunner again, pushing him back a little. "You ready to deal with the consequences of those actions?"

Before I knew what was happening, Gunner had Gabe up against the side of the house, with the butt of his gun pressed against Gabe's throat. "I know it's true because I was there. I saw it go down. I just didn't know what was happening until the bomb went off and pieces of people were flying everywhere. Do you know what it's like to pick up a kid who's missing an arm? To watch as her eyes flutter shut and never open again? I do." He blew out a deep breath. "I do, and I hope I never have to again, but I will not back down or walk out on the people who need me." He stepped away from Gabe.

"I'm there for the people who count on me." He took a couple more steps back and looked up at the night sky.

There were tears streaming down his face. *But he's a rebel,* I thought. *Why is he crying? And are all those things he said true? Security enforcers? Bombs? Children killed? Really? I didn't hear anything in the news about kids dying. All kids are just kids until they're old enough for Enhancement. What if one of those children had the incredible mind that someday would have found the cure for some obscure disease, or created the next symphony that would bring all of humanity to tears, or ...or just grown up to be somebody's daughter, then somebody's mother?*

Green or not, someone had loved and cared about that child, someone had lost a piece of their heart, of their soul when that child died. I knew how that felt, and an immense sorrow swelled up inside of me – enveloped me – sorrow that I had pushed down and shoved away for a long time. Now, I couldn't stop it. It enveloped me.

Tears streamed down my face, too. Tears for that little girl who lost her life. Tears for Gunner, who had to watch that life fade in nothingness. Tears for my mother, who left me far too young. And tears for me, and what I had missed out on. I had tried to be strong since she left me, but I felt weak without her. And always fearful that someone would see my weakness, my fear, my loneliness, and think less of me. *How different would my life be if she were still here with me now?*

"Gunner, I will always be here for you. You know that." And with that statement, Gabe stepped forward and threw his arms around his friend.

"I want it to be like it was when we were kids, Gabe. Eating dinner with each other every night, switching from your house to mine so that our parents wouldn't have a fit because we were gone so much. Making swords out of branches. Pretending to whup the bad guys to save the farm. I miss those days. Sometimes, I just wish we never had to grow up." Gunner's shoulders sagged and he stepped back from Gabe.

There was silence for a couple of seconds. "I can't leave Ana and Ben, Nana Jane and Dad. You know that, Gunner. They need me. They need me more than you do. You're strong. They're not – you know that. Right? You know I have to be here, with them. Right?" Gabe took a step toward Gunner.

Gunner stiffened and stepped back again. "I know. They're family. You got to stick with family. Right. I know."

"Wait, that's not what I meant. You're my family, too, Gunner ... I ...."

Gunner cut him off. "It's okay. Everybody has their place in the new world today. But things are changing, Gabe. Choices are being made, with or without you. You can't just sit on the sidelines and say you're not on either team. It doesn't work that way. Because eventually, it will affect you. And your family. Directly. And because you didn't make a choice, it will be made for you."

He sighed heavily. "Then come find me. I'll be there for you, Brother, and you'll need me. Believe me, you'll need me." There was no malice in the words he said. Just firmness, tinged with sadness.

Gunner put his hand out. Gabe stepped forward and grabbed it. They shook hands, almost awkwardly. Then, Gunner punched Gabe in the shoulder, and said, "You better keep an eye on Ana. When did she go and grow up? Better make sure she hasn't figured out how to sneak out by climbing down that old tree in the back that we used as kids."

The tension seemed to melt away. Gabe grinned. "Oh, don't worry, I pruned that tree way back at the end of last summer when boys started calling the house. Nu-uh. No way. Not my sister. They got something else coming if they think they can sneak my little sister out." Both guys laughed.

A sharp, high whistle came from the field. Gunner turned and stared out into the darkness. "That's Kye. I better be going." He turned back to Gabe. "Take care." He nodded his head. "Take care of yourself and your family."

"I will," Gabe said. "And don't be a stranger. Stop by when you can. Maybe without your bodyguard so you can stay and have dinner."

As Gunner started to walk away, he replied, "Don't write Kye off – he's a good guy. Wrestler, boxer, sharpshooter – he's someone you'd want on your side. Trust me."

"Oh, well maybe if he's so cool, I'll just invite him to dinner next time instead." They both laughed, and I watched Gunner walk into the darkness.

Gabe stood there for a few more minutes, staring off into the dark. In the light cast off from somewhere at the back of the house, I could see the sadness reflected across his face. I wanted to rush downstairs, throw open the door, and run to him.

I wanted to hold him in my arms and tell him that he wasn't alone, and how incredible he was, and that I cared about him. I wanted to put my face against his chest and tell him it was okay, that his friend would be back, that his family would be safe, and that the world would be a good place.

But then, Gabe didn't need to hear anymore promises when I didn't know what the future would hold for any of us.

Chapter 22

I was still sitting in that dark bedroom under the window thinking about what I had witnessed when the door slowly opened. Ana peered around the door, spotted me sitting there, and then, without even turning on the light, she simply walked over and sat down beside me. Neither of us said anything. I think we were both lost in our own memories.

I felt Ana's sadness as well as my own. *She has such a wonderful, loving family, and an incredible big brother, along with this super cool farm. Everyone's so warm and caring. Everything feels right. This is a home, not just a place where people live. Why is she so sad?*

Sitting next to her reminded me of how badly I had always wanted a younger sibling, a little brother or sister. I thought of all the times that Livvy had been so mean to me, and then of how I thought I would have treated a younger sister – so different from Livvy's sarcasm and continual ridicule.

Ana reached up to the nightstand next to the bed and turned on a small lamp. A warm glow filled the room. It softly shone on her face as she stared at me. "I think you should teach me all about going Green so I'll be ready when it's my turn for Enhancement."

Huh, that's interesting. I wonder how her family feels about that.

She must have seen the question in my eyes because she turned away from me and said, "It's been a sore subject in my family. Gabe won't even discuss it with me. He gets angry that I would even consider it. He feels it would be a betrayal to our family since Ben would never be allowed to go Green.

"Nana Jane doesn't see any reason for it here on the farm. And, Dad, he just says that it's an adult decision, and that we'll wait to discuss it when I'm old enough to make it. Nobody understands how I feel. Nobody gets me." She ended with a small, muffled sob. Here was Ana, who tried so hard to be cool and flippant at school, but really had a soft side that I'd never imagined.

I reached out and put my arm around her. "You are an incredible, beautiful person, Ana. You have a family who loves you in a way that I've never experienced. Be patient with them, and be patient with yourself."

That only seemed to make her cry harder. But it wasn't that ugly, look-at-me type of crying. The kind Livvy was famous for, and that usually got her what she wanted. It was more of a quiet, gentle shaking, one that made me want to pull her closer, to protect her, to give her everything I had to make her life better.

After a minute, she sat back and looked into my eyes. She looked younger, so innocent, so hopeful. "When you go back to SciCity, can I come visit you? Maybe this summer?" Her voice was so earnest. This was a sincere side of her that I hadn't seen. No eye rolling, no jokes, no sighs.

"I'd love that, Ana. We'll have so much fun together. I'll take you all around the city, introduce you to all my friends, take you to the coolest stores, and of course, hook you up with the most awesome tech! It'll be just like we're sisters." I took her hand and gave it a squeeze.

"Thanks, Lyssa." Ana's eyes sparkled.

She'll be even more beautiful when she goes Green. And I totally know that I can talk Father into scholarshipping her. I could even work with her on the violin, I thought. *This is what having a little sister is like, well can be like, if you want it to be.* I hugged Ana again and felt her relax against me.

Then I felt a rush of heat fill my face as anger shot through my whole body. Livvy had cheated me out of this. *What kind of person wouldn't want this?* I felt my muscles begin to tighten at the thought.

Let it go, Calyssa. Don't let Livvy ruin this for you, too. I took a deep breath, willed my muscles to relax, put a smile on my face, and pulled back from Ana.

"You are going to have an amazing life, you know," I said to her.

"Oh, Lyssa. You make me feel like anything could be possible. And maybe when Dad and Gabe get to know you better, they'll understand that it's okay for me to go Green, too. Like you." Then she flipped her hair over her shoulder, a gesture I realized I often did.

"If not, you could always run away to the city and live with me." I laughed. Ana just stared across the room.

Chapter 23

We both got up off the floor and stretched. As I reached over to turn off the lamp on the nightstand, I saw a thick, old-fashioned book with a lacy pink cover sitting on a shelf below it. I reached down to pick it up. It was heavier than I expected and I set it carefully on the bed.

"What's this?" I asked Ana. I'd seen pictures of old books with actual pages and stuff, but I'd never held one. And I'd never seen one quite like this. Someone had hand-written in a swooping cursive, "Take time to appreciate the moments that make you smile," on the front.

"Oh, that belonged to my mom. It's pictures, the old kind. She started it when she was a little girl. She always loved taking pictures. Her great-uncle taught her how to develop them like he used to when he was a boy, and she was hooked."

"Why didn't she keep them in a memory bracelet?" I touched mine as I asked. I had hundreds of pictures on it, each catalogued based on who or what was on them so I could pull up any picture at any time I wanted to see it. And with the newest model, of course thanks to Livvy, I could project each of the pictures as a holographic image as well.

"Nana says my mom loved to develop the pictures with her own hands. To watch the image appear on paper from nothing. That it helped her feel each of the moments she photographed all over again." Ana opened the book.

We sat together on the bed, side-by-side, legs crossed in front of us, and casually browsed through the pages. It began with the oldest pictures. Girls and boys played together in some of them, running, swinging, laughing. In others, the same children stood linked arm in arm, posing, smiling, and goofing around. They all seemed so happy and carefree.

"That's my mom, Lydia. Those other kids are mostly her cousins. They all grew up together. She was smart and brave, and Nana says she was always a little wild." Ana stared at the pictures, running her finger along one of the girl's faces, a face that looked strikingly similar to her own.

Several pages later, a teenage Lydia stood with her arms around a beautiful, older woman. The woman looked at Lydia with love and admiration in her eyes. Lydia had her head back and was laughing like the woman had just shared the funniest story that she had ever heard. Even in the picture, I felt the love between the two of them.

"Is that Nana Jane with your mom?" I looked again, knowing the answer before Ana spoke. The smile, the same shade of dark blond hair as Ana, the twinkle in her eye. *Yep. That's Nana Jane.*

"Yeah. They were both so beautiful, weren't they? Mom was Nana Jane's only child. She tried, but she couldn't have any more. I think that still makes Nana sad sometimes. And why she decided to live with us." She sighed.

"Wait a minute. Nana Jane was your mom's mom? I don't know why, but I thought she was your dad's mom. I guess since she lives with all of you. Hmm. Has she always lived with you guys?"

Ana turned back to look at me, and surprise showed on her face. "No, Nana hasn't always lived here. She lived at a house on one of our other farms, the one that Grandpa James helped out with after Mom and Dad got married."

I saw her shoulders sag a little as she continued. "Grandpa James died a few months before Mom did. Something to do with his heart. He was a great big man with a deep laugh. No matter what he was doing, working on the farm, talking with the men, whatever, whenever he saw Gabe and me, he would always stop what he was doing and pick us both up, twirling us around and giving us big hugs." Another sigh.

"I was only four when he died, but I still have lots of special memories of him," she said as she found a picture of him and pointed it out. "Sitting on his lap, watching him smoke his old tobacco pipe, making cool smoke rings with his mouth. He told us stories about when he was younger, working as a forest maintenance supervisor. How he helped bring the forested areas back and how we all needed to responsibly nurture our plant population.

"He was funny and super smart, and," she said as she closed her eyes, "he always smelled like cinnamon and pine." When she opened them, she had a faraway look as she continued.

"I asked him about it once. He said the pine was from years and years of working in the forest, that the sap of the pine trees ran through his veins. And the cinnamon, well, that he said was our little secret. Then he pulled a handful of red candies out of his pocket. 'These,' he said, 'are so your Nana Jane doesn't know I've been smoking that nasty old pipe again.' Then we both popped one of the candies in our mouths and giggled as Nana Jane came around the corner to tell him something. He put his fingers to his lips and I crossed my heart, and we both sat there and tried not to smile."

"It sounds like he was a special man."

"Yeah. I miss him. I haven't thought too much about him in a while. It's good to think about people so that you don't forget the memories you have of them." Ana tried to quickly wipe her eyes.

"Wow. You lost your grandpa and your mom in the same year?"

A tear escaped down her face that she wasn't quick enough to catch.

"I'm sorry, Ana. We don't have to talk about it anymore." I closed the book.

"No, it's okay. They're good memories." She wiped her face with both hands and then opened the book to another section, turning a few more pages. "Look. Here's Mom and Dad with Gabe when he was a baby."

"He was so cute, and so chubby! I can't believe it. He's so – so – fit – now." I could feel my cheeks turning red again. *Seriously, did I just tell Gabe's sister that I think he's "fit?"*

Ana laughed. "You can say it – you think he's hot. I've heard it before. All of the girls at school tell me all the time."

I quickly turned the page in the book to change the subject. "Is that you? Oh my word, you were an absolutely adorable baby!"

"Oh, and what am I now? Are you saying I'm not cute anymore now that I'm grown up?" Ana stuck out her bottom lip, acted pouty and hurt.

I bumped her with my elbow. "Nuh-uh. Now, you're stunningly beautiful, and that's way better than absolutely adorable!"

I turned a few more pages. "That must be when your mom was pregnant with Ben. And there's you and Gabe again."

"Yep. I'm four and Gabe's about seven. That was taken a few days before Ben was born."

I flipped through a few more pages of the book. Pictures of Ben as a baby, of all three kids at various important stages and functions. Nana Jane and Andrew scattered throughout, younger versions of themselves from years past.

"I don't see any more pictures of your mom in here." I looked at Ana. She looked like she knew what was coming, as if she was bracing herself, steeling herself against the inevitable.

"She died giving birth to Ben. There were complications. They didn't know if Ben was going to make it either. He went a while without oxygen, and the doctors think that's what caused his – problems.

"Ben came early and fast. Dad didn't have time to get Mom to SciCity. She didn't have problems delivering Gabe or me, so it was totally unexpected. Mom started hemorrhaging and by the time the doctor got to her, there wasn't much he could do.

"Dad tried to keep Gabe and me out of the room, but we both saw more than we probably should have. I think Gabe understood what was going on more than I did." Ana got up off the bed and paced around the room as she continued to talk.

"I saw a lot of blood, but that didn't really scare me. I mean, we live on a farm; I've grown up seeing cows and hogs butchered. It never occurred to me that something bad might be happening to Mom. I was just excited that the new baby was coming.

"Nana Jane arrived right after the doctor. She brought Ben into Gabe's room to see Gabe and me. He was so small and cute. Totally quiet, just stared at us, content being held. Gabe and I took turns. I didn't even think about why Mom and Dad weren't in there with us, or why we didn't go in with them instead of Nana bringing the baby to us."

Her pacing speed increased. Lines burrowed their way across her forehead. Her voice became more and more strained as she continued.

"I didn't realize anything was wrong until I heard a low, loud moan from Mom and Dad's room. It was scary, not like anything I'd ever heard before. It was so, so sad. Gabe and I both ran to Nana and she held all three of us together on her lap. And she rocked us. She had tears streaming down her face, but she didn't make a sound." A tear slid down Anna's cheek.

"Then Dad's cries filled the house. I don't think I'd ever heard him cry before. Gabe and I started crying, too. Only little Ben didn't cry. He just lay silent in Nana's arms. We all sat that way for what seemed like forever, arms all wrapped around each other, crying together. At four years old, I wasn't sure why we were crying, but I knew it was something bad if it made Gabe cry. He only cried when he got hurt, and not just skinned up, like he and his buddies used to get all the time, but hurt bad like the time he broke his collarbone or when he dislocated his shoulder and Grandpa James popped it back in for him." Ana stopped pacing, put both hands on the windowsill, and stared out into the moonlight.

When she turned back to look at me, I felt her silent sadness. I knew what was coming in her story because I had been in that same situation. I could feel the tears in my own eyes pushing to escape.

"Dad came into the room and we all got quiet. I almost didn't recognize him. His eyes were red, his face was wet and puffy, his hair was all messed up. He sat down by us and took Ben into his arms.

"He said to us, 'Gabe, Ana, this is your little brother, Benjamin. We all have to take real good care of him together because your mama won't be here to help us. She went to live in heaven, but she's gonna be watching us every single minute, making sure that we all watch over little Ben, that we take care of him and protect him just like she would have, like she did for all of us. You know your mama, she will not put up with any slackin' off, and even though she's in heaven, if we don't do our best by Ben, I know she'll find a way to let us know.' Then he smiled, but it was a sad, tired smile."

Tears streamed down Ana's face now. Mine, too. Neither of us tried to stop them.

"Then Dad lay down on Gabe's bed with the three of us. He pulled all of us into his arms, and we went to sleep there together. I woke up later that night and it was just Gabe and me. Dad and Ben were gone. Nana Jane wasn't around either. I crawled out of bed and went downstairs. Dad was sitting by himself in the dark. I crawled up on his lap. We talked about Mom living with the angels and Nana Jane living with us. And it's been that way ever since."

I stood up and walked over to Ana, putting my arms around her and pulling her into a hug. "I know how you feel, and I'm not just saying that to try to make you feel better. I lost my mom, too, when I was five. I think there's been a hole in my heart since the day I lost her, and it still aches just as bad as it did the day I found out she wasn't coming back.

"If I could talk to her one more time, I'd tell her so many things: how much I loved her, how much I appreciated her, how beautiful she was, how incredible her music made me feel, how when she brushed my hair I felt like the most important girl in the world ...." My voice trailed off.

We both held each other and cried. Cried, and remembered all the wonderful things about our mothers, how they sounded, how they smelled, how they made us laugh.

Stepping back just a bit, Ana said, "You may not believe me, but I kind of feel like you fill that place in my heart. The one left by my mom leaving us. I mean, you're not like a mom or anything, but you're like she was. Maybe a sister is just what I needed to fix that sad feeling, the one that the boys and Dad and Nana can't." We hugged again.

"Hold on a minute," I said as I pulled away. "Stay here. I'll be right back." I stepped back and headed out of the room before Ana had a chance to say anything.

Returning just moments later, I held out my hand. "This is for you. I want you to have it."

Opening my fingers, I showed Ana my old memory bracelet. "I want you to have it, to take pictures after I leave the farm so you can send them to me. And I'll send you ones of me, too."

Ana delicately picked up the bracelet and turned it over in her fingers. "Oh, Lyssa, it's beautiful, and it looks really expensive. I can't take this." But she was already trying it on.

I smiled watching her adjust it on her wrist. "It fits you perfectly. I want you to have it. I wear mine all the time," I said, holding my wrist up for her to see.

"It does look good on me, doesn't it?" The old Ana, full of spunk and sass, was back.

"Well, I don't know ...maybe it would look better on me ...I mean you may not be able to work the tech, and ...."

Ana interrupted before I could finish. "Oh no, you can't take it back now. There's that whole thing about possession and the law and all that." We both laughed and she gave me one more quick hug.

I took a minute to show her how to take, sort, and categorize pictures. The process was simple, and for practice, she took several of us together. We set our bracelets to sync on touch so we could share pictures quickly and easily. I also showed Ana how to upload pictures to a shared file so we both could access them after I was back in the city.

Then we heard Nana Jane call up the stairs, "Ana, Calyssa, you young ladies coming back down any time soon? The boys are complaining that they're withering away from starvation. You know Gabe has to eat lots to stay so big and strong – and handsome."

"Nana!" Gabe said in a pleading voice.

Ana and I looked at each other and laughed one more time, then headed down the stairs.

Ana is right. Being here on the farm makes my heart feel a little fuller, too.

Chapter 24

Seeing the front door triggered my memory of the rebels. Ana hadn't said anything. I guess I hadn't asked either. I wasn't sure if I should bring it up. *I'll wait to see if anybody says anything. If not, I can talk to Ana or maybe even Gabe later about it.*

"I think cookies will have to wait," Nana Jane said. "But don't worry, Calyssa, we'll make them tomorrow. Ana, your father asked that you go back out to the barn for a minute and help with a young horse that got tangled up in some thorn bushes. Some of the hands found it and brought it in. Or, I suppose you could stay and help make dinner." Nana smiled.

Ana practically ran toward the door. "Sorry, Lyssa. Gotta bail. Don't be too hard on her, Nana." Then she winked at me and left me standing there. *No talk about the rebels now,* I thought.

Nana Jane looked at the old-fashioned wristwatch on her arm (I'd only seen old ones like that in pictures), then started back toward the kitchen. Looking over her shoulder as she walked she said to me, "Come on, Calyssa. We'd better get something on for dinner. Time slipped away from me. Andrew and Gabe are starving. And you, too, huh Ben, my boy? You ready for some dinner?" I hadn't noticed Ben sitting in the corner of the kitchen as we walked in.

Ben looked at Nana for several seconds and then simply nodded his chin once, and said, "Pizza, please." Then he jumped down from the stool he was sitting on and went across the kitchen to one of the drawers. He started pulling out silverware. He stopped, staring into the drawer. Then he turned and looked at me, and then at Nana.

"Do you have a question, Ben?" Nana waited. Several seconds ticked by. "I won't know your question if you don't ask it." She simply continued to stare at him and wait.

Ben looked at me again. "Is she?" was all he said.

"Is she what?" Nana asked patiently. She stood completely still and kept her eyes focused on Ben. Again, seconds ticked by. I was beginning to feel a little awkward.

Ben looked at me. "Is she having dinner with us tonight?" Then he looked back at Nana Jane expectantly.

"Yes, she is Ben. Please set a place for Calyssa at our table. And thank you for asking. It was very polite of you to think of adding a place for her." Ben nodded his head once and went back to gathering the needed silverware for the place settings. Once he had what he needed, he left the room.

"You have to be patient with Ben. But don't let him off, he's a smart boy." Nana turned and opened the cupboard behind her.

"Do you all sit down and eat together?"

Nana nodded as she moved around the kitchen, gathering various supplies from the cupboards. I was astonished.

"Every night?" I asked. She nodded again.

"All of you?" I knew I probably sounded stupid but I couldn't get over the idea of a whole family sitting down every single night together to eat. Our kitchen was more of a "pass through" area where we'd grab something when we'd needed it, and since Father and Livvy were Green, they simply stopped by for drinks that Lena always had ready for them. I couldn't remember the last time Livvy, Father, and I had all sat down at a table together.

"Wow," I said, eyebrows raised. "That seems like a lot of work. Cooking for your whole family every night without an automate. I've watched Lena, our domicile attendant back in SciCity, whip up stuff for me, but it's nothing like all of this," I said as I glanced around at all the items she was pulling out. "I can't even begin to imagine how you do it.

"And why isn't anyone in here helping you? I mean, you're the oldest one here ...I mean, you're not old, that's not what I'm saying ...I just mean ...." I knew I was rambling. *Seriously, Calyssa*, I thought. *Get a grip on yourself.* Could I have sounded any more incompetent?

Nana laughed. "Calyssa, I cook because I love to. It's something that I've always loved. I've taught all three of the kids to cook as well. Ana does it, but would rather not. Gabe excels in the kitchen when he has time - you should ask him about it. He makes a super beef casserole. Even little Ben can make himself meals when he needs to. He's very efficient, and very careful, too." She had the counter in front of her full of all sorts of items. Things I had never seen before.

I realized again I was lost in this world. Fear and self-doubt began to creep up inside of me. I had no idea what to do or how to do it. *How could I be eighteen years old and so helpless, so useless? All my schooling, all my advanced tech, all the advantages given to me throughout my life – and not a single thing that I can think of that will help me out here.*

Nana laughed and shook her head. *I am so tired of people laughing at me. It's getting old.*

"Oh, Sweetie, don't look so glum. Come over here and help me. If I can teach my three knuckleheads to find their way around the kitchen, I'm sure you'll pick up the basics in no time at all." She grabbed a long cloth with strings and tossed it to me. "Put on this apron so you don't get messy." She grabbed another one. I watched how she pulled part of it over her head and tied the other part around her waist.

Okay, I can do that. I mimicked her actions then looked down at myself. *So far, so good. Maybe this cooking thing will be a snap. After all, I'm a quick learner most of the time at school. I guess we'll see if that translates over to the kitchen.* What would Livvy have said if she saw me now? I didn't think that aprons were very high fashion. Who knew, maybe I would be the trendsetter and start something new in SciCity?

Nana Jane washed her hands in the sink. "Okay, Calyssa, listen up. Here's how I look at cooking. You can't think of it as a chore, like Ana does. Instead, think about it as an opportunity to create. It's a way you can express who you are and how you feel. In a sense, every time I cook something, I feel I'm sharing a part of myself. Food is necessary to support life here on the farm. Everybody has to eat; they need the energy to grow, to learn, to live. If we all have to sit down and take the time to eat, I want us to enjoy it."

She continued, "At a good dinner, you share not only the food, you share your day. It brings us all back together to celebrate who we are. A family. It's easy to get rushed, everybody going in different directions, wanting to do a hundred different things. But Andrew has always made it a priority that we will all sit down together for dinner. In this house, everyone simply has to make the time."

I washed my hands next and thought about what she had said. About how different their lives obviously were from mine. *To sit with your whole family every evening and share your day. Every day. Wow. That would be a lot of listening to Livvy, even more than now, but I think I'd like it.*

That made me a little sad, because in a few weeks, I would finish going Green and I'd never need to sit down and eat again. *Just nutrient drinks, and everybody drank those on the run. Maybe I could convince Father and Livvy to plan time to sit together, to drink our drinks and just talk about our day. Maybe.*

Over the course of the next hour, I learned to wash, peel, and cut up vegetables (becoming an expert at slicing more than dicing). I learned how to make dough for a crust from flour, sugar, salt, yeast, a little oil and water. Then, we had to let the dough rise for a bit. I thought the yeast was just another grain, but Nana explained that it, too, was a living organism, a fungus, that produced carbon dioxide bubbles that would expand the dough, making it light and fluffy.

I learned how to grate cheese (with only a couple of raw knuckles), to slice pepperoni (which I learned isn't a type of animal, but is made from the cows on their farm), and to brown sausage (not an animal either but comes from hogs.)

This is so cool and amazing! I thought. *Why don't we do things like this in school?*

Nana Jane and I laughed and visited. The smells in the kitchen, the laughter in the air, the ease of the conversation. I stopped placing pepperoni on the dough.

This is what it's like to have a grandmother. I had never met my father's parents. Or my mom's. All of them passed away when I was young or before I was born. Funny, now that I thought about it, I didn't know when or how they died. I had never really thought about them before. *No real reason to, I suppose.* But now, after spending time with Nana Jane, I realized once again that perhaps I had missed out on some more important things in my childhood. *To grow up knowing this kind of love, not that Father and Livvy don't love me, it's just a different kind of love.*

I looked up and realized my eyes felt misty. When had that happened? I turned away quickly from Nana and wiped my eyes with my apron. *Why am I crying? And so often here? I'm having a great time. So where are all these feelings coming from? I've only known these people a few hours.*

Nana walked over to me, put her arm around my shoulder, and whispered in my ear, "I'm glad you're here. You remind me of my daughter when she was your age. I think you two would have really liked each other." Her eyes were a little misty, too. She wiped them with her apron and said, "No more cutting onions for us." Then she smiled and started gathering dirty dishes.

I put the finishing touches on the pizzas and then placed them in the oven, which, I learned, gets way hotter than an automate. *Pizza. Hmmm. What an interesting food. It seems to have a little of everything on it. I can't wait to try it. It smells amazing.*

Nana excused herself from the kitchen to go freshen up before dinner. I took off my apron, placed it on the counter, and looked around. *In twenty minutes, I'll be eating the first dinner I've ever made.* Well, helped make. But I was a part of it. My hands cut and rolled and cooked and baked. I was the creator of something besides music.

Chalk it up as another first for me. I think I'm getting the hang of this "trying new things." Bring it on, Staytons. I'm ready.

Chapter 25

Dinner turned out even better than I expected. I looked around as everyone was filling their plates. Piping hot pizza, cool crisp salad, and breadsticks that I didn't even realize Nana Jane had made. *That woman is crazy talented in the kitchen!* I looked at each person smiling, laughing, cramming a bite in here and there as they shared their experiences of the day.

Nana Jane recounted the birth of a calf mid-morning that she and Ben got to see. They had been out on their morning walk when one of the farm hands had called to them from the barn. She and Ben ran over to see what was happening. They got there just in time to see the calf drop. They stayed until it was up walking around. Nana said she and Ben had discussed it and decided to name it Twig because it was skinny and brown. Ben nodded his head.

Next, Ana enlightened everyone about the intricacies of the new digital lockers in the girls' locker room. Apparently, the new tech had been installed last week, and today the combos had been given out. She was disappointed that they had to spend the whole period waiting for each girl to get her new combo so they didn't get to play field hockey.

Ben simply stated that "there were 237 more entrances to the hive today than yesterday." Nana asked him what that meant. He was silent for a few seconds then said that he thought the bees were becoming more active.

Gabe told everyone about a new student he met in tutoring who had recently moved here from Eurasia. He was a sixteen-year-old boy whose father worked in robotic prosthetic development for humans. He had been recruited to SciCity to expand on his work here. Gabe said that the boy, advanced for his age, had moved around a lot in the past few years, so he had missed a few things in his classes. Gabe was confident that he could help catch him up by the end of the school year.

Andrew started his turn by officially introducing himself to me and welcoming me to the farm, and then he went on to share about a meeting that he attended with several other farmers that afternoon. They were proposing some exchanges of livestock to keep the gene pools fresh.

None of the information they shared with each other was riveting, well, except maybe the calf being born, but that didn't seem to be a very big deal to them. They listened to each other, asked questions, laughed, and continued filling their plates and their mouths throughout the entire time. They looked earnestly at whoever was talking, focused on them. So different from my family back in the city. Father and Livvy rarely seemed interested or focused on what I had to say.

I felt a small pain in my chest, a little ache in my heart that I recognized as that loneliness I tried so hard to hide. I looked down at my plate. *Enjoy the moment, Calyssa*, I thought as I took another bite of pizza.

When Andrew finished, he looked at me. "So, Calyssa, what can you tell us about your day?"

Me?

I stopped mid-chew. My mind went blank.

What have I done today? Did I do anything today? Apparently not, because not a single thing came to my mind. I felt myself blush. Everyone was silent. They kept eating and watching me. I swallowed the food in my mouth with an audible gulp.

"Well, um, I ...." I shook my head and looked around, like maybe something would magically appear so I could talk about it. "I learned about cows today."

Okay, that was lame. Really? What was that? Everyone was still looking at me so I tried again. "I mean, I know about cows, but not your kind of cows. I mean, like farm cows, not pet cows. Not that your cows aren't pets, I mean I think they are because they seem to have names. Not that they have to have names to be pets ...."

Um, not any better. One more try. "Well, I mean your cows are just bigger, but have less hair, which means you probably don't have to fix it. Which is good because you seem to have a lot of them and that would be a lot of crimping and curling ...." *Nope, third time's not the charm.* "Uhhh ...." I stopped.

Everyone at the table broke into laughter at the same time. I laughed, too.

"Why don't you tell us about something you enjoyed today?" Nana Jane said. "Ana told me you play the cello, that you two met in a music class. Did you get to play today?"

I smiled. *Nana Jane to the rescue.* "I do play the cello and I did get to play today. In fact, I played a piece for my class that I haven't played for a long time. One that I love. It was written over a hundred years ago, but I think it's just as beautiful now as it was then."

"Will you play it for us tonight?" Ana asked.

"I guess I can if you want to hear it."

Andrew nodded at me. "Absolutely. After dinner then." He turned and looked around the table. "It sounds like everyone had an interesting day. Let's finish up, help Nana Jane clean up, then we'll listen to Calyssa play. It's already getting late, and we have lots to do tomorrow.

"Gabe, I need your help to finish that gate trigger, and if you get a chance, take Ben to the hives. I want to make sure that the numbers aren't jumping around too much. Run a full diagnostics report. Ben, let me know about any differences you notice. Good catch today." Ben nodded.

"Ana, you need to spend time on that new horse. Take it out for a few hours and see how he handles. You can take Calyssa with you." He turned to me.

"Have you ridden before?" I just shook my head. "Well, Ana's a great teacher." He turned back to Ana. "Put her on Blackjack. She's gentle and patient. She'll make a good first ride."

Nana Jane got up. "Bring your plates to the kitchen when you're finished. Gabe, your turn to wash tonight. Ana, you've got drying duty. Ben, clear the rest of the table."

"But Nana, Lyssa is here. Can't Gabe and Ben cover it tonight? Please?" Ana clasped her hands in front of her as she pleaded.

"Nope, but Calyssa can help you." She smiled at me and turned to go to the kitchen. Andrew got up, grabbed his plate, and followed her.

"Nice job, Ana. Score Calyssa some chores on her first night here." Gabe laughed when she glared at him.

"Sorry, Lyssa," she said. She sighed, got up, and sighed again. "I bet you don't have to deal with this kind of stuff at your house. We have all kinds of farm hands. I don't get why we can't have someone come in and take care of the cleaning for us. It sucks."

Andrew leaned his head back in the room. "That's why I had kids," he said. "It's the only free labor I get around here." He smiled, and then he disappeared.

"It's not a problem. I don't mind helping out." I grabbed my plate and followed the others to the kitchen.

I spent the next half hour learning how to "do the dishes." At my house, everything went through the autoclean. But I didn't think this was horrible. The three of us talked about our favorite music, our favorite book, the foods we liked, the teachers we liked, and our plans for next year.

I talked about my music scholarship and plans to attend the University of SciCity. Ana still had a few more years in high school. To hear her tell it, I thought her future was going to be unbearable. Gabe and I just laughed as she complained about her classes scheduled for next year. We both told her that we had lived through them and we figured she'd make it.

When it was Gabe's turn, he got quiet.

"I don't know for sure yet. I may go to the U. I've already been accepted."

What? Gabe's already been accepted at the U?

166

"Our dad went there and still works with the research faculty in the science department, so they're willing to let me attend, even though most of the staff don't like the idea."

He stared into the sink. "But I don't know. It's hard to go if you're not a Green, I mean not hard coursework, but just dealing with people." His frown deepened.

"Even though going Green is a choice, there are a lot of people who simply won't accept others who aren't Green. I don't know if I want to deal with that kind of bigotry. It's bad enough this year in high school." He shook his head and looked frustrated.

I had never thought about myself that way, but looking at it through his eyes, I could see where he was coming from. I mean, earlier this week, I had assumed that since Gabe wasn't a Green yet, that either his family couldn't afford for him to go Green or that he simply wasn't smart enough or talented enough to be scholarshipped. I had assumed that he didn't have anything to offer to make our community a better place.

But now, after getting to know him and seeing what they did here on the farm, I knew how intelligent he was, and I had seen firsthand the projects he had helped with to make not only the farming community, but also the whole world, a better place.

"And I would never leave Ben. I know Nana won't be with us forever. Someone has to be here to look out for him. He'll always need someone to look out for him."

I stopped drying the plate I was holding. "I'm so sorry, Gabe," I said softly.

"I know I was one of those people. But I was wrong. I was wrong about you, and your family, and your life. I wish I knew how to make things better." I set the plate down. I felt helpless, like nothing I could do would make a difference.

I turned toward him. We were shoulder to shoulder at the sink, so when he turned to look in my eyes, we were only inches apart.

"You're different than I thought, too, Calyssa. Better than I expected. I was prepared to hate you." A small smile spread across his lips. His head leaned slightly toward me.

"Oh. My. Word. If you try to kiss her, I'll knock you upside the head. Did you forget I was in here? Hello-o!" Ana snapped Gabe with the towel, and we both jumped away from each other. Gabe's neck was red again. I couldn't see his face.

I bumped him with my hip. With a completely straight face, I said, "It's good to know you don't hate me. It means I've got you fooled." He turned his head sharply and gave me a curious glance.

"You know, you won't be prepared when I wrestle you to the ground, and then kidnap you away from all of this." Then I winked at him. He smiled and shook his head. Ana just looked annoyed.

I finished drying the last plate and put it back in the cabinet. Then I wrapped my arm around Ana's shoulder and said, "How about we go grab our instruments? We can play something together for your family tonight."

Her face lit up. She pushed me toward the kitchen door. As we left, I heard Gabe yell, "Hey, you two were supposed to dry off all of the counters, too!" We just kept going and laughed.

It's going to be a great spring break, I thought. I'm so lucky to be here.

Chapter 26

That night Ana and I played together. Pretty much everything that she knew how to play, I had already learned, so I let her pick the pieces. If I didn't know something, I was confident I could pick it up after listening to a few measures.

Nana Jane sat in an old-style, wooden rocking chair, and Andrew looked comfortably relaxed in an autorecliner. Gabe sprawled out on the floor, his head resting on a large pillow. Ben sat cross-legged on the couch with his hands in his lap. They were a wonderful audience, applauding at the end of each piece, giving words of praise, asking us if we knew certain songs.

After we had played for about a half hour, Nana Jane asked if I would play the song that I had referred to during dinner, the one I had played earlier that day at school.

Was it still that same day? So much had happened. So much had changed.

I've changed, I thought.

I closed my eyes and began to play the Zimmer piece, and within the first few measures, I had left the farm. I was once again with my mom. I saw her face, heard her laughter, felt her touch. And I remembered an evening just before she got sick when we had played together, me on the cello and her on the violin. She had let me choose the pieces that night.

Sometimes, Mom sang when we played songs that she knew. Her voice was soothing, gentle but confident. She praised my efforts, telling me how lucky she was to have such a wonderful daughter. Her smile had made me feel confident; her words made me feel loved. Our fingers danced together on our instruments, making waves created by the music. We twirled and whirled. We mixed the march of a melancholy melody with the wonder of wispy notes. There was peace and love and joy all around us.

As the song came to a finish, and I had drawn my bow one final time across the strings near the bridge of my cello, I opened my eyes. Nana Jane had tears rolling down her cheeks. Andrew and Ana were smiling softly. Gabe had sat up, his arms around his knees, his head leaning to one side, his eyes and face as intense as the music I had played.

And Ben was standing right next to me. I don't know when he'd moved there or how long he'd been there, but he stood there silently staring at my bow. It was odd that I didn't jump when I noticed him, but it didn't startle me. I felt comfortable with him next to me.

"Calyssa, that was truly beautiful. You certainly do have a gift. I've never heard anything quite like that." Nana Jane got up, walked over to me, and gently kissed me on the forehead. Then she kissed each of the other three kids in the same way, and headed for the stairs.

"Yes," Andrew said, as he, too, stood. "Thank you for sharing with us. I hope that we will be fortunate enough to hear you again at some point this week." He looked at Ben. "Come on, young man. It's way past your bedtime." He held out his hand to his youngest child.

I turned my head to the side to look at Ben. He was still looking at my bow. Slowly his eyes rose to meet mine. He didn't say a word. He just reached out, wrapped his arms around me, and hugged me. I was a little surprised at first, but I squeezed him back. Then he dropped his arms and walked to his dad's side. Taking his hand, they walked up the stairs together.

Ana and Gabe were both staring at me. Ana had her hand over her mouth.

"What?" I asked.

They looked at each other, then back at me. Ana dropped her hand. "I've never seen Ben do anything like that. He's not very comfortable touching other people or being touched. Especially with somebody new. It usually takes him a long time to even talk to somebody, if he ever does decide to talk to them."

Gabe shook his head in disbelief. "It's true. And he usually doesn't display any sort of affection. Even rarer that he initiates it. He hugged you. He actually hugged you and he let you hug him." He smiled at me, one of his good, warm smiles. "Nice job. And cool music. Both of you. Great job. You play really well together."

"It's easy when you have a great partner," I said, looking at Ana. She beamed back at me.

"I'm heading to bed, too. Sounds like Dad has a full day scheduled for me tomorrow. Night, Sis. Night, Calyssa. See you in the morning." He got up, stretched and headed up to his room as well.

Ana and I both began packing up our instruments. "Thanks for making me sound good tonight. You totally could have picked songs you knew and played the whole time by yourself."

"What fun would that have been?" I asked as I closed my case. "And don't sell yourself short. You play beautifully. I can't think of anyone else I'd rather play with."

We grabbed our instruments and headed back to our bedrooms. Ana paused outside her door. "Night, Lyssa. I had a great time with you."

"Me, too." We both went into our rooms and closed the doors.

I stayed up for a while longer unpacking my bag. I figured that I might as well move in and get comfortable since I would be here for a whole week. I hung up my clothes in the closet, laid out my jewelry on top of a large chest of drawers, lined up the shoes I'd brought along one wall.

I slipped off my memory bracelet and laid it next to my jewelry. *I have to make sure that I put it on every day this week so I can keep taking pictures here.* Div and Jess were never going to believe this if I couldn't show them pictures to back it up.

Thinking of my friends made me realize that I hadn't heard anything out of my iBud since we got here. I focused intently on the tech. Nothing. I tried again. This time, a soft chime went off followed by a voice that told me I was "out of range" and "to try again later."

I'd have to remember to ask Ana and Gabe about that tomorrow. I wondered if my iBud would work anywhere around here or if we were simply too far away from the city. I knew that Father and Livvy both had extender satellite software on theirs so it didn't matter where they were, but they both traveled for AHGA so they needed it. I hadn't been out of SciCity since I was little so I hadn't thought about asking Father to add it to my iBud.

I took the iBud out and placed it with my jewelry. I couldn't remember the last time that I hadn't slept with it in. It felt weird for it to be missing. I changed into an old t-shirt and shorts, cracked open my window, physically turned off the lamp by my bed (remembering that they weren't automated in this house), then pulled back the covers and slipped in. I usually went to sleep with music playing on my iBud.

Will I be able to fall asleep without it?

I closed my eyes and realized that there was music in the air all around me if I chose to listen. I heard the soft wind rustling through a tree outside the window, along with a rhythmic chirping noise. *Crickets. I think that's what Ana called them when I heard them earlier tonight.*

I relaxed and let my mind drift. My body was tired, but my mind was relaxed. Pictures of Ana, Gabe, Ben, Nana Jane, and Andrew flashed in front of me. For one week, I had a new family.

Chapter 27

The next couple of days flew by.

Every morning, after breakfast, Ana and I would go horseback riding. The first time I was terrified. But true to Andrew's word, Blackjack was patient and gentle. And Ana was a great teacher. She showed me how to use the reins to guide the horse where I wanted it to go, along with using pressure from my legs on the sides of the horse's giant body. I learned to keep my feet in the stirrups, which allowed me to nudge the horse on, and to stand up a little when trotting so I didn't feel like my teeth were going to rattle out of my head. I also discovered that as I leaned, the horse felt my movement and leaned with me.

After I got the hang of it, Ana took us out to an open field. And there, we ran the horses. I had never felt so scared, yet so exhilarated, in my life. Out of control, but in control at the same time. The more we ran, the more I relaxed, and the more fluid we became. Ana said I looked like a natural.

Back at the barn, she taught me how to get the horse ready to ride, to put on and adjust the reins, to place the saddle blanket, to work the saddle with its straps and cinches, to change the length of the stirrups. And how to do it all in reverse, and finish up by brushing the horse down to make sure it would be comfortable and rested. By the third day, I could do it all without any reminders or help. It felt good to be learning new things, things that I could do by myself. I didn't even need any tech!

We'd be done riding and would let the horses out in the field to graze by lunch so we could head back to the house and make ourselves something to eat. Lunch was "on your own" at the farm. I liked that.

Sometimes, we'd run into Gabe, or Nana and Ben in the kitchen at lunch time and we'd eat together. Sometimes it was just Ana and me. I found out that I loved grilled cheese sandwiches and tomato soup, two new items I was definitely adding to my ever-growing "favorites" list.

Afternoons were filled with farm chores, but I didn't mind. I learned to muck out a stall, gather eggs, milk a cow, and feed the hogs. These were all things that Ana did regularly – she said she hated them, but I thought they were cool.

Ana and I talked a lot during "chore time." She asked me about the city, my house, my sister, my father, Lena, even about Lulu. I asked about her family and farm life. We took pictures of each other with our memory bracelets, syncing them every so often to share pictures we thought were funny or cool. We laughed constantly, and the time seemed to fly by.

After chores, I went in and helped Nana Jane get dinner ready. I found that I really enjoyed my time in the kitchen, and I learned how to make all kinds of things, like oven-fried chicken, brandied pork loins, and beef kabobs. I made mashed potatoes, baked potatoes, and scalloped potatoes. I learned which vegetables were best roasted, boiled, or freshly cut up. Nana even shared her secret dessert recipes with me, and although she was right about baking cookies, her chocolate lava cake served with vanilla ice cream had my vote for the most delicious food on the planet.

And every night, as Nana Jane had promised, everyone in the family sat down together to eat dinner and share their day. Andrew always had plenty of questions. He seemed to know just what to ask to draw out forgotten details. He listened to each of his children.

It became the time that I looked forward to the most each day. I loved listening to everyone take their turn around the table. Even me. I was a part of this now, too. I truly felt as if I was a part of this family.

In the evenings, after dinner, Ben would go get my cello. On the second night, I asked him if he would like to play it. In regular Ben-fashion, he was silent for a few moments, then simply nodded his head.

I had him sit directly in front of me. I showed him how to place the cello in its rock stop, and how to hold it. Next, I gave him the bow, and showed him the basic movements, how to push it or draw it across the strings. We worked on finger placements to produce different notes, and I explained to him about pressure and speed, and how they affected the sound of the music.

Ben listened intently to every word that I said. He was persistent and methodical. He would continue to try something repeatedly until it was right. I taught him beginner songs, like "Twinkle, Twinkle" and "Happy Birthday to You."

When Ben needed time to practice, I would work with Ana on her violin. We worked a lot on connection and pressure, and on the feel of the bow in order to produce a certain pitch or tone. Ana was a quick learner, and with the one-on-one time, she rapidly increased her skills. I was proud of both of them. Focused and determined to do well, they were fun students.

After about an hour of music time, Ben and the adults would head to bed. But Gabe, Ana, and I went outside to sit under the stars. I couldn't get over the beauty here. The stars never looked like this in the city. Too many lights shone into the sky, even at night, so it never got dark enough to see what the stars really looked like.

Gabe talked about the constellations, their names and locations, and their locations in the sky at different times of the year. He pointed out Polaris, the North Star, and Ursa Major and Ursa Minor, the Big Dipper and the Little Dipper. And, Ana even told me how to use the Big Dipper to find the North Star.

One night we walked to a stream that ran behind their house. Another night, we lay in the tall grasses and told our favorite stories from childhood. Each night, I went to bed exhausted, but excited to find out what the next day would bring.

And it was at night, when I was alone, that I thought about Father and Livvy, wondered what they were doing, if they missed me, if they missed home. I did miss them, but I didn't really miss the city or even the tech. I wanted to live each day fully, to the minute, because as each minute ticked by, I knew I was one minute closer to the end of this incredible journey.

And that, I realized, made me sad.

Chapter 28

On Tuesday morning, I woke up to face the fact that I was half way through my stay on the Stayton farm. In some ways, it felt like I had just arrived. In other ways, I felt like I had been here all my life. How could I have felt two things so strongly that were so opposite?

I hustled around to get ready, jumping in for a quick shower, then simply throwing my hair back in a ponytail and only putting on a touch of make-up. I glanced in the mirror before I went downstairs. *I would have never done this before,* I thought, *in the city. Leave my house and go see people without full make-up and hair styled to the max.* No jewelry. No crazy search through clothing programs to select the right color and patterns that would emphasize how I wanted to be seen on that particular day. *Here, I'm just me. And I think I'm beginning to like just being me.*

I took the stairs two at a time, then dashed around the corner into the kitchen. Immediately, I knew something was different. There was a solemn, quiet feeling in the air. Andrew and Gabe were seated on stools at a small island counter in the middle of the kitchen, which in itself wasn't that unusual. We only sat at the big table in the dining room for dinners in the evening.

What was unusual was that Nana Jane and Ben were absent from the picture, as well as Ana, although she may have already headed out to the stables. But Andrew and

Gabe weren't eating. They were staring at a portable digital monitor, which Nana Jane never allowed in her kitchen. She always scooted the family off to other rooms if they had something they wanted to watch.

Gabe looked up at me when I came in. Andrew's focus never shifted from the story that was playing out on the news in front of him. His eyes were intense and his face serious. Gabe turned back to the monitor. Neither of them said anything to me, so I quietly pulled up a stool to join them.

The newscaster was a handsome Green citizen who I recognized as another one of the local SciCity favorites. He was standing in a field that was smoldering around him. In the background, several large buildings were on fire in various stages. Most seemed to be under control, but from just a glance I could tell that the damage was devastating. Both Greens and non-Greens moved across the screen behind the man, some running, some walking, some simply taking a few steps and then stopping to stare.

As I took in everything I was seeing, I listened to the report the man was giving. His voice was deep, and he used dramatic, swooping hand gestures as he spoke. Not that he needed them. The true drama emanated from the destruction around him.

" ...here at the Washburg farm. Located only four miles from some of AHGA's most prominent grain engineering fields, firefighters fought bravely to battle back the blaze, to keep it from spreading further, and damaging more homes and property. The fire raged over six hundred acres last night, before it was brought under control. But that's no consolation for the Washburg family. Their homes, their belongings, their barns, and the majority of their equipment were lost to the flames." He turned and looked at the devastation behind him, slightly shaking his head before turning back to the camera.

"And, if that wasn't enough, even more shocking to everyone here has been the loss of two lives. One of Maddy and Tom Washburg Sr.'s sons, Tom Washburg, Jr., twenty-six years old, has been identified in the wreckage, along with his grandmother, Carol Washburg, who was eighty-one. One family member I spoke to said that Tom Jr. rushed back into the burning house, engulfed in flames, when he was told that his grandmother had not made it out to join the rest of the family. Their bodies were found together, his covering hers in the corner of her second story bedroom.

"Tom Jr. was married with two small boys. He and his family lived in a recently built addition here on the Washburg farm, in order to help his father run the family business. Those of us here at Channel 47 want to express our sincerest sympathies to the Washburg family. Rhys Hix, reporting live from the Washburg farm, nineteen miles west of SciCity."

The news coverage at that time switched to a beautiful Green woman sitting at a news desk in the station. "Thank you, Rhys. We here in the studio reiterate that sympathy." She paused, moving her chin to her left, and was picked up by a different camera, so she could still look directly into the eyes of her viewers.

"Although a full investigation is under way, SciCity Security Enforcers' preliminary reports are indicating the fire is related to recent rebel attacks. Xander Cairo, the lead investigator on this case, made a statement that indicates they have found evidence leading them to believe that a small rebel group was heading to the AHGA research fields next to the Washburg farm when an explosion took place.

"Due to recent dry, windy conditions, the fire spread quickly and soon overtook the houses as well as other buildings. None of the family members have confirmed a rebel presence at the farm, but Officer Cairo stated that was not unusual in cases like this." The woman shifted her focus again.

"Officer Cairo told our reporter that the rebel attacks were becoming increasingly more destructive and well-planned, and that once the fire had started, he was sure the rebel group had fled the scene. However, security enforcers did find one rebel fighter in an adjacent field, apparently badly injured in the explosion, when they expanded their search. We've been informed that this rebel never regained consciousness, and died while en route to the hospital in SciCity. At this point, he has not yet been identified."

The reporter turned her head again, focusing on a new camera. "More on this story and new developments as we continue to follow the rebel terrorism that brings violence to the door of our city. Stay tuned in throughout the day for the most current, accurate information." The screen changed to an ad for some new hotel in downtown SciCity. Andrew switched the monitor off.

Andrew and Gabe turned to look at each other. "Didn't you tell me Tom Washburg was at your meeting a couple of days ago?" Gabe's voice sounded shaky.

Andrew took a deep breath, held it for a few moments and then released it. "Yes, he was there, talking about his family and his son, bragging on his two little grandsons any chance he got." He closed his eyes. "Those poor little boys. That whole family. And, Tom. To lose his oldest son and his own mom in the same fire." They both sat silently.

I couldn't move. I just sat there. I squeezed my eyes shut, too.

Death. Loss. Pain.

I knew what was ahead for those little boys, and I wished with all my heart that I could protect them from what was coming.

I opened my eyes and saw Gabe place his hand on his dad's shoulder. "I'm sorry, Dad. I know Tom Sr.'s your friend. I don't know him or his family that well, but I know from everything you said about them, they're good people."

Andrew opened his eyes, covered Gabe's hand with his own. "Thank you, Son." His eyes glistened. He looked down, then wiped them with the back of his hand.

Gabe's hand dropped back into his lap. He looked down at the counter, and his breathing became more ragged. "I don't know what to believe anymore. How do we know that the security enforcers are telling the truth? How do we know that the rebels were responsible for this?"

His voice started to get louder and faster as he went. "I mean, why would rebels be on the Washburg farm? If they were crossing to go to the research fields, they didn't need to go anywhere near the house. Six hundred acres burned? They could have stayed far out in the fields to avoid the chance of anyone seeing them." His eyes looked wild as his voice got even louder.

"And what kind of 'accident' would cause that kind of a fire? The more I think this through, the more questions I have. And come to think of it, how do they know that guy they found in the field is a rebel if they haven't even identified who he is?" Gabe sat there, shaking his head, his face expressing both anger and confusion.

Andrew sat motionlessly, but I could tell he was thinking, processing everything that Gabe had said. "We'll have to wait and see what else they learn as they investigate. Everything's still preliminary right now. We can't jump to conclusions."

Gabe jumped off his stool, knocking it over, causing me to jump in my seat. "Why not? Why not jump to conclusions?" He was yelling now. "That's exactly what they're doing. And they're sure as hell not going to interview any of the so-called rebels to hear their side of all of this!"

"Gabe, that's enough!" Andrew's voice matched Gabe's in volume. He leaned over and picked up Gabe's stool.

Gabe stared at his father for a few moments, then turned and walked out of the kitchen.

Andrew closed his eyes again and just sat there. For at least a whole minute. He didn't move a muscle. And I didn't either.

I didn't know what to say, what to do. Gabe had some valid points, and even though no one had talked about it all week, I knew he must have been thinking about Gunner, too. About the things Gunner said about the security enforcers and that everything wasn't as it seemed, all packaged up nice and neat on the surface for the news.

Andrew finally turned to me. "I'm sorry, Calyssa. This is a difficult topic for those of us who live outside the city. What do you know about the rebels?"

"Um, I guess only what I've heard on the news. Not that much actually. Only about the attacks lately." *And what I overheard Gabe and Gunner talking about,* I thought.

"There is an extreme rebel group out there who truly believes that anything that is genetically modified or engineered is unnatural, and therefore, should be removed from our planet. There are a lot more people outside the city, people like us, like me, who don't believe that there's a need for extreme genetic modifications anymore, but we also feel that everyone has the right to make their own choice on this issue.

"The problem is that as the city grows larger and expands, it needs more room. Companies, like your family's, need more fields and more room for research as well. And the people, who own the land outside of the city right now, don't want to move. So there's significant tension between these two groups. Two groups of good people with opposing views when it comes to science and their beliefs." Andrew kept his gaze steady, watching my eyes.

"Like Gabe, I have concerns. It's difficult to know if these current situations are the extremists trying to rile up the outlying farmers against SciCity's expansion, or if it's the government trying to find ways to motivate the people to move off their lands." He shook his head.

"Either way, the people who are losing the most aren't the rebel extremists or the government officials. They're people like Tom Washburg. People who work hard every day to do their best for their family and their neighbors. Who keep to themselves but are willing to lend a hand to those who need it. They're good people stuck in the middle of a bad situation." Andrew sighed and looked away from me. He stared out a window that looked across his fields. His land.

The Staytons are pretty far out here, I thought, *but how many years before the growth spreads to here?* The thought of the Staytons losing their farm was unbearable.

This farm. Our farm. It may be the only farm I've ever been on, but now that I've been here I can't imagine it being gone.

I placed my hand on Andrew's shoulder and gave a little squeeze. He continued to stare out the window.

I got up quietly, turned, and walked out of the kitchen.

What can I do? I thought. *How can I help? Who would listen to me, a Green girl on a farm that produced its own food and energy? How do you stop something when you don't feel you have any power?*

Chapter 29

I didn't see Gabe for the rest of the day. I did all the same things, riding horses, cleaning stalls, helping with dinner, but everything seemed somber and quiet. Ana and I didn't visit as much. Mostly, we worked in silence to finish the chores. An unsettled feeling hung in the air. Even Nana Jane wasn't her usual talkative self as we worked together in the kitchen making dinner.

I didn't mind the silence. I wasn't the type of person who needed to talk all the time, so it didn't make me uncomfortable, but I missed the laughter. There was still a comment here and there, and politeness as farm hands passed, but it was obvious that events on the news from last night and this morning weighed heavily on everyone's minds.

After dinner, Ana told Ben we weren't going to play the instruments tonight. Instead, she and I went up to her room and sat on her bed. I could tell she wanted to talk, so I sat there quietly, waiting. After a few moments, she got up and began to pace.

"All this stuff with the Washburg farm is terrible," she began. "It makes me want to cry to think about those two boys that are going to have to grow up without their dad now. I just don't get it. Why don't they put a stop to all of this?" She looked at me, anger flashing through her eyes.

"The government just needs to send the security enforcers out to kill all those crazy rebels. It's ridiculous. They have the power. Why don't they use it and end this?"

I felt my mouth drop open. *Kill the rebels?* I was confused.

"Ana, I don't think that killing anybody is going to stop the problems. In fact, people dying is what's making all of this worse."

She turned and looked right at me. "You don't get it, Lyssa. In a couple of days, you get to go back to your cool house with your awesome tech, and in a few more weeks, you'll be completely Green. In a few months, you'll be going to the university, hanging out with your Green friends." She looked angry. Angry at me.

Why is she angry with me?

"But I'll still be stuck here. On the farm with people who don't understand progress and the future and ...and what I want. And the worse this whole rebel thing gets, the more Dad is going to look for ways to stay out of everything. Because that's what he does. Stays out of things, stays wrapped up in his own little world that he's created to protect us from all the big, bad stuff outside." She looked away from me for a moment, then whipped back with even more intensity in her eyes and her voice.

"But that's where I want to be. Outside of this crappy little world, with all its boring people, trying to find lots of new ways to play it safe. I don't want safe! I want adventure, and freedom, and excitement! I want your life, Calyssa! You don't know how lucky you are!" Then she turned toward the wall and smashed her fist against it.

I got up off the bed and walked over behind her. As I put my hand on her wrist, our memory bracelets touched and chimed, a signal that picture syncing was about to begin, but Ana just scowled at me and shrugged my hand off. I tapped my memory bracelet to cancel the sync, then looked back her. I didn't know what to say to make her feel better. She walked away from me, over to a window and stared off into the night. I walked over and stood beside her again. She stiffened but she didn't leave.

"You're right, Ana. In a few days, I have to leave. But I'm not excited about that. You might think I'm crazy, but it's hard for me to imagine leaving all of you, even though I know I have to. Your family has shown me a completely different life here. And I've discovered it's a life I love.

"You look at my house, hear about my family and my life, and you think you're the one missing out, when the opposite is true. It's what you've got that I've wanted all my life. A father who really listens to you. Siblings who love you and respect you. A grandma who would do anything for you.

"What do I have? A father who is so engrossed in his work that I often don't even talk to him for days. A sister who ridicules me whenever she gets the chance. And that's it. I don't have any other family." I had to stop for a few seconds. I really meant the words I said, and it wasn't easy to say them out loud.

"So I get to go Green. So what? What does that mean? What good does it do for me? Will it make me a better person? It didn't make Livvy a better person. I just don't know." I ran my hand through my hair.

"Why did I do this, the whole Green Enhancement, if I didn't need to? I've found things here at the farm that I love. Like food — real food, not just automate imitations. I love cooking, making things that I enjoy, that others enjoy. I love sitting down at the dinner table with all of you, eating together, listening, sharing. And guess what? In a few weeks, there won't be any reason for me to ever do that again. Ever. Any of it."

I closed my eyes. *Going Green had never seemed like a choice that would force me to give up anything. But now ....*

Ana turned toward me for the first time since I had started talking. "It's worth it. You'll see. You'll see just how lucky you are." Then she turned and walked back to her bed. She lay down and rolled over so her back was to me. I just stood at the window and listened until her breathing became slow and regular.

When I knew she was asleep, I slipped out of her room. I walked over to Gabe's room, but the door was closed and I couldn't see any light coming from under it. I sighed and went back to my room.

I closed the door behind me, opened the window to let the cool breeze in, and sat in the dark on my bed. I realized I had a lot to think about. Talking with Ana made me recognize that I was unsure about so many things in my life.

Was it only last week that I looked at myself in my mirror and thought that my life couldn't get any better than it was on that day?

What a difference one week can make in someone's life. I wasn't sure what I'd say right now if I was once again standing in front of that mirror, evaluating myself and my future.

I felt restless. I got up and looked out the window. The farm was truly beautiful at night, maybe even more than during the day. The night held a softness here, one that insulated all it held with tranquility and serenity.

Then, out of the corner of my eye, I saw a movement. I almost looked away thinking I had imagined it, but I saw it again. *There's someone out there.*

Chapter 30

I dropped to my knees and continued to watch. The dark figure came right up to the house, one window over from mine, looking up, seemingly studying the second floor. Then it picked something up and tossed it at the window.

Clink. It bounced off the window. *Gabe's window*, I thought. Clink, clink. Two more tosses, not hard enough to be trying to break it, but loud enough to notice. *What's going on?*

I heard Gabe's window slide up. I couldn't see him, but I knew he was there, in the darkness, just like me.

"Who's there?" His voice was low, but it held a harsh tone.

"Gabe?" A man's whisper.

"Who is it?" Gabe's voice was a little louder this time. That caused the man below to look around. He glanced back over his shoulder, and moved closer to the darkness of the house. I felt my breath catch.

"It's Kye, Gabe. I need to talk to you. Now. Come down."

A few seconds of silence and I heard Gabe's window slide shut. After a few more seconds, I heard his bedroom door open and soft footsteps head down the hall.

Kye.

Gunner's friend. But why is he here without Gunner? He didn't even seem to know Gabe the last time he was here. I got a bad feeling in the pit of my stomach.

I jumped off my bed and pulled on my shoes. Thankfully, I was still fully dressed. I slipped out my door and headed for the stairs. Just as I got there, I heard the front door click softly shut. Gabe wasn't far ahead of me.

I have to catch up so I don't lose him in the dark.

I hurried down the stairs and opened the front door, pausing only long enough to look up to make sure no one had heard me. The rest of the house was completely silent. I slipped out the door and pulled it softly shut behind me.

I ran close to the side of the house, rounded the corner, and immediately dropped to my knees. Gabe was motioning for Kye to follow him, then he headed across the yard toward the closest barn. Kye followed, still looking around, scanning the yard and fields beyond, as if he expected to see someone else. I waited until they were almost to the barn and then sprinted after them.

By the time I reached the barn door, they were already inside. But they had left the door slightly ajar, and I slipped in. I heard hushed voices, but I couldn't make out what they were saying. Sliding silently along the wall, I stopped when I could see them standing at the edge of one of the empty stalls. I moved closer until I could make out their words.

"Why?" Gabe asked, his voice still hushed but harsh.

"Believe me. This is not what I want to be doing right now." There was a brief pause, and then Kye continued. "Do you get the risk I took coming here? There are security enforcers everywhere, in case you haven't noticed. And they're not asking questions with those loaded guns they're carrying." Kye's voice was just as hard as Gabe's. This wasn't a friendly conversation.

"Then why come here? It's a risk for you. And, we don't need people linking us to you rebels."

"You rebels? That's what you've got to say? Man, I should walk out of here right now. I knew this was a mistake. Damn Gunner."

"Gunner?" A change in Gabe's voice. Concern. Urgency.

Kye paused again for a second, like he was trying to decide what to do next. He took a couple of steps away from Gabe and I couldn't see him anymore. "Yeah. That's why I'm here. Did you hear about the incident at the Washburg place last night?"

My heart was pounding in my chest. *No*, I thought, *not Gunner*.

"Yeah." Gabe's voice was even quieter now. He stepped in the same direction Kye had gone. I leaned forward, but I couldn't see either of them without moving around the stall wall.

"Gunner was there. And he got hurt, Gabe. Bad. I don't know if he's going to make it. He lost a lot of blood. I carried him back. He's with the camp doc right now. Last thing he said before he passed out was that he wanted to see you." Silence. Seconds ticked by.

Finally, Kye's voice continued, "That was last night. It was close to daybreak before I could get him back to our camp. He never regained consciousness and I had to carry him over some rugged terrain. Then I had to wait until nightfall again to come here."

"He's alive?" Gabe sounded alarmed. His voice was getting louder. I heard horses beginning to make noises in some of the other stalls.

"He was when I left. I didn't tell anybody I was leaving. I snuck out and came straight here. Gunner is a good man. I felt I owed him that. To come tell you what happened." Kye's voice was less harsh now, more tired, softer.

"Did you ride here?"

"No, I couldn't get a horse out without raising too much attention. And the vehicles are all under guard with everything that's happened. I just ran."

"How far?"

"Not sure. Maybe ten, twelve miles." More silence.

"Okay. Let me saddle up some horses. My truck will be too loud. We can stay in better cover if we take the horses back to your camp anyway."

Then Gabe came back around the corner of the stall ...and ran directly into me.

Chapter 31

"Calyssa!" Gabe looked surprised, but only for a second. Then anger began to spread across his face.

"Gabe...I ...uh ...." I didn't know what to say. I was still reeling from the news.

"Who's this?" Kye was now standing next to Gabe. His gun pointed directly at me.

I heard a gurgle come out of me. Not a sound that I'd ever made before, and not one that I wanted to ever hear again. I felt nauseous. A gun pointed right at my chest. I looked at Gabe. My mouth moved but no actual words came out.

"Whoa, Kye. Relax. This is Calyssa. She's a friend of mine staying here at the farm over spring break."

"Oh." Kye lowered the gun and replaced the scowl with a smirk. "Staying with you for spring break, huh? Must be nice."

"What?" *Is he inferring what I think he is?* Even though I still felt like I was going to throw up, I looked him straight in the eyes. "He said friend." I closed my eyes and shook my head. *Guys. Seriously.*

Kye laughed. My eyes snapped back open and I glared at him. *Funny how anger makes you feel a little braver,* I thought as I noticed that puking feeling subside. He just laughed a little harder. I clenched my jaw and felt my face begin to flush.

"Calyssa, knock it off. This is not the time or place. Get back to the house now," Gabe said as he turned to walk away.

I grabbed Gabe's arm, pulling him back. "Really? You think you can send me to the house? I heard what you heard, and I am not letting you go anywhere alone with this guy. Not a chance."

Gabe shook off my grip. "I don't have time for this. Go back to bed. This isn't about you. It doesn't even have anything to do with you. Go. You're wasting time that my friend may not have." Worry was back in his eyes again.

I crossed my arms.

"The way I see it," I said, "is you have two choices. Let me go with you and we leave right now. Or, send me back to the house, and I go wake your dad up and tell him exactly what's going on."

"Or I knock you over the head with this gun, and we leave you here. I vote for the third option," Kye said with a sneer.

"Stop it, both of you. Calyssa, you're being impossible. You can't go. You could get hurt. You'll just slow us down." Gabe started to walk away again.

Once again, I grabbed his arm, and this time I jerked him hard back toward me.

"I can ride as well as you can now. I'm not going to slow you down. You don't know where you're going or what you're walking into. This is my decision. My choice. Not yours, Gabe. I'm going." I let go of his arm and walked toward the saddles. I grabbed the one I had been using, and within seconds, I was saddling up Blackjack.

Both guys stood staring at me. They looked at each other.

"I don't care if she goes or not as long as she doesn't slow us down. I'm already going to have some explaining to do when I get you back to camp, so I don't think that bringing one more is gonna get me in any more trouble than I'll already be in. But we've got to go now." Kye pulled the strap of his gun over his head and slipped the gun around his back.

Gabe sighed. "Fine. You slow us down, we leave you. You screw up anywhere along the way, we leave you. You get lost ...."

"Yeah, yeah. I know. You leave me. Quit wasting time and get your horse saddled up." That got a smile from Kye.

Now Gabe scowled. He grabbed a saddle and tossed it to Kye. "Know how to use one of these?" He pointed to a big black horse. "Take that one."

Then, he grabbed another saddle and put it on a chestnut horse. Gabe was fast, and he and I mounted at almost the same time even though I had started saddling up first.

We rode out the back of the barn where a huge door stood open to the field behind.

"Wait a minute," Gabe said. He jumped down and ran back inside. He came back out about a minute later with a gun slung over his own shoulder. He jumped back up on the horse and we all took off.

We rode the horses to the fence at the back of the field. Gabe jumped off again, punched a code into a panel, then mounted back up on the horse. We all rode through, the gate closing automatically behind us.

As soon as we were clear of the farm, Kye took the lead, and urged his horse to a full gallop. Gabe fell in behind him, and I followed Gabe. It was pitch black in the forest and I couldn't even tell if there was a trail we were following, but Blackjack seemed sure of what she was doing, so I leaned forward and urged her on.

We ran the horses on and off for the next hour as the terrain allowed. Riding by moonlight was beautiful, but at the speeds we were traveling, I rarely got to look around. We came to a large river and paused for a couple of minutes to let the horses get a drink.

"We're only a few minutes away," Kye said, finally speaking. He turned toward us. "When we get there, follow my lead. Don't talk to anyone. Don't say anything. Act like you know what you're doing, and that you're supposed to be there."

He looked at Gabe. "I'm telling them you're his brother. In his eyes, you are. That'll get you in to see him."

He looked at me and smirked. "And I'm saying you're Gabe's wife. I don't want any questions about why you're with us. Any problems with that?"

Gabe shook his head.

"Fine by me," I said. "Mrs. Stayton it is." Gabe shot me a warning glance. Kye laughed.

"Get into your role, man. The Fitting brothers are in camp right now. Nothing can smell fishy or you'll find yourself strung up."

I didn't know what that meant exactly, but it didn't sound good.

We walked the horses now, still single file, along the riverbank. Up ahead, beyond Kye, I saw light. A minute later, there were voices. Then a couple of guys appeared. Kye walked right up to them. Gabe glanced over his shoulder back at me, and our eyes held for a second, then he turned and followed Kye's lead. We handed the reins off to a guy after a hushed, but obviously heated discussion.

"We walk from here." Kye started up a path through dense trees. In a few minutes, the forest opened up and we stepped into a clearing. I looked around and noticed that even though it was the middle of the night, there were people everywhere with guns. Big guns. Mean looking people. Nobody smiled.

Automatically, I slipped my hand into Gabe's as I walked by his side. He looked surprised for a second, then pulled me closer to him. It made me feel safer to walk right next to him, to have him holding my hand.

No one else stopped us as we walked through the camp. It was huge. Tents everywhere. Campfires spread out with people standing around them. Everybody watching us. Everybody with his or her hand on a gun. Except me. *I think I might be the only person in this entire place that doesn't have a gun.* I wasn't sure that was a very reassuring thought.

A big tent was off to the right in front of us. Kye stopped and talked to the men at the door. They all looked at us. One of them ducked inside. He came back a few seconds later. "Okay," he said, "but only for a couple of minutes."

He pulled back the flap of the tent and we followed Kye inside.

It was incredibly bright in this tent and it took my eyes some time to adjust. Gabe was pulling me along. As I looked around, I saw makeshift hospital beds. About a dozen of them. Each one with a person on it with some sort of injury. Broken arm. Leg elevated in a cast. Head bandages. Scrapes. Cuts. Burns. But I noticed that even though we were in the middle of the woods, this tent had a white floor, and the patients and the beds were clean. We were probably the dirtiest things in the room.

I heard Gabe gasp before I actually saw Gunner. That's when I knew it was going to be bad. I squeezed his hand and looked around Kye. Most of Gunner's face and body were covered with white bandages. His eyes were closed. But I could see his chest moving.

I let out my own breath. At least he was alive. We had made it and he was alive. I felt Gabe relax, just a little, as he leaned over to see Gunner better. "He's breathing," he said. I nodded.

A tired looking man in a long, white coat hurried over. Kye intercepted him on the way. They talked for a moment, then Kye turned to us, and said, "I'll meet you outside in a couple of minutes. The less people in here the better. Infection and all that." He turned and left the way we had come in.

The man introduced himself as Dr. Garreth. "Your brother was in an explosion. He had a piece of metal that was jammed through his ribs, into his chest. It punctured one of his lungs, but it missed his heart. Fortunately, Kye had the good sense to leave the metal in him. Gunner would have bled to death for sure if he had pulled it out."

The doctor turned and looked at Gunner. "He has some burns, but those are mostly superficial. I've stopped the bleeding by sealing up the arteries that were hit. Thank God, I have some of the new surgery tech here. I was able to seal his lung as well. He lost quite a bit of blood, but I'm feeling much more confident tonight that he's going to make it.

"It was touch and go through the day, but he seems to be stabilizing now. I have him on some serious pain meds, but he should be at least somewhat awake by the morning. Come back then and we'll talk more."

"Thank you, Dr. Garreth." Gabe shook his hand. Then we turned and left the tent.

Kye was waiting for us outside. "Come on. I need to get you two put away until I can spread your cover story around a bit." Kye took off and we followed. He came to a small tent.

"Get in. It's Gunner's and mine. You can stay here tonight. I'll bunk with some other friends. Don't come out. I'll come get you first thing in the morning. And be quiet. Don't want you newlyweds drawing any attention to your honeymoon suite." I shot Kye a look, and then, even in only the light of the moon, I noticed Gabe's face turn red.

I followed Gabe to the tent. "Goodnight, Kye."

He smiled at me and disappeared back down the path.

"We should probably head in for the night," Gabe said, reaching to find the zipper on the tent flap.

But even as I nodded, I could hear lots of voices, some sounding agitated. "Maybe we should go check out what's happening," I said. "If it's trouble, like security enforcers, or something, we won't know in time to do anything if we're in the tent." It sounded plausible, but really, I was a little nervous about this whole sleeping arrangement.

Gabe looked toward the direction of the voices. I could tell he was thinking about what Kye had said and weighing it with what I had pointed out.

"Okay. But just for a minute. Until we can figure out what's going on. And stay close. We don't need to get split up."

"Don't worry about that," I said, grabbing his hand again. "I have no intention of being anywhere around here without you."

Chapter 32

I followed Gabe down a trail that led toward the voices. As we got closer, I saw a large group around an enormous fire that lit up the whole area. People seemed upset, restless. We tucked into the back of the group and worked our way up a little closer to the front, where several men were engaged in a serious conversation.

Someone in the crowd yelled out, "What do you think about it, Joshua?"

A man rose and walked toward the fire. A silence fell over the crowd. Every face focused on his slow, deliberate movement. Even the crackle of the fire seemed to hush in his presence.

When he first began to speak, his back was to us. I couldn't see his face, but it didn't matter. His power was in his voice.

"As I stand, on this very spot, I am a free man. I live the life I choose. No one tells me what I have to do, where I have to go, if I have to eat, who I have to love. Those are my choices, mine alone.

"But my heart is heavy. For so many stand blindly, bound by a society which thinks no more of them than what they can give. Which tells them that their value is based not on who they are but what they can become. That they are not enough, that they must *become more* in order to *mean* something."

Joshua turned as he spoke. The fire reflected in his eyes as if fueling his passion and his volume as he continued.

"They tried to force their ideals, their attitudes, their restraints upon us. They call us 'Drones.' Like the bees in our colonies that have no real purpose for living. They believe we are mindless, that we have nothing of real value to contribute to society.

"Does that sound like you? Have you not been the tireless workers of your communities? Have you not given and given until you simply had no more to give them? And when it wasn't enough? Some of you refused to give more and ran, some of you revolted and were punished, and some of you gave in and were broken.

"But by God's grace, each of you made it here today. Take a good look around, Brothers and Sisters. See what your society, your community, the false gods governing the Green Commonwealth have taken from you. Your homes, your land, your jobs, your spouses, your parents, your children."

He paused, and I did as he commanded — I looked at those around me. Across the fire, I saw a woman crying. Silent tears running down her face. And I felt a wave of incredible sadness wash through the crowd, seeping from person to person as they remembered loved ones who were no longer with them, houses that they had called homes, lives that they had somehow, somewhere lost along the way, circumstances tossing them into this camp as easily as a wave tossed sand on the shore.

"I have felt enough, heard enough, seen enough suffering to last me a lifetime." Joshua's eyes glistened. He closed them for a moment and dropped his head. Seconds ticked by.

And when it felt like the weight of all the terrible things that had happened in our world just might crush us, Joshua lifted his head, standing up so straight that he seemed to grow six inches right there in front of the fire.

And his voice was no longer sad. It carried a far different feeling this time.

"Enough. Enough feeling sorry for yourself. No more tears. Take that sadness, that hopelessness, that weakness, and mold it into something useful. No more standing on the sidelines. No more feeling inadequate. Because you are not inadequate. You are not a failure. You do not need to be anything more than you are today. You are enough. Enough to rise up and take back what is rightfully yours." His voice continued to rise with each sentence, and people were beginning to nod their heads, to stand up a little straighter, too.

"Genetic engineering threw us headfirst into a crisis that almost wiped out our planet, our entire population. Unrelenting scientists and corrupt corporations pushed and prodded and forced nature to do unnatural things. And our beautiful, incredible planet struggled and fought, frail, on the brink of devastation, extinction, total annihilation ...only through God's grace, it slowly found a way to return to us.

"But look around and don't be fooled by what you see. We find ourselves as a human race back on the same path we have already once taken. One that almost wiped us completely off the planet. New corporations, more powerful than ever, and new scientists more willing to prove that they can be their own gods, creating their own organisms in any form they choose, have risen up and taken hold of our world once again."

What? What is he saying? There was so much more to the PK years. It wasn't that simple. We all knew that, I mean, everyone had to know that, right? So many positive things had come from genetic engineering. But people were beginning to agree, to yell out their support, standing up. And Joshua, his eyes now wild, scanned the crowd, slamming one fist into his other hand over and over to emphasize his points.

"It's time to stand up and fight for what is right, what is natural, for our planet and for our people! It's time to take back our lands, to remove all of the GMOs that have been forced on us, to rid the world of anything unnatural!"

Everyone was up, on their feet, yelling, fists pumping the air. The overwhelming sadness that I had felt earlier had been completely erased and replaced with a fierce, almost out of control anger. Feet were stomping, bodies were swaying, everyone pushing to get closer to Joshua. I felt Gabe's arm tighten around me.

"Everything genetically modified on this planet has to go! Nothing can remain! We must purify our planet so we can start over, fresh, new, uncontaminated by the evils of science and genetic engineering!"

A voice rang out, over the top of the others, "What about those who have chosen to go Green? What will happen to them?"

Joshua held up his hands, and silence once again spread through the crowd. His breathing was heavy, and he took a few more steps toward the fire. His next words seethed with anger.

"I never said that doing what is right would be easy. It's not a path for cowards. But those people that *chose* to be genetically modified knew what they were doing. They made their choice. They are no longer of this earth. They cannot produce children that are Green. As a species, they would die off without science intervening. They cannot be allowed to continue to contaminate our world."

"But wouldn't that be murder?" another voice yelled out from somewhere in the back.

Joshua's eyes turned hard. His jaw clenched. Every muscle in his body tensed.

When he responded his voice was low and slow, as if he disliked the taste of each word he spat out. "Murder is the killing of another human. Humans are born naturally on this planet every day. The Greens are not born, they are created in labs, by scientists. To kill one is no more murder than putting down a diseased dog. Both slaughters protect our families and bring safety back to our communities."

Again, he paused, and looked slowly through the crowd. Piercing eyes – I swore he could see me, that he knew I was there. Sheer terror froze me in place. I knew I should run, but I couldn't move. My feet, my legs, my body ...nothing followed the commands of my brain.

"Search your hearts, search your souls. Look inside you for what you know is right. Tonight I ask that those who hear the call deep inside themselves, those who no longer are willing to be shackled by science's stranglehold on nature and man, step forward to join me and the others who chose to take this fight to the cities, to the Green Commonwealth, to the corporations who have already taken so much from us!"

At first, no one moved, but low murmurs began to stir through the crowd. Then, about a dozen people, a mix of men and women stepped right up in front of Joshua. He smiled at them. And, again, a silence fell.

"The choice you are making is not for everyone, only for the incredibly brave, the deeply committed, only the true believers – those of us who know we are the only ones who can make a difference, who will put our lives on the line for our brothers and sisters, our mothers and fathers, our children and our children's children. With this knowledge comes great power, and with great power comes great sacrifice, for you must leave your families, your friends, and the safety of your camp. But in return you will become a part of the greatest war this planet has seen, the only one that truly matters, because it is the fight to save humankind."

Two other men joined Joshua. "Kneel," he commanded to the people now standing in front of him.

He continued to speak while the other two men placed something around the neck of each person kneeling. "As a symbol of your commitment, I give to you the 'Lost Star,' for we have been lost far too long, and it will remind you of the way home, back to nature and a time before science tampered with the true perfection of our world. Welcome, Brothers and Sisters. Rejoice tonight with your friends and family, for tomorrow at dawn we leave to join others at the front line."

My heart was racing. What in the hell was I thinking coming to this place? I had to get out of here. What if someone found out who I was? What I was? I leaned over to look for a way out of the crowd, back to the tent. And with that small movement, I lost my balance. But more importantly, I lost hold of Gabe.

Chapter 33

I turned to look where Gabe had been, but people were rushing now toward Joshua and his new recruits, and I didn't see Gabe anywhere. I had to get back to the tent. My heart felt as if it could burst out of my chest at any moment. I couldn't breathe.

I had to get out of this crowd. *Now.*

With my head down, I pushed against that massive surge of people that were all fighting to move closer to the fire. For every step I tried to take, I felt as if I was being pushed two steps back, but somehow, I finally made my way past all of the people, and broke out into the open.

Taking a big gulp of fresh air, I half sprinted toward the trail that I thought led to the tent. At that point, I didn't actually care where I went as long as it was away from that man.

Who was this "Joshua?" How could he be so full of anger and hatred? And, why were all of these people listening to him? Some of the things he said may have been true, but others were just plain crazy! And those people, they were right there with him, being carried along by his tirade. I shuddered when I thought about what might have happened if someone had found out about me, that I was one of the unnatural evils that he was talking about.

Wiping a cold sweat from my forehead, I stopped to figure out exactly where I was. I could still hear people talking, but I could no longer understand what they were saying. As I continued to walk, the sound became a faint hum in the distance.

A twig snapped from up ahead and I instinctively dove off the path, scraping my hand and banging my shin on a big rock. "Ouch!" I said, more loudly than I intended to.

"Calyssa, is that you?" A forceful whisper from just ahead of me.

Gabe.

"It's me. I'm right here. You startled me," I said as I scrambled to get back to my feet.

He grabbed me and pulled me into a tight hug. "I thought I had lost you, and then ...I started to think about what would happen if they found you, and ...." His voice trailed off.

"I'm okay," I tried to say, but it came out weird because it was muffled since my face was totally squished into his chest.

"Oh, sorry." He awkwardly stepped back from me.

I reached out and grabbed his hand again. "I'm just happy you're here now."

We took off, and in a few minutes, we were back at Gunner and Kye's tent.

Inside the tent was a small digital light that must have been set to motion-sensor because it lit up softly as soon as we went in. Somehow, just being inside the tent made me feel safer. Like I could breathe regularly again. Like maybe, I wasn't in a camp full of crazy maniacs bent on taking over the world.

The tent wasn't very big. Gabe couldn't even stand all the way up in it. It had some blankets folded up and stacked in one corner, and a couple of duffle bags in the other. A few pieces of clothing thrown to the side. And there were a few pictures pinned to one of the walls, about halfway up.

I squatted down to get a better look at them. Gabe noticed, too, and dropped down beside me. Some were recent photos, and others were obviously older. Several were of Gunner and Kye together. I noticed pictures of Gunner when he was younger, too. I was sure it was him - same mischievous grin. Some were with a man and woman. *Probably his mom and dad*, I thought. In the others, him and another boy. I looked closer.

"That's you!" I smiled, looking at the younger versions of Gabe.

Gabe slumped all the way to the floor. He put his arms on his knees and his head in his hands.

"Gabe, are you okay?"

"No." He looked up at me. "Look around this place. Gunner has nothing. This is it? Some blankets, a bag with a few clothes, some old pictures." He shook his head as he looked around again.

"How could I not know he was living like this? I should have paid more attention. I should have insisted that he move in with us when his parents died. I should have ...done something. Anything." He dropped his head and rested it on his knees.

"But I didn't. I failed him. My very best friend in the whole world. I looked the other way. And now, he's here. In a rebel camp with nothing but all of these irrational people.

When Kye came, I'd thought it might be bad, but I didn't know it would be this bad. Those people would have killed you tonight, Calyssa, if they had known who you were." Gabe slammed one of his fists into the ground.

I sat down next to him. "I know. Believe me, I was terrified. But we don't know who that guy was or if Gunner even knows him. It doesn't sound like he's actually a part of this group." I pulled his other arm away from his face. His cheeks were damp. "Gunner made his own choices to be here, Gabe. You can't blame yourself for choices he made."

I was still holding onto his arm, and I gave it a little squeeze. "And you're here now. You're here to make sure he's alright. You're risking a lot to be here for your friend."

And so am I.

"But where was I when he needed me? Maybe if I had been there I could have done something. He came to me, Calyssa. That was him at the door on your first night at the farm, when we sent you upstairs."

"I know," I whispered. "I saw him inside from the top of the stairs. And then again, outside the window of Nana's bedroom. I overheard your conversation."

"Then you know he asked for my help. But I was selfish and turned him down. And now he's here, in the middle of nowhere, in a makeshift hospital being cared for by a guy that I don't even know is a real doctor." There was true anguish in his eyes.

"If he dies, it's my fault."

"Oh, Gabe." I placed my hand on the side of his face and gently pulled it over so he would look at me.

"This is not your fault. You are the least selfish person I know. You couldn't go with Gunner, your best friend, because you couldn't leave your family. You put their needs first. You had to. Ben, Nana Jane, Ana, even your dad. They need you." He started to look away, but I pulled his face back toward me again.

"Because that's who you are, Gabe Stayton. You're the most incredible guy I know. You love your family and give everything you've got to them, for them. You're a hard worker. You're a loving brother, son, grandson." I paused, took a breath, and continued, looking straight into his eyes. "You're a very special person." I smiled softly at him. "I wish you could see yourself the way I see you."

"Yeah, I'm a real saint. But I'm a total loser as a friend." He pulled his head away from my hands and dropped it again.

I leaned against him, and put my head on his shoulder. "I don't think so. You just traveled by horse, in the middle of the night, over ten miles to check on a guy that you were fighting with a few days ago. Because he's your friend." Gabe sat silently.

"It's okay to be scared. I'm scared, too," I said. "And it's okay to be angry. But don't beat yourself up. Gunner's going to need you to be strong in the morning."

I slid my arm around him. "Gunner's lucky to have you as his friend."

We stayed seated that way for a long time. My arm around him. My head on his shoulder.

Finally, he took a deep breath. "We better get some sleep. It'll be sunrise soon."

Sunrise. Dawn. Morning!

"Umm ...what is your family going to think when we're not there when they get up in the morning?" A little bit of fear raced through me. I didn't think that Andrew Stayton was a man that I wanted upset at me.

Gabe looked at me, and for the first time since we got to the rebel camp, he smiled and let out a little laugh. "Don't look so stressed. When I went in to grab my gun, I wrote Dad a quick note saying that I decided to take you camping for a night or two. I said we wouldn't go too far and that we'd be careful. I go out camping all time. He probably won't like it, but at least he won't call out a search party for us. I hope." He smiled again.

"And, I'm sure we'll have to sit down and have a 'talk' when I get back about how it's inappropriate to take a young woman camping by myself. Not to mention that Ana is going to be incredibly pissed that I took you. That might be worse than the talk with Dad."

I laughed. "Great. There's gonna be all kinds of rumors about us sleeping together. Good job, Gabe Stayton. Thanks a lot." He laughed, too. It was good to feel some of the tension leave, even if it would only be for a little while.

"We do need to do it," he said. I felt my eyebrows shoot up.

"Go to sleep, I mean." Another half-smile.

He grabbed the blankets and laid them out, one on top of the other.

"That's it. Sorry, only a bed. No pillows. I know it's not what you're used to. Do you think you can rough it here for the night?"

I scrunched my nose and pretended to look overly skeptical.

"If not," he said, "I can check with Kye. I bet he'd let you snuggle up with him tonight,"

I pitched off my shoes and jumped under the top blanket. "You coming?"

He stood there for a few seconds, hunched over in the tent, looking down at me.

"Really, you shouldn't make a girl ask twice." I tried to keep my face serious, but a smile kept trying to slip out.

In a blink, he tapped off the light, kicked off his shoes and was lying next to me under the blanket.

"No pillow does kinda suck, though," I said.

"I knew you'd be high maintenance." He sighed. "Come here. Rest your head on me." He pulled me up against his chest. "I know I'm all muscle so I won't be too soft, but at least maybe it'll get you to stop complaining."

I tucked into his side, nuzzled my head on his shoulder with his arm wrapped around me.

"Nope. It's fine. I don't feel any muscles at all, just soft and squishy." I poked him in the side. He grimaced.

"Hey, down-and-out guy here, remember? Careful with the cutting remarks. I'm sensitive." I couldn't see his face, but I could hear the smile in his voice.

"Right. I'll keep that in mind." I closed my eyes and snuggled in toward his chest. It really was comfortable. And I was tired, more than I'd realized.

I lay there, next to Gabe, listening to his breathing, feeling his heartbeat on my cheek. I did mean all the things that I'd said to him. *He's an amazing guy.*

I thought about the others guys I had thought were amazing. Like Ashton. *Really?* Boy, my standard of amazing was definitely a lot lower before I met Gabe. Ashton didn't even compare. He was gorgeous, but that was all he cared about. Looks. Connections. What other people thought about him. He didn't want to be with me because he liked me. It was all about who I was, well almost was, because he didn't want to be seen with me until I was Green.

It's going to be interesting back at school, I thought. I was glad Gabe was in my science class. That DeBeau had put us together for that project. That I had the chance to get to know the real him. Because he was right, I hadn't known who he was then. But I was getting there now. Gabe Stayton was definitely a person worth getting to know.

Chapter 34

I opened my eyes when I felt movement. It was light outside. Gabe was putting on his shoes. He looked over and our eyes met.

"Good morning, Sleepy Head. Might want to wipe that drool off the side of your face." He smiled.

Drool? What? My hand automatically went to the side of my mouth and I wiped it on my shirtsleeve. *Yuck!*

"I'm starting to hear some voices outside the tent. I'm thinking Kye should be back any time to get us." He unzipped the tent a crack so he could look out.

I stretched, rolled over, and put my shoes on, too. I wanted to be ready when Kye came. And, I didn't want to be anywhere in this camp without Gabe.

Gabe and I folded the blankets and put them back in the corner of the tent. I also folded the clothes that were lying on the floor as well and laid them on the bags.

Hearing the zipper move, I turned around to see Kye opening it, motioning us out. I followed Gabe.

"Morning," Kye said to Gabe. Gabe nodded.

As I stepped out of the tent door, Kye looked at me. I smiled. Then a weird expression flashed across his face, and Kye pushed me roughly back into the tent. Hard enough that I fell right on my butt as I went though.

"What the ...?" I heard Gabe say, and I saw Kye shove him through the door as well. Then he followed us in. Three in this little tent was definitely a crowd.

Gabe stepped forward so he was in Kye's face. If it hadn't felt so tense it would have been comical. Both guys hunched over, nose-to-nose.

"Back. Off." Kye growled and turned around, zipping the tent back shut. "Are you purposefully trying to get me killed?" he asked in a low voice.

"What are you talking about?" Gabe asked.

I was struggling to get back on my feet. There wasn't a lot of room so it was making it tough to get back up again.

"Are you serious? You had me bring a *gimp* into this camp? Think about that for a minute. Are you nuts?" Kye glared so harshly at me that I froze. Gabe turned to look at me, too.

"I didn't even think about that ...I ...Calyssa's different ...she's ...."

"She's a gimp. Plain and simple. Nothing else is going to matter."

"Wait a minute," I snapped. "A gimp? Come on, Kye. You don't have to be a jerk. Grow up."

"Are you kidding? You have no idea just how much trouble you would have been in if the Fitting brothers had found out you were in the camp ...."

I cut him off, "The Fitting brothers? I've heard them mentioned on the news ...." I paused as the pieces began to fall into place in my mind. "Oh my god, was that the guy talking last night at the fire?"

Kye threw a nasty look at Gabe. "You were there last night? At the fire? With her? After I told you to stay in the tent?" He was fuming. "I should just turn you both over right now to the camp council. Joshua Fitting and his brothers may have taken off this morning, but there are still people here thinking about joining them. And yeah, that's who you heard last night. Joshua, the oldest of the Fitting brothers."

"Now wait just a minute," I stammered, trying to move away from Kye in that tiny tent, "Gunner sent for us, remember? You did this as a favor to Gunner, your friend. What would he say if he found out you turned us over to that crazy guy?" I was starting to sweat again. Memories of last night were racing through my head.

Kye sighed and sat down on the floor. He rubbed his eyes. Gabe and I sat down, too. Kye looked at Gabe and shook his head. "This is trouble."

Gabe turned to me. "Out here, calling someone a gimp isn't just 'name-calling.' A gimp is a genetically modified person. You heard first-hand last night what they believe when genetic modification is involved. Genetically modified people are no exception."

I stared at both the guys, the realization of my situation once again hitting me like a punch in the stomach. "But I'm not totally Green yet."

"You've started. Anybody can see it. You've got the eyes." Kye looked stressed now.

My eyes. My incredible, green eyes. The ones that I had waited eighteen years for. Today, they just might get me killed. I swallowed hard. This was unreal.

"What do we do?" Gabe asked. "Can't she stay in the tent all day? Then we can sneak her back out tonight. We can say that she's sick or something?"

Kye was shaking his head. "That won't work. People saw her last night when you guys arrived at camp and went to see Gunner. The doc saw her, too. Thank God he was preoccupied with all his patients. But today, out in the sun, with everybody checking you guys out ...not everyone, feels the same as Joshua Fitting, but with him and his brothers in camp last night, people are considering his ideas more closely."

I had a sinking feeling. I started to panic. I looked around. The little tent started feeling a lot smaller. I was breathing harder, but I couldn't catch my breath. I felt dizzy.

Gabe reached out and steadied me. "Look at me, Calyssa. I won't let anything happen to you. Give us a minute. Kye and I will figure this out."

Kye jumped up and unzipped the tent.

Gabe jumped up, too. "Where are you going?" He looked worried.

"I'll be right back. Don't go anywhere."

Right. Like we're going to take a stroll around the camp.

I heard the tent zip back up and Gabe sat back down with me again. I was still breathing hard. I started to rock back and forth. "This is bad, Gabe. I shouldn't have come. I shouldn't have pressured you to let me come. You tried to tell me. But I wouldn't listen. I'm so stupid."

Stupid enough to get myself killed. And Gabe has a family that needs him, and now I've got him wrapped up in this, too.

"Calyssa." Gabe grabbed my shoulders and shook me, hard enough to snap me back to reality.

"Calyssa, listen to me. It's going to be okay. Kye will come up with something. Look at me. I'm telling you it's going to be okay."

I looked into his eyes. "I'm so sorry." I felt a tear slide down my cheek.

"Damn it, Calyssa. Don't you give up. I wouldn't have made it last night without you talking me through everything. You wouldn't let me give up on myself then. Don't you give up on me now." He leaned in close to me. Wiped the tear from my cheek.

"I won't let anything bad happen to you. I promise." He leaned in closer. "Tell me you believe me."

"I believe you," I whispered.

The zipper moved and we both jumped. Kye stepped through and quickly zipped it back up. I noticed a small bag in his hand. He pushed Gabe over a bit and sat down directly across from me. "Start praying right now that this will work."

He unzipped the bag and took out a small rectangular container that had two round screw tops on it.

"This is from one of the supply tents. Sometimes when we send people into SciCity, we try to make them look different if we're worried they'll be recognized." He held out the container.

"You're going to have to put these in your eyes, Calyssa. They're colored contacts. I don't know how well they'll work to cover that green, but anything is better than what you have now."

I hesitated. Kye grabbed my hand and slapped the plastic container in it. "Do it," he said. "And do us all a favor – don't take them out until you leave here."

"Uh ...I ...How?" My vision was great. I'd never had to wear glasses or have corrective surgery or anything. I didn't know what to do.

"Put one of the contacts on your fingertip, then open your eyes wide and look up. Touch the contact to your eyeball, slowly. When you feel it set, relax your eye and look down. It'll slide into place." I opened one side of the container.

I looked at Gabe. He nodded.

I gently picked up the thin contact, noticing it was a dark brown. I thought about what Kye had said, then carefully placed it in my eye. It felt awkward, but it didn't hurt. *One down, one to go.*

Unscrewing the other side, I took out the second contact and placed it in my other eye. I blinked a few times, then looked at both the guys. "Well, did it work?" I asked as I tucked the small plastic case in my pocket.

"It's better," Kye said. "Here put these on, too." A pair of glasses. Small, black framed. I put them on and noticed right away that they were simply glass. Another rebel prop. *That's good,* I thought. *I don't want to be stumbling around because I can't see when I'm running for my life.*

"I think that'll work. Between the contacts and the glasses, less of the green stands out. More of a hazel color now," Gabe said. I let out a breath.

I grabbed a hair band from the bag as well and pulled my hair into a ponytail, then looped it through to make more of a messy bun. "Does that help?" I tried to keep my face relaxed as I looked from guy to guy. *I can do this, just relax, slow down the breathing.* One more long breath out.

"Kind of got that sexy teacher thing going now," Kye said.

Gabe shot him a look.

"What?" Kye's smirk was back on his face.

"I don't think you should be talking about my 'wife' like that if we're going to pull off this cover story you've made up." Gabe looked serious. That made me laugh, and some of my tension disappeared. He shot a look at me, too. I tried to stop smiling.

"No worries there. Oh, that reminds me." Kye reached back into the bag. "Your cover story is in place. I've been spreading it around all night. Put these on." He handed each of us a thin gold ring. "You'd be surprised how differently people treat you when they think you're married. You can gain their sympathy talking about your spouse or kids, gain access to places and end up with some pretty interesting information."

Gabe slipped his ring on his left hand. I looked at mine. It brought back the seriousness of the situation. This wasn't play time here. It wasn't a joke at school. *If we can't pull this off, if they figure out I'm a Green citizen ....*

I slid the ring on my left hand as well.

"Let's go." Kye stood up, leaving the small bag on the floor of the tent. "I stopped by the med tent on the way here and checked on Gunner. He was awake, but kind of out of it. I told him you were here and about the cover we came up with, but I don't know how much of it he got. Keep your fingers crossed that he remembers it."

He turned, unzipped the tent again, and stepped out. We followed behind him. There were way more people walking around than last night. Which meant even more guns.

Chapter 35

Kye led us back through the camp to the large tent we had visited the night before. A few people looked at us, but most kept to themselves. New men stood at the door of the tent. They waved us through when Kye approached.

Dr. Garreth was leaning over another patient, checking a bandage. This morning there were a couple of other people walking around, checking on the patients, too. Probably nurses or techs. We waited until he noticed our arrival before moving further into the tent. He simply nodded and tipped his head toward Gunner's bed. Kye led us back.

Gunner lay in bed, his eyes closed.

"Hey," Gabe said softly. Gunner's eyes fluttered open.

"Gabe." Then a smile. "So I hear my brother went and got married on me and didn't even bother to invite me to the wedding." He looked at me. "Nice score for a farm boy."

Gabe smiled. "Good to hear you approve. Actually, it's just good to hear you, period." He sat down on a bench next to Gunner's bed. I sat beside him. Kye stayed standing.

"Gunner, this is Calyssa. Calyssa, Gunner."

"Nice to be formally introduced," I said. "I saw you last night, but you weren't in any shape to visit."

"Yeah. It's been a rough couple days from what I hear, but I don't remember anything after the explosion."

Kye shook his head. "Not here, Gunner. I'll fill them in later."

Gunner sighed. "You're probably right."

Then he looked back at Gabe. "I warned you that things were getting bad. I just didn't realize I would be right in the middle of it." He coughed, grabbed his side, and grimaced. "I forgot. No coughing."

Dr. Garreth walked over to the bed. "Substantial improvement this morning. Good to see you visiting with your brother." He turned to us. "I don't think we formally met last night." He held his hand. "Ryan Garreth."

Gabe reached out and shook his hand. "Gabe Stayton. And this is my wife, Calyssa." I smiled as I shook the doctor's hand as well.

Gunner let out a little laugh that quickly turned into a cough, ending in a moan.

"I think we better let Gunner get some more rest. You can stop back in later this afternoon. What he needs now is lots of sleep." The doctor reached down to check one of Gunner's bandages.

"And lots more great pain meds," Gunner added. Another grimace. "Take care of them, Kye, until I can get out of here."

Dr. Garreth pulled a small vial out of his jacket pocket and pressed one end against Gunner's neck. Gunner's eyes fluttered shut. "Morphine infuser," the doctor said, and then he went on to check Gunner's vitals.

Kye motioned for us to follow him and we left the med tent. Once outside, we started to walk back toward our tent.

"Now what?" Gabe asked.

Kye looked at both of us. "There's a meeting I have to attend. You two can walk around a bit. Get the lay of the land. But try not to draw attention to yourselves. Stick to the story. People here like Gunner, so I don't think anyone will give you any problems. I'll come find you when I'm done. Oh, and don't mention to anyone else that you're a Stayton. The doc's not from this area, but lots of people know your family. A first name is good enough for introductions here." Kye turned to leave.

Gabe reached out and grabbed his arm. "Thanks, Kye. I don't think I've said that yet. I really appreciate everything you've done. I know that Gunner would have died if it hadn't been for you."

Kye simply replied, "He would have done the same for me," then turned and walked off.

"Where to now?" I asked.

Gabe looked around. "Let's take a walk back toward the river. I'd like to see if we can figure out where our horses are." He held out his hand and I took it.

We walked silently hand-in-hand for the next couple of minutes. As we got back down by the river, I noticed a woman watching over a group of several children playing. *Why would she bring her children to a rebel camp?* I thought.

"Why don't I hang out here for a bit? That way, if you run into someone who asks you what you're up to, you can say I wandered off and you're looking for me. Less obvious that you're poking around." *Besides, I think I should stay away from the crazies in the camp.*

Gabe looked hesitant. "You'll stay right here until I get back?"

I smiled. "Don't worry. This is the only place I've seen since we've been here that doesn't have guns everywhere." He still looked unsure.

"Really," I said, rolling my eyes. "I'll be fine."

I leaned over and kissed him on the cheek. "Off you go, Honey. Get to work." I was nervous, but I wanted Gabe to find the horses and know how to get out of here if we needed to make a quick exit.

He shook his head.

I ambled away toward the water so Gabe wouldn't catch on that I was playing "brave." As I got closer to the river, I watched the six kids playing there. The oldest looked about ten or eleven. The youngest child, led by several of the others, seemed to be around two. The woman's eyes looked tired, but her smile appeared sincere.

"That your boyfriend?" she asked, looking after Gabe as he walked away.

"Husband," I answered, holding up my hand to show her the ring.

"Oh," she said softly. "You new here?" I nodded. "Any kids?"

"Nope, I don't think we're quite ready yet." *Now there's the understatement of the year.*

She seemed nice. Not like the wacked-out people from the fire last night. I was sure that they all couldn't have been at that meeting, and since she was still here, it probably meant she hadn't chosen to leave with the Fittings.

"I'm Leah, by the way."

"Calyssa," I said. "These little ones all yours?" I walked over closer to where she sat on the ground.

"Yeah. There's six of them now. The oldest is Josie, after my husband, Joseph. Then there's Luke, Daniel, Conner, and Michael. And little Sara." She smiled again.

"They're sweet." I couldn't help but laugh a bit as Sara splashed her older brothers.

"Usually, but with six, they can't all be sweet all the time. Conner, don't you throw that mud in your hand at Michael. I don't want to change his clothes again." She shook her head, and one of the boys bent over to wash his hands out in the river water.

"Nice catch on the mud. I didn't see a thing. Do you mind if I take some pictures of them? They look like they're having a great time," I said.

"Go ahead." She continued watching the children, and I raised my memory bracelet and tapped it a few times to record the images.

"Is your husband back up at the camp?"

Her face darkened. "No. He died about a year ago."

I started to stammer something, but she held up her hand. "It's okay. He was a good man and a hard worker. We used to own a farm north of SciCity. Nothing big. Just a nice place to raise our kids." She sighed and turned back toward the river, watching the kids play. A smile again on her lips, but this time, a sad smile, one that didn't quite make it across her face.

"This group has taken care of my kids and me for the past year. Given us a place to live, food to eat. And we're not the only ones. There are more people here with stories similar to mine. We're all just trying to make it together. Everybody pitches in and does their part. There's plenty of work gardening, cooking, and washing. There's even school for the kids. An older woman who used to teach in a small rural school ended up here, too. She's great with the children."

Josie walked up carrying Sara. "Hey, Mom. I think we need to take Sara back and change her. She doesn't smell too good." She wrinkled up her nose. Leah and I laughed.

"All right. Boys, it's time to go. Come on now. Maybe I'll bring you back down later." She smiled at them, but the sadness was still there in her eyes.

"Would you mind helping me up?"

"Not at all." As I helped her up, I noticed that her lower leg and foot were twisted at a funny angle. She started to walk away slowly, with a pronounced limp. "Run along kids. Mama's right behind you." Then she turned to me and simply said, "Nice meeting you, Calyssa."

"You, too, Leah."

She turned back toward the chattering children and followed them up the path.

I sat down, looking out over the river, and I wondered what events had led Leah to a rebel camp to raise her six young children.

Chapter 36

I sat there, lost in my thoughts, waiting for Gabe to return. About twenty minutes later, Kye showed back up.

"Where's Gabe?" he asked as he sat down beside me on the riverbank.

"Out scouting the place and looking for our horses. Just checking things out, I think." I turned toward Kye and studied his face. I had thought that he was much older than I was, but up close, I saw he was about my age, maybe a year or two older, but not much.

"Kye, I met a woman, Leah, and her kids earlier. She said they lived here, in the camp, and that her husband had died last year sometime. Do you know her?"

"Yeah. We all pretty much know each other here. You get to know the people you depend on. It's like a big family."

I looked back toward the river. "What's her story? Leah's, I mean. Why would she want to raise six young kids here? I don't get it. I mean, I understand you and Gunner, but kids? Here?"

Kye looked at me. "There are lots of people here because they don't have anywhere else to go. No family. Some have lost everything. Or had it taken from them. Like Leah."

"What do you mean?" I asked. He had my full attention now.

"Are you sure you want to know about this? It's not a pretty story. I won't fancy it all up like they do for SciCity news." His eyes were hard again. It made me feel uncomfortable, but I still nodded.

"One night Leah woke up and her husband, Joseph, wasn't in their bed. She went outside but she didn't see him anywhere. She wanted to go searching, but she was afraid one of her kids would wake up and she didn't want them wandering out of the house at night." Kye looked back at the river.

"When she turned to go back in the front door, she heard a strange noise, and followed the sound around the side of the house. Joseph was on the ground. He was beat up really bad, and it looked like when he hit the ground, he'd knocked his head on something hard. There was blood splattered everywhere." He picked up a stone and skipped it across the river. He paused for a few seconds, long enough that I wondered if he was going to continue.

"Joseph was mumbling. Leah said it was hard to make out what he was saying, something about security enforcers. She thought he wanted her to call them so she ran inside to grab their satphone. She said she was hysterical, screaming for someone to come help. When she ran back out to him, he was already gone. She said she could see it in his eyes." He looked back at me – the hardness was gone from his eyes, replaced with sadness.

I reached out and touched his arm. Kye stiffened, but didn't move away.

He continued, "She didn't have any family around, and with all those kids, she knew she couldn't manage the farm.

A few days after Joseph died, some big company from the city sent a rep to talk to her about selling their land. She was still in shock, and I guess she went kind of crazy on him, telling him that it was her farm and he couldn't have it, even though she knew there was no way she'd be able to keep running it.

"The Green guy got ticked off, told her she wouldn't get a better offer, and that she should take what he could get for her now before the farm wasn't worth anything. She continued to refuse so he left." He shook his head and sighed.

"About two weeks later, when things were actually starting to get really bad, Leah woke up and smelled smoke. She ran out of her room and down the hall. Her whole living room was engulfed in flames. She said she screamed, running through the house, throwing open the kids' doors, pulling them out of bed. She grabbed Sara, the littlest one. She was frantic, and the fire was getting worse. She said it was so smoky, she could hardly see." Again, he paused. I remained silent.

"Leah got a bedroom window open and helped Josie crawl out, then started passing the younger kids out to her. The fire was at the doorway by then, flames licking into the room. She said the heat was unbearable, her lungs were full of smoke, and she felt like she was losing it.

"She started to crawl through the window herself when she heard Josie screaming, 'Where's Steven? Mom, where is Steven? He's not out here with us!' She said she turned to look at her kids and counted six. One was missing. Luke's twin." Kye picked up another stone, and rubbed it between his fingers.

"She scrambled back in, but the fire was everywhere. Her kids were crying for her to come back, but she jerked a thick curtain off the wall, wrapped it around her, and ran through the fire back to the hall."

Kye turned toward me, his voice low, but forceful. "She said she knew that must be what hell is like, that she could feel the fire burning the curtain, burning her skin, but she didn't care, that she had to find her little boy." He turned away and threw the stone into the river.

"As she started down the hall, the ceiling collapsed in front of her. She got disoriented, and somehow ended back up in the living room. Then she said the front door flew open and a man ran in, grabbed her, threw her over his shoulder and carried her out. They rolled on the ground when they got outside to put out the flames, but she was screaming at him to let her go back in, that her son was inside.

"The whole house was engulfed by then. She said that even as she was screaming, she knew it was too late. That her little three-year-old Steven was with Joseph." He hesitated, looking back up the trail. When no one came down, he continued.

"She saw other people around. People trying to put the fire out, but it was a lost cause. She looked at the man who had saved her life, and realized he was a friend of Joseph's from their school days. His name is Peter. I know him. He's a good guy. He told me he just held her as they watched the fire. Someone else brought her kids over to them. She sat there on the ground and pulled her kids into her, crying." Kye took a deep breath and blew it out.

"Peter also told me that about an hour later, security enforcers showed up to investigate the cause of the fire. Within a few hours, they told him and Leah that it was rebel retaliation. That they had done some investigating after Joseph's death, and that they already knew Joseph had said he was going to help the rebels, but when he didn't follow through on his word, the rebels had decided to make an example out of him. That they killed him, and then came back to finish off his family, too. That rebels had set the fire that killed Steven." He shook his head again.

"Leah didn't know what she was going to do. Within a couple of weeks, her life had completely changed. Her husband was dead, one of her sons was dead, and her house and every single item they owned were gone. But Peter scooped them all up and loaded them into his truck. And brought them here."

I was confused. "But I thought the rebels were responsible for her husband's death, for the fire. Why would she want to come here?"

"Once Peter got them back here, and she got the kids settled into a tent, Leah spoke with several of the people who lived here, including Peter and me. We talked a long time that night. Peter told her rebels didn't start the fire, that this was a "rebel" camp, that he was a part of this group. He knew it was all a lie. He said that the security enforcers killed Joseph and started the fire. That they were working for the company that wanted her land. Joseph wouldn't sell so they roughed him up, and accidentally killed him. And that when she refused to sell as well, they had set the fire. One way, or another, they were going to get her land."

Kye turned his whole body toward me. "Peter had several others back up his story. He had been working undercover in SciCity gathering intel when he heard about Joseph's death and the attack that was planned for the farm. He went straight there, but it was too late. The fire had already taken over the house. He heard the kids screaming for their mother, and he ran inside to find her." Kye looked angry now, his muscles tight, and his eyes hard once again.

"And hey, guess what's on her land now? Research fields." I felt the horror on my face. *Research fields? No. It couldn't be any of our fields, could it? No.*

"How do you know that was the truth? Maybe Peter was lying." I couldn't stop myself. The words were tumbling out.

"Leah said she thought about that. A lot," he said. "But then she said she remembered what Joseph had said that night she found him. She thought he wanted her to call the security enforcers, but now she thinks that he was trying to tell her who had hurt him. She said that thinking back, she could tell by the look in his eyes. He knew he was going to die. He wasn't asking her to call anyone." I shuddered as I thought about what Kye had said.

"And her leg?" I asked. "Was that from the fire, too?"

"Yeah, that happened in the fire. But the doc here is good. She didn't think he would be able to save it, but he did." He turned, and skipped one more stone across the river. We sat in silence.

A twig snapped, startling me, and I noticed another guy coming down the trail. "Hey, Kye. They need you at the auxiliary tent for a minute."

Kye jumped up. "Stay here, Calyssa. Wait for Gabe. I'll be right back."

I looked out over the river again, picked up a stone and threw it as far as I could. And then I cried.

Chapter 37

I was still just sitting there when Gabe arrived back at the river. He walked over and sat down next to me. I scooted close to him, leaned my head on his shoulder, and said quietly, "I need to tell you about the woman I met today."

He nodded his head, and I told him all of it. He didn't say anything. He just listened. And when I finished, we both sat in silence, watching the water drift by.

"Hey. I'm back." It was Kye. When we turned to look at him, he stopped. "Is everything okay?" We looked at each other and nodded.

Kye stood there for a minute, as if he was unsure of what he wanted to do, then walked over beside us. It was beautiful and peaceful, but I didn't feel at rest.

"Tell us what happened to Gunner," Gabe said. Kye looked from Gabe to me. I nodded. Kye blew out a long and slow breath.

"Not here. Let's take a walk."

After a minute or two of walking along the river, Kye paused. He picked up a few stones and started skipping them across the water. Gabe reached down and grabbed a couple as well. And we all just stood there, the three of us, looking normal, hanging out, skipping stones across the water.

"I'm sure you heard what the news is reporting, about the 'incident' at the Washburg farm. Their 'version' of what occurred two nights ago." Gabe and I nodded. Kye shook his head.

"Well, there were rebels at that farm, but not for the reasons that they said on the news." He shook his head again.

"Let me say first off that most of the 'rebels,' the people in this camp, are good people that are looking for a safe place to live. Most of us don't want to fight, but we will if we have to. Most of us have lost loved ones, and we're just trying to find others who will care about us, accept us. Saying that all rebels want to kill every genetically modified organism on this planet is like saying that all scientists want to genetically modify every living organism on the planet just to be able to say that they can. Two extreme ends of the same line."

Skipping another stone, Kye continued, "People call us rebels because we don't want what the city wants. And we don't want to give up what we have so they can have what they want. I guess most of us are 'rebelling' against 'mainstream' Green Commonwealth ideas. We're scared of what happened in the past and don't want to have to live it again in the future." Again, he paused.

Turning back to us, he said, "So five of us from this camp, including Gunner and me, went to the Washburg farm two nights ago. We weren't heading to the research fields, and we didn't have any explosives. We were going there, to that farm, to meet with Tom Jr. to discuss some trading.

"One of our guys had known Tom since they were kids, and had kept in touch with him. The last time he and Tom spoke, Tom told him he was looking to start expanding his crop rotations. We have access to lots of different crop seeds and Tom had livestock he was willing to trade. It would have been a good deal for both sides." Kye rubbed the back of his neck and leaned forward, staring at the ground.

"We were supposed to meet Tom that night after dark out in his barn. We had the sacks of seed he wanted, and we were going to take some cattle back with us. It should have been quick and easy. When we got there, we headed straight to the barn."

I felt my heart begin to speed up. My mouth felt dry. My stomach felt queasy.

"We weren't there for five minutes when something exploded inside that barn. Tom was right at the barn door when it happened. Knocked him back about thirty feet. He got up dazed and ran to help us.

"Gunner and Levi, he was another guy who went with us, were the closest to the explosion. Gunner looked the worst, but Levi's head was bleeding pretty badly. I was with two other guys, at the other side of the barn, looking at some of Tom's new harvesting equipment. The three of us had been knocked off our feet by the blast. We had lots of scrapes and scratches, but nothing life-threatening."

Kye rubbed his hands over his face. For a second, I wasn't sure he was going to continue. But then, he looked back up and went on. "Tom and I found Gunner on the floor. We got him up. The other two guys helped Levi up.

He could stand, but he wasn't too steady. The barn was on fire so we headed for the front door.

"As we stepped out, a single shot hit the door frame. Somebody was shooting at us! We ran back inside, and Tom showed us a side exit that we could use, one that couldn't be seen from the front. He got us out and sent us toward the fields when he noticed the fire was moving toward the house.

"Tom yelled for us to go, that he would get his dad and they would take care of his family. Once we were in the field, we all split up, saying we'd meet back here. I could see Tom and his family outside, and neighbors were coming to help fight the fire. I knew I had to get Gunner out of there, especially since it seemed that there was a sniper around somewhere."

Kye closed his eyes. "We wouldn't have left Tom if we hadn't thought he had things under control. Gunner couldn't run, so I picked him up and started running. I just focused on the path, on getting him back. I was so scared he was going to die in my arms." His voice had lowered, but it was soft, vulnerable, so different from any other time I had heard him talk.

"Later, we found out that the wind kicked up, and the fire whipped around from the grass to trees and buildings with incredible speed. That in a matter of minutes after we left, flames were everywhere. But we couldn't see it from the forest. And it wasn't until the next morning that we figured out that Levi hadn't made it back. Doc said it could have been internal injuries or head trauma, but obviously he never made it out of the field."

"Why didn't the rest of the family tell the media what you guys were there for? Why wouldn't they tell the truth?" Gabe asked.

"We only dealt with Tom Jr. His dad didn't like the idea of getting mixed up with 'rebels,' but they were short on cash, and Tom had traded with us before. So I don't think the family lied. I think they just didn't know we were there."

"And then Tom died in the fire and couldn't tell anyone," I said. Kye nodded and looked away.

"Somebody set you up." Gabe had that angry look in his eyes again.

"I think so, I mean, a barn doesn't just blow up by itself. And I don't think the Washburgs knew anything about it. Tom seemed truly shocked when it all happened. I don't know who knew about our meeting, or how, but I'd like to find out." Kye looked angry now, too.

"Joshua thinks the security enforcers were already there. That they found out about the trade somehow, waited for us to arrive, blew up the barn, and shot at us. Their new advanced drone technology could have easily created that blast. He thinks they killed Levi, too. But I don't know about that. He wasn't in good shape when we left the barn."

Kye stood silent for a few moments. "Not much we can do now but wait." He readjusted the strap on his gun and looked back up the trail. "Let's head back to camp. I'm getting hungry and something was smelling good when I left. We've got some great cooks here."

After we ate lunch, Kye had things to do, so we told him we would meet him back at the med tent that evening before dinner to see Gunner again. Gabe and I walked around the camp.

I was nervous at first, but it was different from what I expected. It wasn't just a bunch of crazy people bent on murdering Green citizens.

We met many people, heard their stories, how they ended up there. One guy referred to it as a "community for lost souls." Some people had lost their land because they couldn't pay their bills. Others were tired of the city life, just scraping by there. We met people who didn't believe in the system, who wanted to be off the grid. Some people, like Leah and her kids, were here because they didn't have anywhere else to go.

I was asked to help in the kitchen area for a while and, of course, said yes. We were told that here, in the camp, only females worked in the kitchen. Gabe told the women he'd leave but they'd be missing out on a mean beef casserole, which got him a few weird looks. He just laughed and told me he'd be back by dinner and then we'd go see Gunner. He kissed me on the cheek before he left, a nice little show for the women there who all thought he was wonderful.

As I peeled, chopped, and sliced, I listened to these girls and women talk about the changes in the weather, disagreements with spouses and loved ones, who they thought were cute or jerks, and what everyone wanted to make for breakfast tomorrow. They were ordinary people living their lives.

Once all the men had left the area, the conversation changed to the Fitting brothers. I learned there were three brothers: Joshua, the oldest, followed by Jonathan, and

Jesse, the youngest. These three men worked their way around camps like this one that were sprouting up all over the place, talking about their solution for a society that had gotten out of control and taking new recruits with them along the way. The brothers believed in the eradication of all GMOs. Plants, animals, humans. It didn't matter. Not everybody here agreed with them, but it sounded like more and more people were listening to what they had to say.

I brought up the "Lost Star" and one of the women explained it was a symbol used by the Fitting brothers' group to identify their followers. It was two triangles interlaced with each other forming a perfect star with a circle connecting the six points.

The triangle with point facing down represented humankind – men, women, and children. The triangle with the point facing up represented nature – earth, water, and fire. She said the Fittings explained that all six were required for harmony on our planet.

Apparently, the necklace they wore ensured their safe passage as well as needed rest stops in camps throughout the countryside, because, honestly, no one wanted to mess with the Fittings. A few nervous looks passed between some of the older women, but everyone continued working.

The Fittings also apparently talked a lot about the security enforcers being the right hand of the big scientific corporations. According to the Fitting brothers, it was these corporations that "brought the PK virus into the world." Corporations that "almost killed all the plants on our planet through their extreme experimentation." Corporations that "continued the same research and development today." Corporations that "were leading humankind right back down that same twisted road we traveled a hundred years ago."

It was scary to listen to. People here were considering that maybe the Fittings were right. That maybe it was the only way for the world to be safe again. People were scared. They were looking for someone to trust. Someone to believe in.

Gabe came back with the men when dinner was ready. We all ate together. When we'd finished, Gabe stood up and reached for my hand. I said goodbye to the women. They thanked me for my help, and some even hugged me.

"You must have made a good impression," Gabe said as he smiled at me.

"Kye was right. They're good people." I smiled, too.

Gabe reached for my hand. "I love it when you smile. Your whole face lights up and it makes me feel good."

I leaned in and whispered in his ear, "You better watch out, Gabe Stayton. With lines like that, a girl might get the idea that you were actually falling for her."

He leaned over, whispering in my ear, "Maybe I am."

Chapter 38

We met Kye in front of the med tent and went in to see Gunner again. This time he was sitting propped up in bed. Some of the bandages were gone. Bruises and scratches covered the majority of his exposed skin, but overall, he looked like he was feeling better. We went straight back to his bed and sat on the bench. Kye pulled up a chair on the other side of the bed. Gunner smiled at all three of us.

"Doc says I'm healing up great. May not be running a marathon anytime soon, but I should be out of this bed in the next couple of days."

"That's awesome, Bro." Gabe leaned in closer and lowered his voice a bit. "How soon before you think you can travel?"

Gunner looked surprised. "Travel where?"

"To the farm. With us. I want you to come back with me. Stay with us while you heal up. For as long as you want." Gabe was all smiles.

"I'm not going anywhere, Gabe. This is my home. Here with Kye and the others. Why would you think I'd want to leave?"

"You're living in a tent, Gunner. Sleeping on the floor between blankets. Out of a duffle bag, Dude." Gabe's eyebrows shot up as he was talking. "Come with me. You'll have your own room, a cushy bed, and all of Nana Jane's home cooking you can eat." Gabe lightly punched Gunner in the arm. "Just like old times. Me and you hanging out at the farm."

Gunner's smile dropped. He looked at Kye and then back at Gabe. "This is my home, Gabe. I care about these people. I like it here. I don't need any more than I have. The doc has a cot they'll move into our tent. The blankets are plenty warm. And have you tried the food here? It's phenomenal." A small smile returned to his face.

"Come on, I just want what's best for you." Gabe put his hand on Gunner's arm.

"Lay off, Gabe," Kye said brusquely as he stood up. "Gunner says he doesn't want to go. He's his own man. He certainly doesn't need your approval. Or advice. I came and got you because Gunner wanted to see you. You saw him. Your obligation is finished here. So now you can take your girlfriend and go back to your 'cushy' bed on your 'cushy' farm and your daddy's 'cushy' money, and forget about Gunner again. Just like before."

Gabe stood up so abruptly that he almost knocked over the bench we were both sitting on. Startled, I scrambled to keep my balance.

Gabe's glare was harsh, his shoulders tight, as he leaned across Gunner's bed toward Kye. "You don't know anything about my life or Gunner's. We've been friends for fourteen years. How long have you known him? A year? Maybe two? Not long enough to really look out for his best interests. If you were, you'd get him out of this hell hole and back to civilization!"

Kye leaned over the bed as well, closer to Gabe. In each other's faces, again. "You taking this somewhere?"

Gabe leaned in more. Just inches apart now. "Anywhere you want to go."

I stood up. "Guys, come on now – that's enough."

They both turned and glared at me.

And Gunner burst out laughing. And that made him cough, which made him grab his side and moan, which made everyone sit back down. When he finally quieted, he looked back and forth with an angry glare ...which suddenly turned into a sheepish grin.

"Oh, boys," he said in his best girlie voice, "I don't want ya both fighting over little ol' me now. I couldn't stand to be the one that split us all up." He batted his eyelashes.

That made Gabe and Kye scowl even more, and Gunner and I broke out laughing. But Gunner didn't laugh quite so hard this time. He was still holding his side from the last coughing attack.

"Guys. It's okay." He turned to Gabe. "I'm staying here. People count on me here like people count on you at the farm. People care about me here, and I care about them, too. I've made this my home, and I like it here."

Then he turned to Kye, placing his hand on Kye's arm. "Gabe is my oldest friend. I owe you for bringing him here for me. I thought I was done. And I don't believe for a minute that he only came because he felt obligated. He came because he's a real friend." Then he turned back to Gabe.

"And Gabe, I trust Kye completely. For God's sake, he carried me – I don't even know how many miles – to save me. He saved my life. I think we can all agree that he's got my back here." Gunner sighed, his arm dropping back down and wrapping around his side once more.

"It comes down to the fact that I have two incredible people who would do anything for me. Most people are lucky to have even one of those in their whole life. Gabe, it was you and me, best friends for as long as I can remember. Now I live here with Kye by my choice. That doesn't mean I can't or won't come see you, but if you're my friend, my brother, you have to respect my decision."

He looked at all of us again. "So guys, how about it? Play nice and share?" He smiled at both of them, and winked at me. "And Gabe, if you ever divorce my hot sister-in-law over there ...."

They all three looked at me. "I can't help it," I said. "It's that sexy teacher look I got going on." The tension broke.

"Kye, thank you for getting Gabe and bringing him here. And Gabe, thank you for coming. I think just seeing you here helped me realize I would be okay. And Calyssa, thanks for marrying my brother because I'm not sure anyone else would put up with him."

Right about then, Dr. Garreth came over to the bed. "Sorry. Time for Gunner to get some sleep. He seems to think he needs to be out of this tent this week, so as his doctor, I've got to try to meet his expectations." That last comment was rather sarcastic, but the doc was smiling.

We all stood. "I think Calyssa and I will be heading back bright and early tomorrow morning. We'll stop in and see you before we leave," Gabe said.

Then he turned to Dr. Garreth, "Thank you again for everything you've done for Gunner." They shook hands, and we walked out just as darkness was beginning to fall.

Gabe and I said goodnight to Kye and headed back toward the tent, our tent for just one more night.

"Want to go for a moonlit walk down by the river?" Gabe asked.

"Absolutely."

He held out his hand. I took it. *Funny how that seems natural now*, I thought, holding his hand as we headed down the path. We walked along the river for a while in silence. When we came to a small clearing, Gabe stopped. "Up for a little star gazing?"

"Always." I smiled. We lay down in the grass by the river and he quizzed me on the stars and constellations from earlier in the week.

"I can't believe that I'll be going home soon." I looked over at Gabe.

"I know." He continued looking at the stars.

"You and your family have changed my life. I'm a different person than I was just last week. I can't believe that I didn't even know you then."

"I know," he said again, still looking up.

"I want to keep hanging out when we go back, and not just in science class. You're a lot cooler than I originally thought."

"I know."

"Boy, you sure do know a lot, don't you?"

"Yep."

"More than me?"

"Yep."

"Like what?"

Gabe was quiet for a minute. I was about to give him a hard time for not being able to come up with anything, when he rolled over so he was lying right next to me. He put his arm over the top of me and ran his fingers through my hair.

I turned and looked into his eyes. "Gabe, I ..."

He interrupted. "Just listen, Calyssa. Let me tell you about what I know."

He took a breath.

"I know that I've always thought you were beautiful. Before you even knew who I was. Back when your eyes were the most incredible shade of brown.

"I know that I can't wait to see you in the morning. That my day doesn't start now until I can make you smile.

"I know that when you play the cello, you play for you, not for anybody else. You lose yourself in your music. By not trying to impress anyone, you impress everyone.

"I know that Ben hugs you, which is something truly special in itself because it means he trusts you completely.

"I know that Nana Jane looks at you like she used to look at my mom. And my mom was the kindest, most caring person I've ever known. And I've never known Nana Jane to be wrong about anything.

"I know that you shared with my sister that you lost your mom just like we lost our mom. And that made her feel like she wasn't so alone.

"I know that you'll try new things even if you're scared because you don't want anyone to think you're afraid.

"I know that you have a tender heart and you look for the best in people, which brings out more in them than they even knew they had.

"I know that every time I look at you, my heart skips a beat, and that every time I hold your hand, my breath catches.

"I know that you, all by yourself, Calyssa Brentwood, have turned my entire world upside down."

He paused.

"And, I know that I'm falling in love with you."

Then he slowly leaned his head down to mine, and brushed my lips with his.

And then he rolled back over, and looked back up at the stars.

I couldn't move. I couldn't breathe. I couldn't even think in complete thoughts.

After a few seconds, I rolled onto my side and stared at his face. "Gabe, I ...."

"Nope," he interrupted me again. "Tonight was about what I know." He turned his face toward me. "Your turn tomorrow night. And just so you know, I'm expecting something really good because I rocked that." He winked at me. Then he stood up and held out his hand.

"We should be getting back. Come on." I gave him my hand and he helped me up. Then he put his arms around me and hugged me. I squeezed him back for all I was worth.

I don't think I've ever been this happy in my whole life.

Chapter 39

We walked back silently to the tent, once again hand-in-hand. We didn't need to say anything. Gabe unzipped the tent, we stepped in, and he zipped it back up. We spread the blankets back out on the floor. Then we sat down, took off our shoes, I removed my glasses and let my hair down, and then we both crawled under the top cover.

I rolled over and placed my head on Gabe's chest. He rolled toward me and enveloped me in his arms. And then, without saying a single word, I fell asleep.

I woke to light streaming through the sides of the tent. Gabe was gone. But I wasn't worried. I knew he hadn't left me. I knew it in my heart. *Because last night, he told me he was falling in love with me.*

It was the first time in my life that someone loved me who didn't have to. I mean, parents have to love their kids and siblings have to love each other (even if they don't like each other very much sometimes) because they're family. Beyond that, there's no rules. Nobody has to say that they love anybody else. But Gabe had said it to me. He had chosen me.

I sat up in bed and smiled. Tonight was my turn to tell him how I felt. I had to come up with something really good. I wanted to make him feel as special as he made me feel.

I stretched up and to the sides. I felt great.

I tossed the covers aside, put on my shoes and glasses, checked to make sure my contacts were still in place, and redid my hair in the bun. Then I stood up and folded up the blankets. I looked around to make sure everything was tidy since we would be leaving today, and Gunner and Kye would be moving back in here soon.

I unzipped the tent, stepped out, and zipped it back up, making sure that everything was done up nice and tight. Then I took off down the path to find Gabe.

I thought I'd try the med tent first, and I was right. I went in and saw Gabe sitting with Gunner. They both saw me and smiled. I walked back and sat in my usual spot beside Gabe.

"Good night last night?" Gunner asked me. Gabe shot him a warning look, but I just laughed.

"I think so," I said.

"I was telling Gunner that we'll head back to the farm soon. We'll ride the horses back, and I'll tie the horse Kye rode to mine to lead him along. I don't think Dad would appreciate it if I left his horse here with the rebels."

"His horse, as in all the horses on the farm belong to him, or his horse as in 'his' horse?" I asked with raised eyebrows.

"It's his horse as in his favorite." Gabe smiled. "Hope he's in a good mood when we get back." Gabe looked over at Dr. Garreth.

"I'm going to talk to the Doc one more time, just to make sure everything is good before we take off." Gabe got up and walked across the room.

"You know he's got it bad for you, right?" When I turned, Gunner was staring at me. "I may not be going back with you guys, but I need to know that you understand he's not messing around here. I don't know what you did, or how you did it, but he's head over heels. I've never seen him like this before. Ever." Gunner's expression was serious.

"I don't know what I did either. But I know that he makes me feel different than anyone else I've ever been around. I feel special and safe, and just good about everything, when he's with me." I smiled at Gunner.

"He told me about your Enhancement. What's your plan?" Gunner still wasn't smiling.

I hesitated.

"I don't know yet. This is all so new to me. I need to talk it through with Gabe. He's such a good listener. I'll be Green in a few weeks, and then ...."

Gunner interrupted. "You know he'll never leave Ben. And he'll never expose him to the people in the city who might make fun of him."

"I know."

"Then let me give you some advice. If you're not willing to leave the city to be with him, break it off now. It's already going to break his heart. But once you tell him you love him, it's like the point of no return. So don't say it to him if you don't mean it. Think about what you want because it's going to affect both of you."

"I ...." I tried to say something, but Gunner interrupted me again.

"I don't need you to reassure me or say anything, just think about what I've said." There was a pleading in his eyes, so sincere and so genuine that it brought a real smile to my face.

"You're a good friend, Gunner. Thank you for looking out for Gabe. He's lucky to have you." I leaned over and kissed him on the cheek.

"Hey now." Gabe walked up to the bed. "I leave for one minute and you're already trying to move in on my wife – at least wait until she's available." He winked at me.

"Doc says you're continuing to look better all the time. Beyond his expectations. So I think we'll be taking off. I want to take Calyssa home a different way than we came so she can see some of the amazing country out here." He put out his hand and Gunner reached for it.

Gabe pulled him in gently and hugged him. "Don't ever scare me like that again. Once in a lifetime is enough, okay?" He smiled at Gunner.

Gunner flashed a huge smile back. "Okay."

"And come back to the farm to see us when you feel better."

"Okay."

"Take care," I said, and I leaned over and gently hugged him, too.

"You do the same, Calyssa. For both of you."

Gabe and I turned and left the med tent. For the last time. Gabe led the way down a different trail and we ended up at a horse pen. Kye was there with our three horses saddled and ready.

"Not gonna waste any time getting us out of here, huh?" But Gabe was smiling.

Kye smiled back. "Didn't want to let the gate hit you in the butt on your way out. Just trying to help."

Kye and Gabe shook hands and Gabe mounted up. I gave Kye a hug. "Thanks again for taking care of Gunner," I said. Kye simply nodded. I hopped up on Blackjack and we headed down the trail with the extra horse following behind.

"Safe travels," Kye called after us.

We spent the majority of the morning winding through wooded areas. We saw waterfalls and wild flowers. We stopped to sample blackberries and smell mint leaves. I learned how to catch crayfish with my hands and identify the differences between a pine tree and a fir tree. I was happy that Gabe wasn't in a rush to get back. It was nice spending time alone together.

Around noon, we stopped in a little meadow, and Gabe pulled a small sack from his saddlebag. "Kye grabbed us some lunch for the road from the cooks in the kitchen." He pulled out bread, cheese, and cut up fruits and veggies along with a couple of bottles of water. We let the horses wander through the meadow as we ate. When we finished, Gabe sprawled out and I laid my head on his stomach, watching the clouds float across the sky.

Suddenly, Gabe sat up and looked at the horses. They were making some snorting noises, moving around impatiently, agitated. And they were all turned, looking in the same direction. Then they went silent. I could tell they were listening, but I didn't hear anything.

"What is it?" I asked Gabe. He put his fingers to his lips, and got up very slowly. He motioned for me to do the same.

We walked slowly and silently over to where the horses were standing. Gabe grabbed the gun hanging from his saddle and threw the strap over his arms. Taking the reins of all three horses, he began to lead them toward the edge of the field. I still hadn't heard anything, except for us moving through the grass.

As we reached the edge, Gabe pulled the horses back behind some bushes, and looped their reins over a low tree branch. Then he moved back through the brush toward the field and ducked behind a couple of fallen logs. I followed him and kneeled down on the ground.

Not more than a minute had passed when we saw a young man and a woman run into the field. Their clothes were torn, they had scrapes and scratches on their skin, and they were breathing hard. When they got to the middle of the field, they looked back for a minute, then stopped to talk. I looked at Gabe.

"What's going on?" I whispered. Once again, he placed a finger on his lips. In the next couple of seconds, a handful of men in security enforcer uniforms descended on the field from all directions. One passed less than thirty feet from us. I dropped down even lower. I looked at Gabe. His focus was intense on the man and woman in the middle.

The two had their hands up. They were saying something but I couldn't make out what it was. One of the security enforcers yelled at them to put their hands on the top of their heads and to drop to their knees. Both of them complied. The security enforcers moved in.

This wasn't right. Something was really wrong here, I felt it in my stomach. I whispered to Gabe that we needed to do something, but he shook his head. Six of them and only two of us. I looked down.

My memory bracelet. I still had it on. I held it up between two branches on the fallen trees and started snapping shots. One right after the other.

One of the officers said something again. The man turned toward the woman, slowly reaching into the front of his shirt.

Another officer yelled, "Stop! Don't move! Keep your hands where we can see them!"

As the man brought his hand out of his shirt, metal caught the rays of the sun, and for half a second, it reflected a brilliant flash across the field. And, in that moment, as my eyes locked on his hand, I saw in his fingers a Lost Star.

And in the next second, all the officers fired at once, and the two bloody bodies crumpled to the ground.

Chapter 40

I threw both of my hands over my mouth.

The shots startled the horses and one of them let out a frantic whinny. A security enforcer turned toward us. He said something to another one, and they both began to walk in our direction.

Gabe grabbed my chin, turned it toward him, and then whispered, "We have to get out of here right now. We're going to crawl slowly back to the horses. If I yell for you to run, you get to Blackjack, mount up, and make her run as fast as you can. Head out to the path over there on the left where the trees are the thickest.

"Do not look back. Do not stop for anything. Keep running. Keep her running until she can't run anymore. Do you understand me?"

I was terrified but I nodded.

"Those guys just killed two people. We saw them do it. I don't think they're coming over to ask us questions. Do you understand what I'm saying?"

Again I nodded. I thought my heart was going to pound right out of my chest. I don't know if I had ever been that scared in my entire life. Gabe leaned forward and kissed me. "Be brave, Calyssa." Then he adjusted his gun under his arm and we began moving back to the horses.

The ground was hard and the low brush was thick here. It ripped at my clothes and scratched at my skin. I felt it draw blood on my arm and my cheek, but I kept pressing through. I was almost to Blackjack when I heard one of the officers shout, and then Gabe yelled, "Run!"

I jumped up and in two steps was on Blackjack. She seemed to immediately sense my urgency and took off at a dead sprint. I heard shots fired and saw the bark on a tree next to my head splinter as I passed it. *Keep your head down and the reins loose. Lean forward. Trust the horse to know the path. She's a runner. Let her do what she does best.* Ana's words from our time together on the horses rolled through my mind.

Mostly, I just held on. I think my eyes were closed for the majority of the time. I kept urging Blackjack forward. To keep running.

I don't know how long we ran. Time seemed to stand still. We could have run for ten minutes or ten hours. I had no idea. We ran and ran until Blackjack couldn't run any more. She slowed to a trot and then a walk. She was breathing harder than I had ever heard her breathe. Her body was soaked with a lather of sweat. She stumbled a little and I knew it was time for me to get off and give her a break.

I jumped down and almost fell myself, finding my own legs unsteady. I could hear a creek. We walked toward the sound of the water. I sat down at the edge, and while she drank, I splashed the cool water on my face and arms, realizing that somewhere along the way I had lost my glasses. I rubbed my eyes and discovered the contacts were gone, too. More water on my face helped stop the burning from the sweat in the scratches.

I'd made it out of there. My mind was replaying the images of the bodies of those two people crumpling to the ground over and over again. Why were they shot? They didn't have guns, but the officers shot them anyway.

And suddenly my chest tightened. Where was Gabe? Why wasn't he here yet? Had he made it out? Had he even made it to his horse? I searched my mind for the answers but they weren't there. As soon as I had heard him yell to run, I'd never looked back.

What if he didn't get away? What if he had been shot? A muffled sob escaped from my throat.

I got up and ran back to the path. Where was he? He had to be all right. I wanted to yell for him, to scream from the top of my lungs, but I was afraid the security enforcers might still be after us. I dropped to my knees and began to cry. Where was he? *Come on, Gabe. You have to make it. I need you to make it.*

And that's when I realized I loved him. I thought I did before or that at least I was falling in love with him, but now I knew it. I knew it with all my heart.

I crawled over to a big tree and pulled my knees up to my chest. As time went on, my cries turned to sobs. I didn't know where Gabe was, where the security enforcers were, or how to get back to the farm. I cried until I couldn't cry any more. And when the tears stopped, I just sat there.

I thought about Leah and her kids, about Gabe and his family, and about Father and Livvy. I thought about change, about happiness, about decisions, and about consequences. I thought about all the crying and laughing I had done in the past week. One week. A lifetime.

And that's when it hit me. Lies. All the lies told to me. My whole life I had been lied to. Everything that I had grown up believing was a lie. Everything I thought I had known. Lies. And not just simple lies, but lies upon lies spun into an intricate web that looked beautiful and solid, but was only an illusion.

I looked around me. This was real beauty. This was real strength. This was, well, ...real.

But if my whole life had been built on falsehoods and half-truths and illusions, what did that make my life?

And for the first time, I thought about who I really was. Not whose daughter, or sister, or girlfriend. Not what I had. Not what I looked like. Not what I could be. *But who I am today, right now.*

I thought about how Gabe saw me. About what he had told me. About the person I had become because of him and his family. I placed my head on my knees and I closed my eyes. And I waited for Gabe to come back to me.

Later, I'm not sure how long, I heard my name, like from a long way away, like in a dream. Then I felt a hand on my cheek. And I jolted upright. Gabe's face was in front of me. Scratched up, some bleeding, but he was here, in front of me. I shook my head to make sure it wasn't a dream.

Then Gabe laughed. And I knew he was back. No illusions. He was alive and he was back with me. I jumped up and threw my arms around him, knocking him backwards down to the ground. But I didn't care. He was here. He had made it. We both had made it.

We both laughed. Together. It felt incredible. He rolled over so we were both on our sides. He brushed my cheek with his fingertips. I wiped some dirt from the end of his nose.

"I thought I'd lost you," he said to me. "The path split a bunch of times and I wasn't sure which way you went. I kept looking, backtracking, moving forward and then starting all over again. I didn't know Blackjack could run this far." The horse nickered at the sound of her name.

"I just did what you said. I ran her until she couldn't run anymore. How long has it been? Since we split up?"

"Several hours. I'd say you probably ran her for at least an hour and covered more than twenty miles. She had to be exhausted."

I looked over at Blackjack. "She was. By the time we made it here, she could barely walk."

I looked back at Gabe. "What happened with the security enforcers? I know they were shooting at us."

Gabe looked uncertain. "I didn't stick around to find out. I took a different trail, hoping they'd follow me, or that I'd at least split them up. I've kept an eye out for them, but haven't seen anything. I'm sure they've taken off by now."

I stared into his eyes. "I had a lot of time to think. A few hours is like forever when you're all by yourself in the forest, not sure if anyone will ever find you." I paused.

"You know what I figured out?"

He shook his head.

"I love you, Gabe Stayton."

I leaned in and kissed his lips, and he kissed me back, both tender and passionate. And then he pulled me into his chest and held me. Until Blackjack walked up and nudged us.

"I think she wants to go home," I said. Gabe laughed and helped me up.

"Okay, then let's go home." Gabe turned to mount up again, but I grabbed his shoulder.

"Gabe, I don't want to go back to the city. To all the lies. To a family who doesn't believe what I believe. I want to stay with you, on the farm."

He simply said, "Okay," and smiled at me.

We both mounted back up on the horses, and continued down the path. Gabe had a general idea where we were, and when we came out of the forest, he recognized some landmarks. "The farm is over there," he said, pointing toward some rolling hills in the distance. "It's about a half hour from here."

We kept the horses at a brisk walk most of the time, occasionally breaking into a trot or a gallop. We talked a little, but mostly, I think, we just rode side-by-side, together.

It was dusk when the house came into view. The horses sped up as we got closer to home. They were ready to eat and rest. I was, too.

As we got closer, I noticed an odd vehicle in front of the house.

"I wonder who's visiting Dad," Gabe said.

I had a bad feeling again in my stomach. I recognized the car. It was a Ferrari Matrix 700 Series. The kind the executives for AHGA drove.

I looked at Gabe. "I think it might be my father." Gabe slowed his horse to a stop. I pulled up next to him.

"It's okay, Calyssa. I'll be there with you." He leaned forward and kissed me again. Then he smiled. "Let's go. I'm ready to meet your dad."

Chapter 41

We rode straight to the barn. One of the farm hands met us and took the horses. "You better hustle up to the house. Your dad's been pretty worried," he said.

Gabe took my hand and we walked to the front door. Taking a deep breath, he opened it and we walked in. Everyone jumped up when we entered the living room.

"You're okay!" exclaimed Ana as she ran to us, hugging us together. I threw my arms around her, almost knocking all three of us over in the process. As we untangled, our bracelets got snagged together and began to chime. Ana and I laughed as we pulled apart, Gabe trying to duck out the middle.

Then, just seconds later, Nana Jane was there hugging us, too. She ran her hand through Gabe's hair, looking at the scratches on our faces and arms. "What happened to you two?" There were tears in her eyes.

"It's a long story, Nana. We're okay. We're both okay." Gabe leaned forward and kissed her cheek.

Andrew's voice interrupted the reunion. "Gabe, we'll talk about all of this later. But right now, Calyssa, this man needs to speak with you. He says it's urgent." Andrew looked to another man, standing at the side of the room. I hadn't noticed him there until now.

He was a Green citizen, dressed in a suit and tie. Very official looking. Very AHGA. "Miss Brentwood?" He held out his hand and I shook it.

"You may not remember me, but we've met at AHGA. I'm Jaxx, Chayston Jaxx, head of your father's security program. There's been a – development. He needs you to come home immediately."

A development? Come home? Immediately?

He pulled out his credentials pack, a special micro-scanner with a screen that all AHGA security members were required to carry. "Here's my identification to confirm who I am." His picture came up on the screen, along with information about him and his position at AHGA.

"Why didn't Father come himself if it's so important?" I asked.

"I'll explain more on the way. We need to head back right now. I've been waiting for a while, and your father is expecting you."

"Wait a minute. What's going on?"

At that moment his iBud must have gone off because his hand flew to his ear and he frowned as he obviously communicated with someone on the other end. Then he looked uneasily around the room. "I don't believe this is the time or the place for further discussion. I am to bring you back now. I've let them know you've returned. We need to leave immediately."

"Really?" I looked around, too. "These people are my trusted friends. If it's that important, they can hear what you have to say. I'm not leaving until you tell me what's going on." I stepped closer to Gabe, reaching for his hand again. He gave it a little squeeze.

Nana Jane and Andrew exchanged a look, and Andrew said, "Calyssa, maybe you should go with him."

"No," I said, looking defiantly at Jaxx. "Andrew, I trust your opinion. I want you to hear what is so important that I need to be whisked away at a moment's notice by a man I barely know."

Everyone turned back toward Jaxx. He seemed to be weighing his options, and I knew he wouldn't want to go back and face Father without having me with him. I saw that realization cross his face.

"Mr. Stayton, I'm going to ask that you have the children leave the room." His voice was grim.

Andrew looked at Ana. "Take Ben upstairs. Now."

His voice was no-nonsense, and I could see that although Ana wanted to stay, she knew better than to push her dad right then. She grabbed Ben's hand and led him up the stairs.

"I'm staying here with Calyssa," Gabe said, pulling me a little closer to him. Andrew nodded.

Once the kids had disappeared, Jaxx held up the credential pack. "Your father recorded a message for you." He pressed a few buttons and held the screen out flat in his hand. "You'll need to run your fingerprint in order to activate the message."

I placed a finger on the screen and a second later, a small holographic image of Father appeared above it.

"Calyssa." It was Father's voice, but it was odd to be hearing it from the tiny version of him. "Naleeva was emergency medevac'd to AHGA last night. What I'm telling you right now is classified information. This is not available to the general public yet. We don't need a panic on our hands."

What? Livvy? She's on vacation ....

The holographic image continued, "Neleeva was out in a newly developed area, a resort that recently opened up. A couple of hundred miles from SciCity. She's very sick, Calyssa. You must return immediately." Then the image disappeared.

Jaxx looked uncomfortable, glancing toward the door. "We have to go now."

"What ...I ...how ...what?" I was stammering. I couldn't get my thoughts straight.

"Now, please, Miss Brentwood." Jaxx put the credential pack back in his suit pocket. He stepped forward and placed his hand on my arm.

I jerked it away, his touch searing my skin. My voice elevated in both octave and volume. "What's the matter with her?" I dropped Gabe's hand and stepped toward Jaxx. "Tell me!" I was almost screaming now.

Gabe grabbed my hand again and turned me so I would look into his eyes. I could feel myself getting hysterical. "Just breathe, Calyssa. I'm here." No one moved.

Get it together, Calyssa.

I turned back to Jaxx. "What happened to her?" I repeated.

His hand went back to his iBud. After a few seconds, he said, "I've been told that I can tell you that your father and his scientists have identified Naleeva's sickness as being caused by a virus. They believe that it's a newly mutated form of PK, one that attacks the modified chloroplasts in humans." He went silent as I absorbed what he was saying. Nana Jane's hand went to her mouth. Andrew and Gabe looked at each other.

"What? That's not ...it's not ...that can't be right. PK only killed plants. Are you sure?"

"He's afraid that your sister may die, Calyssa. Right now, she's conscious, asking for you. That's why you need to get your things and come with me. We need to leave right now."

I stood there for a minute. I felt like I couldn't move. I didn't know what to say or do – my mind just went – blank.

Andrew walked across the room, put his hands on my shoulders, and looking into my eyes, he said, "You need to go see her. And your father. It's family. Go get your things." Then he stepped out of my way.

I turned and began to walk toward the stairs.

"I'm going with you," Gabe said.

"No." Andrew's voice was strong. "This is something Calyssa needs to do by herself, Gabe. Your place is here."

Gabe turned to his father. "I'm going with her, Dad. You're not going to stop me."

I looked from Gabe to Andrew and then back to Gabe. "No, Gabe. It's okay. I'll be okay. I promise."

Gabe started to say something, then he stopped and walked over to me. And kissed me. Right there. In front of his dad and grandma. Without hesitation or reservation. And that gave me strength.

I looked up at him and smiled, then I turned and ran up the stairs to my room. Grabbing my stuff, I turned to leave. Ana and Ben were standing behind me in the hall.

Ben looked up at me and softly said, "Don't leave, Calyssa."

I dropped my stuff and threw my arms around both of them. "I'll be back. You'll see."

"It's okay," Ana said, looking away from me. "I understand. I'd choose Green over the farm, too."

"No, that's not it at all ...I ...."

Jaxx's voice carried up the stairs. "Miss Brentwood, we need to go. Now."

I kissed both the kids on the cheek, grabbed my things, and ran back down the stairs.

And in a brilliant flash of light, the front door exploded into flames.

Chapter 42

I woke up on a white couch in a small office. It was deathly quiet. Minimal lighting. No one else in the room.

I sat up and immediately wanted to lie back down.

Why does my head hurt so badly?

It all flooded back. The farm, Father's message, Jaxx ...and the explosion. What had happened? Where were the Staytons? Where was Gabe? I jumped up and then had to reach out to grab the wall to steady myself. My head was pounding, and when I thought about what had happened, my chest hurt so bad I could hardly breathe. I had to get out of this room and find out what happened.

As I stumbled toward the door, it swung open. In came Jaxx, followed by a man in a long, white lab coat.

The doctor stepped around Jaxx, grabbed my arm and guided me back down to the couch. It all happened quickly and I felt disoriented.

"What happened? Where are the Staytons? Is everyone all right? Where's Gabe? How did I get here?" I wasn't waiting for answers. I just kept spewing questions.

"Miss Brentwood, please sit still and let the doctor finishing checking you over. If you'll be quiet for a minute, I'll answer your questions the best I can."

I closed my mouth and turned toward the doctor. He placed a scanner on my wrist, read the screen, reached in his pocket, and pulled out an infuser, similar to the one I saw used on Gunner.

"Wait a minute!" I shouted. "I don't want you to put me to sleep! I ...."

The doctor interrupted me. "It won't, it will just help you relax and make sure that none of the scrapes or burns you have will get infected. All your injuries are minor. You're a very lucky young woman, Miss Brentwood.

His eyes darted toward Jaxx, whose jaw tightened with a small, barely perceptible nod of his head. The doctor pressed the infuser against my neck, and I felt calmer almost immediately. The headache started to go away. I reached up and rubbed the spot on my neck.

Then I jolted and jumped up. "What about the Staytons? Is everyone okay? The explosion? I need to talk to someone at the farm!" I felt panic rising again.

The doctor looked at Jaxx. "I'll handle this," Jaxx said. The doctor nodded and left.

"Be quiet, and just listen. I'll tell you what I know, what we've pieced together. But I won't talk to you if you can't keep calm. Do you understand me?"

I sat back down and nodded my head. I didn't trust my voice.

When Jaxx seemed assured that I was going to be calm, he continued. "First, you can't call the farm. There's no communication with the outside on this level of the complex for security reasons. So that's not a possibility. Second, it looks as though there was a rebel attack on the farm."

I started to interrupt, ready to tell him that was impossible, but he held up his hand. "Do you want me to continue?" he asked.

I nodded.

"There was an explosion. Do you remember that, Miss Brentwood?"

I nodded again.

"You were just coming down the stairs when an explosion took place at the front door. You were thrown off the stairs. Knocked unconscious. A secondary explosion went off, taking out my car. I picked you up and requested a hovercopter to evacuate us from the location and bring us to AHGA."

"What about the Staytons? What ...?" Again, Jaxx interrupted me with a hand.

"Let me finish. I don't know all the details, but I do know that two of the Staytons were injured in the explosion. The father and a younger son. Other family members were getting medical attention for them. My focus was on getting you out of there quickly and safely. Security enforcers were already on the scene by the time our hovercopter arrived. They took over. I assured the Staytons that you were in good hands and that I would deliver you to your father."

"What? Andrew? And Ben? Are they okay? What happened ...?"

"I know that they had medical attention. I know that no one died, and that when we left, things were serious, but it looked like everyone would make it."

Jaxx stood up. "That's all I know right now. Miss Brentwood, you've been out for over two hours. We wasted time waiting for you, trying to get you back here. Your sister is in the critical unit. She's been asking for you. Or did you forget that?" His voice was harsh, almost mocking. And it snapped me back to the present.

"No, I haven't forgotten." I stood up and glared at him. "Please take me to Livvy. Now." My tone was just as harsh with him. He smirked and turned back to the door.

Without speaking, Jaxx led me straight to an elevator, swiped a card, entered a command code on the panel, and the elevator door slid shut so we could descend. All the way down. I had never been down to this level. Red clearance only. Strictest level of security.

The door opened to a swarm of activity. It reminded me of the hives on the farm. Everybody moving quickly, efficiently. Nobody talking.

Jaxx took off and I followed, bumping into a woman who was getting on the elevator as I was getting off. She was writing notes on her digital tablet and didn't even bother to look up. I paused as I stepped out. Something caused me to look back at her, a familiar feeling, a trigger of a memory just out of reach, but the elevator door slid shut before I could get a second look.

Jaxx took off down the hall, and I picked up my pace to reach him. He led me to an unmarked door toward the end of the hall where he punched in a code on the panel. The door slid open and he stepped out of the way. "You'll need to wear one of the 'blue suits.' It's highly specialized, air-tight, and designed to prevent contamination. Do you know how to put one on?"

"Yes."

"Good. When you're dressed, go into the next room. It's an air lock. Wait for the door to close behind you. That'll make sure that none of the air from your sister's room can move into the room we're in now. We're not positive about how this virus is spread yet, so we're taking every precaution to keep it isolated."

He looked at me. "Any questions?"

I shook my head.

"Get into a suit. I'm going to locate your father and let him know that you're up and around." He punched in another code on the panel, the door closed, and he was gone.

I turned to the suits on the wall and grabbed one. I had worn the suits a couple of times before when I had come in with father to look at some new genetically engineered baby animals. The researchers liked to get a "child's view" for an interest rating on the odd combinations they put together. It made me wonder now what they did with the ones we didn't like. "Feline turtle" mixes that I didn't think were cuddly enough. "Owl mutts" that looked like dogs but had feathers and could twist their heads all the way around. Those gave me the creeps.

I slipped the full hood, with an air purifying respirator attached, over my head, and fastened the latches to the suit. I heard the seals connect with a swoosh of air. A small green light went on in the upper corner of the mask on the front of the hood that let me know the suit was operating correctly.

Then I stepped up to the airlock and hit the button on the wall. Another door slid open, and I stepped into the small room. It automatically slid closed behind me. A red light on the ceiling came on, and I heard the hissing of air all around. After about ten seconds, a green light came on and the door on the other side of the airlock slid open.

I stepped into the room. Not a very big room, but jammed with all kinds of equipment. And in the center of all of it, looking very small and helpless, was a silent and motionless Livvy.

Chapter 43

I approached the side of Livvy's bed cautiously. All kinds of monitors were connected to her. Wires and tubes going everywhere. She was an odd, yellowy-green color. Her breathing jagged and uneven. Her face gaunt and tight in the harsh lighting of the room.

I reached out and touched her arm with my suited hand. Her eyes quivered and opened slowly. She looked exhausted and confused. I leaned forward so she could see me better through the clear mask in the front of the hood.

"Hey, Livvy. It's Calyssa. I'm here. I came as soon as I found out what had happened."

"Lyssa? Oh ...Lyssa. You're ...here." Her voice was soft and slow. So strange, so un-Livvy-like.

"Of course I'm here." I rubbed her arm, wishing I could touch her skin, give her some reassurance that it was me. "How are you feeling?"

"Azra is ...dead, Lyssa, and ...two other people, too. This is all ...crazy. And they won't ...tell me much." Disjointed words accompanied the trembling hands that reached for me.

"I need you to ...know something." Staring at me, her breathing became heavier with the strain of talking.

"Stop," I said. "Rest. I'm here."

"No ...you have to listen to me. I knew you'd come ...come back for me. You're always here for me ...no matter what. You always have been." She began to cry softly.

"No matter how ...how badly I've treated you. No matter what I've ...I've said." She looked away from me.

I rubbed her arm some more. "Stop. Just stop," I said gently. "None of that matters. You're my sister. I know you love me, Livvy."

"But it does ...matter." She paused, closing her eyes, and for several seconds, I thought she had gone to sleep. But then her eyes opened, and when she spoke, it was even softer, barely audible, but smoother and more connected.

"I've said horrible, mean things, but I always knew you'd still love me because that's who you are. You're the only person I can always count on to be there for me, no matter how badly I've treated you. The only person who would always love me no matter what. I'm sorry, Lyssa. I'm so, so sorry."

She began to cry harder, and her breathing became more jagged again. Tears flooded down her cheeks and I tried to wipe them away, but it was difficult with the glove.

"I love you, too, Livvy. It's okay. Things can be different. I want us to be friends, to share our lives, to listen to each other, to help each other. To laugh together. To cry together. To just ...be ...together."

Like the Staytons, I thought.

"That's what I want, too, Lyssa. For you and me and Dad ...and Mom ...together ...like it used to be." Her words and thoughts were fragmenting again. Her eyes fluttered.

I nodded my head. "I miss her, too," I said.

"But that's ...that's just it ...Lyssa ...she's here. I saw her." Her words were starting to slur. She was mumbling, like she was having difficulty getting them out.

"Who's here Livvy? Who did you see?"

Livvy's eyes were glassy now as she looked jerkily around the room. "Dddddidn't you ...sssssee her? I mean ...she wwwwwas just ...over there ...I think ...I mean ...where did she gggggo?"

I shook my head – she wasn't making any sense, and she was getting harder to understand. *Maybe I need to go get someone. Father. A doctor. Someone.*

"It's okay, Livvy. It's just you and me. It's okay." I tried to reassure her but she struggled, trying to move in her bed to get a better look around the room.

"But ...she wwwwwas just here ...she was, Lyssa ...and she was bbbbbbeautiful ...just like I remembered ...her." She laid her head back on the pillow. "I wwwwwish you could have sssssseen ...Mom." Then she closed her eyes again.

What? Mom? What was Livvy talking about? Was she that out of her mind right now? "Livvy, Mom wasn't here. She died a long time ago, remember?"

No response. I touched her arm, shook it a little, and she sighed. But no more words and her eyes stayed shut. I didn't know if she had passed out or gone to sleep, but at least she seemed to be resting now.

I turned to walk out of the room, but whipped back as I heard Livvy whisper something – she looked funny, like she was trying to remember something but it was just out of her reach. Her words were choppy, but not slurred this time.

"Something is wrong here, Lyssa. It's ...it's ...don't ...don't leave me. I'm afraid. I'm ...I ...it's...." Her voice faded as she looked away from me and I noticed strange, rapid tremors in her left hand.

She looked back at me, confused. "There's something about ...this virus ...the mutation ...whispers ...secrets." For a second her eyes got very clear again, like the old Livvy was back in there, struggling to tell me something important.

"I'm not sure all of this was an accident. I'm scared, Lyssa." Then the confusion and fuzziness were back. She blinked her eyes a few times.

"Dddddon't ...don't ...leave me. I lllllove you." Her eyes fluttered shut. I reached out and held her tremoring hand. I felt her close her hand around mine. And then it went limp.

"Livvy. Livvy!" I shook her shoulder. She mumbled something softly, but her eyes stayed closed. At least she was alive.

I felt confused. Half of what Livvy had said didn't make any sense. Mom, the virus, whispers, secrets? What was she talking about? She probably didn't have any idea what she was saying. Probably it was just the meds.

I turned to look at her face. Livvy needed me. She had never needed me in her whole life. Now, she not only needed me, but she wanted me.

And what if what she was saying was true? What had she actually seen? Had she heard the doctors talking? That it wasn't an accident? Or was that just the confusion talking? The virus playing havoc with her mind and body? I'd find Father. He'd have the answers.

Livvy continued to mumble, but her eyes stayed closed. Her breathing slowed down. But, I kept hold of her hand and stayed with her. So she wouldn't have to be alone.

She floated in and out of consciousness for the next hour, never really making any sense, not really talking to me. I never let go of her hand.

She had dozed off again when I heard a tap on the window. I turned to see Father standing there in his white lab coat. It had been a long time since I'd seen him wear one of those. I thought he had traded in his lab coat for a business suit long ago.

It was time. I got up, heading for the airlock. Father and I had to talk.

As I moved back through to the main room and started to remove my suit, more scientists and doctors came in and began suiting up. Father was barking orders about tests he wanted completed, lab work that needed to be updated, vitals that needed to be recorded. He looked haggard with lines on his face I didn't remember seeing before, and he sounded irritated. No one else was saying anything, only nodding and grabbing whatever was needed to complete the task given to them. When all seven people were suited up, they entered the airlock, and then it was just Father and me. Alone.

He continued to look at the chart in front of him for another minute. Finally, I said, "What's happening with Livvy?"

He looked up, lost for a second, before realizing it was me. "Calyssa. We need to talk. But not here. Let's go to one of my offices." Then, without waiting for a response, he walked out of the room. I shook my head and followed. While some things might have changed, others certainly had not.

We went down the hall, made a few turns and stopped in front of another door. Father punched in the code and went in. Once again, I followed. There was a large desk with two seats in front of it as well as a small couch and a wing-backed chair at the side of the room. Books lined one wall from floor to ceiling. Two framed pictures sat on his desk. One of Livvy and me taken last year at an AHGA function. I didn't even know he had that picture. The other was of Mom.

I wished she were here right now. She would have known what to do, what to say, how to make me feel like everything was going to be okay. That old, familiar ache was there in my chest again.

Father walked briskly around and sat behind his desk. He set the papers down that he had been carrying, and pushed them carefully to the corner, lining up all the edges. He straightened his pictures, adjusted the digital pad sitting in the center. I sat down across from him.

What is he doing? Why is he stalling? The longer he sat silent, the more anxious I got.

Finally, he looked up, directly at me, and asked, "Why would you go to the Stayton farm? What possessed you to think that was even remotely, possibly acceptable?"

I blinked a couple of times and stood up. "Really? Livvy is in the room down the hall dying, and this is what you want to talk about. Right now? I can't believe this. No, actually, I can. It's so typical of you." I shook my head.

Father sat silent, looking stunned. And I realized that I had never, ever talked to him that way. I was actually a little shocked at myself, too.

I sat back down. "I'm sorry. I'm just so worried about her. She doesn't look good. And she sounds so different. Not just her voice, but the things she said to me. I'm really scared for her."

Father rubbed his face and ran his fingers through his hair. "I'm worried, too. We're trying everything right now. At least she's still here. We couldn't save the others." He closed his eyes.

"How'd this happen? Jaxx said it was a mutated PK virus. How is that even possible? Where did it come from?"

Father opened his eyes. "Calyssa, I don't want to worry you with details. Leave the medical part to us. Just be here for your sister."

"Livvy said some pretty crazy things, Father. That maybe the virus mutation wasn't an accident. She said she overheard things. She said she saw Mom in her room." I leaned back.

Father looked at me and I could tell that he was trying to decide how much to say.

"Why aren't you denying it?" I stood up again. My heart was pounding. *Why isn't he denying it?*

Chapter 44

"Sit down, Calyssa. Your sister is highly medicated right now. I doubt she'll even remember talking to you. She doesn't know what she's saying. The doctors said she's been incoherent more often than she's been coherent since she got here. You're making this into something sinister when it's not."

He rubbed his forehead again. "I'll tell you what we know right now. Livvy and her friends went to a new resort in a previously undeveloped area. I've been told that early in the week, they went hiking, found some sort of natural spring, went swimming, had lunch, and then returned. That was on Monday, I think.

"By Tuesday, all four of them were ill, and by Wednesday, someone finally had enough sense to make a call to get some help out there. Livvy got them to call me. I was still in Eurasia on business, but they caught me during a break. Whomever I talked to just said that my daughter and her three friends were very ill and the resort had a doctor on staff, but didn't have the facilities to treat them there.

"Within the next hour, while I was trying to make arrangements over a satphone to get them home, I got another call. This one said that one of the patients had died. A young female, but they weren't sure of the name. The person didn't have more information, only that we needed to hurry. AHGA immediately sent a couple Sikorsky

X15 Hovercopters to pick them all up. I flew back here to meet them. One male died en route to AHGA. Jaxx called me to let me know that Livvy was still alive, but that she wasn't doing well. In the time it took me to get here, the second male died."

Father drew a deep breath and went on. "When I saw her for the first time..." his voice caught. I started to get up to come around to him, but he stopped me. "Sit back down. I'm okay."

"What's happening with Livvy right now?" I knew that keeping him focused on the science of the situation would keep him talking to me. I didn't want him to close up, in typical Father-like fashion, and send me on my way. I needed answers.

He straightened some of the papers again on his desk. "We identified that the virus is related to the original PK virus, but now it's only affecting the genetically modified chloroplasts in humans. We tried infecting plants in the lab, but nothing happens. We also believe that the virus was transferred through water. Livvy and her friends probably picked it up when they were swimming, ingesting small amounts of the water there. The spring has been quarantined until we can do further research. We don't know how it got there or where it came from.

"Even though we haven't found any other method by which this virus can spread, we're not taking any chances. That's why Livvy is in that room, and we're using the 'blue suits' as a precaution. As far as we know, it hasn't infected anyone else. But then, we've never seen this before, so we don't know if there are any other cases world-wide."

"But why is it making Livvy so sick? I mean the chloroplasts just make her food. Couldn't she start eating again and get better?" It seemed logical to me, but Father shook his head.

"When the virus attacks, the chloroplasts stop working and that seems to trigger the other organelles in the cells to stop functioning. If the cells stop functioning, then the tissues stop working, and the organs fail, which ultimately will lead to death. That's what we're working on right now. We seem to have stabilized your sister, but we don't know how to fix this, or if we even can." Father crossed his arms, and sat back. He glanced across the room, then unfolded his arms and began to look through the papers.

"Then this virus came from wherever Livvy went?"

"That's the assumption we're making. There's a lot of testing going on as we speak."

Father had to be right. Livvy was confused, sick, exhausted. AHGA would find a way to cure her. *That's what they do, right? They make the world a better place?* Why was I questioning AHGA – I never had before.

When Father looked up, there was anger in his eyes. It surprised me and I sat back further into my seat. "And then I couldn't find you," he said. "Which compounded the situation. No one – no one knew where you were. I had people looking everywhere. Do you have any idea of the thoughts that went through my head? About what might have happened to you?" His voice was controlled but I could hear the anger there as well. "Then I found out that you were at the Stayton farm."

I was reeling. I had figured that he'd be a little upset about me going to the Stayton farm for spring break, but with everything going on, I guess I'd just thought he'd be more focused on Livvy.

"I'm sorry. I know I should have contacted you. Things just got a little mixed up after you left. And the Staytons are good people. I was safe. I was never in any ...." And then I stopped. *Danger?* Was that really what I was going to say? Never in any danger? Because now I was going to have to tell him about witnessing two people being murdered. That was actually about as dangerous as my life had ever been.

But he interrupted my thoughts. "I know Andrew Stayton. Well, not personally, but I know of him. What I can't fathom is why would you go to that farm, leave the city, after all the rebel trouble lately? How many times have I told you how dangerous it is out there for you? That there are fanatics who would kill you in an instant because you've chosen to go Green. Have you heard the talk going around about the Fitting brothers?"

He shook his head. "Try to help me understand what you were thinking. Really, Calyssa, how could you leave the city? How could you put yourself and that family at such risk?"

I was spinning again. I had put the Staytons at risk?

"What do you mean, that I put them at risk? What are you talking about?" I started to get up again. I felt like I couldn't breathe.

"Sit down." Father got up instead and slid his hand in front of a panel on the wall near his desk. It slid open, revealing a cooling station, and he pulled out two bottles of water. He walked back and handed me one. "How do you think we found out that you were at the Stayton farm?"

I looked around the room. I didn't know what to say. I hadn't really thought about it. "I don't know. I guess I just assumed that you got my message that I left at the house."

Father shook his head. "I haven't been to the house since I got back into the country. We got a ransom demand for you, Calyssa. One saying that the rebels knew where you were. That they had taken you from the Stayton farm. That they were going to kill you if I didn't pay."

"What? That makes no sense. I ...." I couldn't believe what I was hearing.

"I sent Jaxx to check it out immediately. He called it in that you weren't there. On some camping trip with a boy. By yourselves. Again, what were you thinking?" But it wasn't really a question.

"It couldn't have been the rebels, Father. The rebels wouldn't hurt me ...or the Staytons ...." I stopped mid-sentence. Father was staring at me, his mouth open, ready to take a drink from the bottle he held, and I realized the mistake I had just made.

"I ...I ...." I couldn't think of what to say.

Father looked angry again. Really angry. "We wondered how they knew you were there. Are you really that naïve, Calyssa? Did that Stayton boy introduce you to rebels? Is that family allied with those terrorists?" He stood up, slamming the bottle down on his desk. "I think we need to make a report to the security enforcers."

I jumped up. "Stop, Father. Listen to me. No. The Staytons are not allied with the rebels. It's just that no one knew I was there. I ...."

"Well, somehow they knew you were there. We believe that they were watching the farm, simply waiting for you to return. Then they saw Jaxx there. Probably figured they could just go ahead and take out an AHGA person while they were at it. Fortunately, Jaxx had the sense to know something was off." Father shook his head.

"You're lucky Jaxx doesn't believe that the Staytons had anything to do with the attack, or they'd have all been taken in by the security enforcers by now."

"That they had anything to do with it?" I was hysterical, screaming at him now, breathing heavily between bursts of words. "Jaxx told me that Gabe's dad and little brother were hurt in that explosion! And you think they had something to do with it? I care about those people! And they care about me! Are you crazy?" I pounded my fist down on his desk.

Father just stood there, staring silently at me.

When he spoke again, he spoke slowly, his voice low and the words harsh. "That attack on the farm was because of you, Calyssa. Those people were hurt because you chose to be in a place where you shouldn't have been. You made the commitment to go Green. You made that choice. You can't keep acting like a child. Every choice has consequences."

I couldn't move. I couldn't speak. What if he was right? Not necessarily about the rebels. I wasn't sure I believed that part. But if the rest was true? What if that explosion

293

went off because I had brought "Green issues" into a home where they had chosen to stay out of all of that?

What was it that Andrew had told me? That people like him didn't believe that there was a need for the genetic modifications anymore, but he also felt that everyone had the right to make their own choice on that issue. So he hadn't judged me. He had let me stay in his home. And now – now ....

At that moment, something caught my eye. On Father's desk, tucked under his stack of papers. Only an edge was sticking out, probably from the last time he picked up a few papers and moved them around. I grabbed my wrist and looked down. My memory bracelet was gone. Well, not actually gone, because it was sitting there on Father's desk.

Chapter 45

"Why do you have my memory bracelet?" I walked over and grabbed the bracelet, holding it up so Father could see it.

Father looked from the bracelet to me, then shrugged his shoulders. "The pilot of the hovercopter brought it to Jaxx. He said he found it on the floor. Jaxx brought it to me. I hadn't really given it much thought since he gave it to me. I didn't realize it was yours." As quickly as Father got angry, he also got over it. Back to no expression.

Looking down at the bracelet, I remembered the couple in the field. "Father, I need to show you some pictures on my memory bracelet." As I said it, I turned it to the link I had used in the field.

"I don't have time to look at your vacation pictures right now, Calyssa." He didn't even bother to look at me.

"These are *not* vacation pictures," I snapped back at him. That caused him to look up. "They're pictures of a murder. Well, two murders, actually. At the hands of our security enforcers. Do you think you have time for that?"

I glared at him. I felt like I was on an emotional roller coaster. Angry, sad, confused, helpless, angry again. At least when I felt angry I felt like I had some control.

"What in the world are you talking about? What pictures?" He looked at me.

I thought about where to begin.

I thought about telling him about school last week, about being partnered with Gabe, about what a jerk I had been making assumptions about him and his life.

I thought about telling him about Livvy's call, and my friends' conversations with their parents, and Ashton's rejection of me because of how I looked.

I thought about telling him about Ana and how talented she was, that we had music classes together, and about her making the offer to come stay, when no one else could.

I thought about telling him about going to the farm, and meeting Nana Jane, Andrew, and Ben, and how truly incredible each one of them was.

I thought about telling him about the cows, and the horses, and the bees.

I thought about telling him about making pizza and baking cookies.

I thought about telling him about Lydia, the Staytons' mom, how they had lost their mom, like we lost ours, and how I was able to share my sadness and that it was okay.

I thought about telling him about Gunner, Kye and the rebel camp, about Leah and her kids, and about how Gunner had ended up in the hospital.

But in the end, all that I told him about was what Gabe and I had witnessed in the field.

When I finished, he sat there, silent, processing. Now, when he looked at me, his eyes held disbelief.

He stood up and paced around the room. "This is an incredible story, Calyssa. One that I'm afraid I'm having a difficult time believing."

I stood up. "Why, Father?" I could feel my voice rising. "Because I'm the one telling you? Not Livvy? Or Jaxx? Or someone who you actually believe is important? Why would I lie to you? Why would I make up this story?" I felt fury building inside of me.

"Because I'm looking for attention? Because I want you to love me the way you love Livvy? Because I want you to love me for being me?" I was yelling now, but I couldn't stop myself. It was as if a dam broke and the waters were flooding out.

"Calyssa, I ...." This time, I threw out my hand and cut him off.

"I'm just a liar now. Is that what you think? And I'm sure that Gabe is a liar, too, right? Just some stupid kid who doesn't even actually care about me. He'd back up my story – why? Not because it's the truth. That's far too hard to believe."

Breathing hard, I shook my head and the next words came out with so much venom, it surprised me. "And how about that couple? The man and the woman in the field. I didn't even talk to them ...but they couldn't lie to you. Because they're dead. Dead. I got to watch them die. But hey, I'm sure they're liars, too, right?" I wasn't even sure I was making sense anymore. Now tears started down my cheeks, and that made me even madder.

"Calyssa, I ...." I shot a glare at him and he stopped.

I swatted the tears off my face. "They didn't do a damn thing except give up. And those security enforcers shot them in cold blood." I looked down. My memory bracelet. I looked back at my father. "And I've got the pictures to prove it. You're a man of science. You want proof. Well, I've got it."

I activated the link from my time at the Stayton farm and scrolled forward and back several times before I realized the awful truth. My last picture was of Ana on her horse. No pictures of anything past that point.

No pictures of the murders.

And, another realization hit me. No pictures of any of my time at the rebel camp. Not that I had taken a lot, but they were all gone. My mind raced. What had happened? Could they somehow have been erased in the explosion? No. The rest of the pictures on that same link were fine.

Someone had erased them.

I looked up at Father.

"Well, where are these horrible pictures that you have to show me?" His voice flat, his lips and jaw tight.

"I don't know what happened ...they're gone. They were here just a few hours ago, but now ...I don't know." I looked back down at the bracelet, and felt a new fear begin to grow inside of me. What if it was him? What if he had erased the pictures? But why? Why would he do that?

When I looked back up, his eyes were hard again. "So no proof to back up your claims? Perhaps you hit your head harder than you thought. I'm not sure what I can do, with only the word of a high school girl, but I'll check into your story. If there are dead bodies out there, it shouldn't be too hard to find them."

I scrolled through the pictures one more time.

"What's wrong, Calyssa? Are there other pictures missing as well?"

My head snapped up. My eyes met his. Neither of us spoke. Seconds ticked by in silence.

I closed my eyes. "No," I whispered. When he looked questioningly at me, I continued, "I'm just worried about Livvy, and I'm not feeling so well myself."

Father sat back down behind his desk. "Let me get back to working on Livvy's situation. You should go get some rest. And, Calyssa, if there are rogue security enforcers out there, they need to be held accountable for the chaos they caused. I'll see to that."

What did that mean? Father didn't control the security enforcers. And what did he mean by "rogue"? And chaos? Murder was just chaos? My mind was reeling. I suddenly felt sick to my stomach, for real this time. The implications here …my mind refused to take the next steps.

The door opened and Jaxx stepped into Father's office. "You needed me, Sir?"

"Yes, Mr. Jaxx. We have a new issue that needs to be dealt with. We'll be meeting with the head of the SciCity Security Enforcers."

"Yes, Sir." He nodded curtly.

"And I want to thank you again for the part you played in saving both of my daughters this week. We owe you more than I'll ever be able to repay." Father paused.

"Just doing my job, Sir. I'm thankful that I could be in the right place at the right time." He turned toward me. "I think that Miss Brentwood has been under a tremendous amount of stress. The doctor said she took a pretty hard knock to the head. I've had that happen before. Maybe she should be getting some rest."

Father's hand went to his ear. "They need me at Livvy's room. Calyssa, why don't you just rest here for a while?" I looked up at him, feeling sweat roll down my back. He waited for me to nod.

"I'll make sure she has what she needs, Sir." Jaxx stepped out of Father's way as he left the room.

No way. I wasn't staying in this room with Jaxx. I got up and started to follow Father out. But Jaxx grabbed my arm and closed the door. Then he turned back toward me.

"Sit down, Calyssa. I think we need to have a talk."

Chapter 46

Jaxx motioned toward the couch on the other side of the room. I shook his hand off my arm and abruptly brushed past him.

"My job here is to protect your father and your family, no matter what the cost. Do I need to go back to that farm and make sure there are no rebel connections there? Because I can."

Jaxx stepped up to me, so close that I could feel his breath on my face. "And if I do, I will look into every single aspect of their lives. All of them. It's amazing the kinds of things that can show up when you look at people hard enough. It would be a shame to ruin that farmer and his family's lives." I couldn't say anything. I just shook my head. Jaxx stepped back.

"After all the problems there, if you're going to stay in contact with them, I'll need to go through a very thorough protocol. To make sure *all* of you are safe."

I sat down on the couch. My heart raced. I was sure Jaxx could hear it trying to pound its way out of my chest. My hands shook. I clamped them together hoping to make them stop.

Thoughts about Gabe and his family filled my mind, and then Gunner and his "family." What if Jaxx made the connection? What if Jaxx had the pictures from the rebel camp? I was pretty sure that I hadn't taken any of Gabe while we were there. Just Leah's kids and the river. But what if the Staytons were linked to the rebels? What would happen to them? Because of me.

Choices.

Consequences.

I closed my eyes, took a deep breath, and then looked straight at Jaxx. "No, that won't be necessary."

"Good." He started to turn away but then he stopped and turned back. "Be careful, Calyssa. With the rebel attack on the Brentwoods, I realize now that we need to keep a better eye on the family. That was my mistake. It won't happen again. We'll definitely be increasing security."

I wanted to say something, to scream at him that he was wrong, but I knew better.

"Part of growing up is learning that you can't always have everything you want. Adults have to make sacrifices. You have no idea how much your father has sacrificed for you and your sister. You never know when something terrible could happen. Just look what's happened to Livvy. It's important to keep family close." Then he turned and walked out the door.

I sat alone, thinking over everything I had just learned. I wasn't sure my father was the man I thought he was. I wasn't sure that AHGA was the company I thought it was. My sister was dying. My boyfriend's house and family had been blown up, probably because of me, and I had no way to contact him. And the more I thought about it, the more I felt Jaxx had been threatening me.

I walked over to the door and found it locked. Not surprising. I was sure that Jaxx would be keeping me under lock and key here. I tried the access panel anyway, but none of the codes I knew worked. Pacing around the room, I replayed the conversations from the last hour over and over again in my mind. Finally, exhausted, I sat down on the couch and turned on the digital news monitor in the corner of the room.

A picture flashed across the screen before the news transitioned into an ad for new automates.

"Replay!" I yelled at the screen. Nothing happened. The voice software must have been deactivated. I scrambled for the remote sitting on a small table next to the chair, accidently sending a lamp sailing across the room and shattering against the floor. I fumbled with the remote to re-enable the voice software.

"Replay!" I yelled again.

Saxony McClefe's voice filled the room, her face animated as she stood in the middle of an empty field. My field. The one Gabe and I had just been in. The one where the murders had taken place.

" ...right here at this location. Security enforcers have confirmed that the bodies are those of Jesse Fitting and Elaina Johnston. Jesse was one of the notorious Fitting brothers, the youngest of the three fanatic rebel leaders, and Elaina has been confirmed as a rebel insurgent as well. Both were wearing what is now recognized as a symbol for the rebellion, a gold six-pointed star."

A large picture of a Lost Star filled the screen. "The Green Commonwealth High Council has asked that everyone be aware of this symbol, and report any sightings immediately to your local SciCity Security Enforcers."

A new picture flashed on the screen, and Saxony's voice continued, "Citizens, please be advised that the following photo is very graphic in nature." The picture, which up to this point focused in closely on grass in the field, began to pan out.

"We were able to obtain this photo showing Jesse Fitting with the gun still in his hand that he fired at security enforcers, leaving them no choice but to defend themselves. An officer at the scene said that fortunately no security enforcers were injured in the exchange of fire ...."

Saxony's voice continued but I no longer listened to the words she said. My eyes were glued to the picture. It was impossible, but it was right there.

It was my picture. One I had taken in the field. From the exact viewpoint that Gabe and I had witnessed the murders. With one exception.

Jesse's hand held a gun rather than a Lost Star.

Chapter 47

Father and I spent the next few days at AHGA. I was right — there were living quarters on one of the levels. I spent most of my time with Livvy, and the rest of it thinking about my conversations with Father and Jaxx, about my time at the Stayton farm, and about happiness, love, choices, and sacrifices.

The head of one of the security enforcer units came to talk to Father and me. With Jaxx in attendance, of course. Father wanted it kept discreet. To have our name kept out of it. I didn't care. Father told him I had stayed with "friends" on a farm and had wandered off, lost in an unfamiliar area. He never mentioned Gabe. Neither did I.

I told the officer I never saw a gun. He said that I'd probably missed it in my panic. When I started to disagree, Jaxx shot me a warning look. The officer told us there would be a thorough investigation. I wasn't sure who to believe anymore.

Over the next few days, Livvy seemed to stabilize. At least she wasn't getting any worse. But she still had a long way to go.

After a week, I went back to the Stayton farm. I told Father I had left a few things out there. He made me go with Jaxx. I agreed on the condition that Jaxx would stay in the car. It was a long, silent drive. Lost in thought, I barely noticed all the splendor of nature that flashed by my window.

When we arrived, I saw the front of the house was charred, but a new, solid door was there. I wasn't sure what I had expected, but I was relieved not to see a gaping hole.

Ana, Ben, and Nana Jane came out to the front porch when we pulled up. Ben's arm was in a cast, but other than that, they didn't look too bad. Probably not any worse than me.

I hugged each one of them. Nana Jane caught me looking around, and told me Gabe was out working at the hives. Then she and Ben went back into the house. Ana said she wanted to go with me to find Gabe, but I told her I needed to go alone. I watched her eyes grow sad.

"This is it, isn't it, Lyssa? You're leaving for good this time aren't you?" She looked at the ground.

"Ana, I..." but she cut me off with a shake of her hand before I could say anymore. An awkward silence hung in the air. "Ana..." I tried again.

She looked back up. "Don't say anything. It's okay. I told you before I understand. We talked about choices. You've made yours – you're choosing the city, the Green life. Soon, I'll be old enough to make my own, too. I'll miss you, but one day, we'll both be Green."

Slowly, she slipped the memory bracelet that I had given her off her wrist. She reached for my hand and placed the the bracelet in my fingers. "Take this back with you."

"But, Ana..." I stammered.

"Honestly, Lyssa, I can't look at what you have and not get angry all over again. When I'm Green, maybe I'll feel different, but right now, it's just too hard."

I couldn't think of what to say, of how to explain it to her so she would understand. So I just stood there. Silent.

Then, without saying anything else, she turned and went back inside the house, closing the front door behind her. Closing my eyes to fight back the tears, I slipped the bracelet in my jacket pocket.

Slowly, I turned and walked away from the house, feeling the sun on my face as I looked for Gabe. Nana was right. I found him out by the beehives.

I watched him as I walked toward him – the grace in his movement, the steadiness of his hands, the strength that radiated from him. Looking at him made my heart feel full and ache at the same time. He looked up and saw me, a smile spreading across his face. And then he rushed over to meet me.

He grabbed me, picked me up, twirled me around, then he set me down and kissed me. He leaned his head down so his forehead rested on mine and said, "I'm sorry I haven't called. I tried the first couple of days, but they told me you couldn't be reached at AHGA. Dad's been in the hospital. He hurt his neck and back in the blast, but we're supposed to be able to pick him up and bring him home tomorrow.

"I've had to help out more with Dad gone, but I've missed you like crazy. I knew you'd be back as soon as things were better with your family." When he stopped, he stepped back, and still holding my hands, he looked into my eyes.

"What's wrong? Is it Livvy?" he asked softly.

"No. She's really sick, but Father believes she'll make it."

"Then what's wrong?"

I was silent. *Be strong, Calyssa.*

"Calyssa. Talk to me. What's wrong?"

"I can't come back to the farm again, Gabe. Today is my last visit."

A look of shock filled his eyes. "Why? You said you wanted to move here. To be here with us. With me."

"Gabe, look at me, I mean look close." I held one hand up in the sunlight. The slightest hue of green reflected from my skin.

He dropped my other hand. "So? You're turning Green. We knew that would be happening soon. You know I don't care."

"But I can't be Green and be out here, on the farm. Look at what happened already. What happens when I'm fully Green? I can't put you and your family in that kind of danger."

"Calyssa, we don't know what caused that explosion, not for sure ...."

"Gabe, whether it was rebels or enforcers, it doesn't matter. It's not safe for any of you when I'm here. I just don't know how to fix things right now. I can't be here knowing it puts all of you at risk." He tried to look away, but I gently pulled his face back to look at me.

"Please try to understand, Gabe. "

"But I could protect you here. Out there ...out there you could die – the virus – it could kill you."

"I could die from the virus anywhere. I have the chloroplasts in me already, remember? That's a done deal. I'm trusting my father to take care of that part of things. I have to. It's out of my control." I closed my eyes. When I opened them, Gabe was staring intensely at me.

I continued, "But I can control some things. I can try to keep you and your family safe. And, I told my father about the field, Gabe. I said I would testify against the security enforcers who killed those people." Gabe tried to interrupt, but I stopped him with a finger to his lips.

"Don't say it, Gabe. You can't testify. I can't let you. Think of your family. Your farm. With everything we know now, with everything that's happening, you can't be the one to come forward. Not when you live here." I looked around at the vast beauty that surrounded us. An ache filled my chest, familiar and new at the same time.

"I'm not afraid, Calyssa."

"I know you're not, but you have to think about your family, Gabe. And Gunner. You have to trust me. That I'm making the right decision."

He took a step closer to me. "Even if it means leaving me?" He paused, and a deep sadness filled his eyes. "You said you loved me."

"Oh, Gabe," I cried softly, and the tears that I had tried so desperately to hold back now spilled down my cheeks. "I will always love you. For who you are. The most incredible guy I've ever known. And for who you've helped me become.

"And you can't leave your family to come to the city, can you?" But even as I said the words, I knew what his answer would be.

He shook his head. "No. I can't leave them. I can't go to the city."

"But right now, I have to be in the city. Livvy needs me there. And you have to be here, where your family needs you. If I stay here and someone dies, I'd never forgive myself." I swallowed hard and looked away from him.

"I've thought about this a lot, Gabe." I turned back and watched his eyes fill with anguish as he realized that I'd made up my mind. Then tears rolled down his cheeks. He didn't try to hide them.

"Goodbye, Calyssa." He turned and walked away.

And I stood there and watched him go. It was the hardest thing I'd ever done. My heart broke with each step he took. I wanted to run after him, to kiss him, to tell him that I was wrong.

But then I looked down at my memory bracelet. And I turned and walked toward the car to go back to the city – to go home.

Chapter 48

As I got in the car, Jaxx turned to me. "Did you say your good-byes?"

I hesitated a second before I commanded the car door to close, then I turned to look at him. His face was expressionless.

"Yes." My voice was so soft that I could barely hear my own answer.

"Good." Jaxx didn't say another word as he drove home. He didn't even look at me.

And I simply stared out the window. Lost. I had just given up everything that I knew I wanted. I was headed back to a place of uncertainty, fear, anger, rejection ...but I still knew in my heart that it was the right choice, the only choice I could make. With each mile we drove away from the farm, my heart felt a little heavier.

How can doing something that is right feel so incredibly, utterly, totally wrong? How can I live my life now knowing what's out there that I can't have? How can I live without Gabe?

When I closed my eyes, I saw Gabe's face, his sadness, his disappointment in me. A couple of times, I thought about telling Jaxx to go back, that I had been wrong, that I didn't care about the consequences. But then I remembered the bodies in the field, the picture on the news, and my conversation with Jaxx. I cared too much about the Staytons to selfishly go back.

And, I knew that I loved Gabe too much to risk his farm, his family, his life so I could indulge in my own happiness.

On that trip home, I realized several things: growing up sucked, being an adult was far more difficult than I'd ever imagined, and a broken heart ached like nothing I'd ever felt before.

So my tears continued in silence. The sun set. The day ended. Darkness fell. And I just stared out into the night at nothing.

Epilogue

It's been five months since my last trip to the Stayton farm. I didn't go back to school after spring break because of Livvy's sickness. Father brought in tutors so I could finish at home. Divya and Jessalyn stopped by quite a bit at first, but it felt different with them. They tried to be supportive, but I didn't share with them everything that had happened. I couldn't risk it.

If I told them about how wonderful the farm was, about how incredible my time with the Staytons was, about how I felt about Gabe, they'd want to know why I wasn't going back. Then I'd have to explain about the shooting and the rebels and how I knew what I knew. Soon, they'd stopped asking about what happened.

But when they'd tried to talk about school and what was happening there, I felt like I couldn't connect anymore. Their conservations about the crazy things going on in their lives seemed so trivial now.

The last time I had seen Divya, we'd ended up arguing about a new theater that was considering only allowing Green patrons on opening night. She had said that it made sense, that Greens would appreciate the art, the concepts, the "pizazz" more. I told her that was one of the most ridiculous things I had ever heard.

"Come on, Lyssa. What's gotten into you? You know Greens are simply at a different level than non-Greens. It's not a big deal. It's just the way it is."

I shook my head, and smiled, but only a partial, half-hearted smile. "No, Divya. You're wrong. And I know because I have met some truly exceptional non-Green people. Incredible, beautiful, caring, intelligent people, and the color of their skin cannot change that."

Divya looked skeptical. "You've changed, Lyssa. I know Livvy's illness has been hard on your family. I'm worried about you. Have you talked with your dad? Maybe you should be going to some counseling or something."

"I'm okay, really. I finally just see things as they are. Please, don't limit yourself. Take some risks this summer – expand your circles and meet some new people. But not based on their skin. Don't underestimate the non-Greens. Try being the bigger person and taking on a new role – who knows, maybe you'll be surprised if you give it a chance."

"I can't believe it. The world possibly has gone mad – you're giving me advice about taking risks." She laughed, but not long after, she'd gathered her things and left.

Jessalyn had come once more, by herself, a few weeks later, after their graduation.

"Lyssa, you know we love you, right? Div and I. Even if she doesn't always know how to tell you."

"I know. I love you both, too."

"Not everyone feels like Div. I want you to know that there are those of us who don't base our evaluation of others on their color."

So she knew about the discussion that Divya and I had. I started to say something, but she stopped me.

"It's okay. Remember I haven't always assumed I would be Green. No one else in my family is Green, and they're all smart, wonderful people. Well, except maybe for my cousin, Edward." She wrinkled her nose. I laughed.

She continued, "What you said to Divya needed to be said. I don't know if anyone has stood up to her before. About 'Green' topics. And after she was done being mad about it, she actually did start considering the things you told her, in her own roundabout Divya-sort-of-way. I think it's important. If you can change the way Divya thinks, I think you could influence just about anybody.

"And, someday, when the time is right, you'll tell me what happened on spring break, at that farm. You don't have to say anything now. I don't want you to. But when you're ready, I'll listen."

I hoped that was true. I wanted to have someone to share everything with.

For now, at least I had Livvy. We were getting to know each other again. And, she was getting a little stronger every day. I had asked her several times about our conversations in the hospital, about Father, about the role of AHGA and the virus, about Mom ...but she told me she didn't remember any of it, or anything else from her time in the critical care unit at AHGA, just that she was happy to be home. She still spent most of her days in bed, but occasionally she felt strong enough to sit out in the sun with me for a short while.

As I suspected, the security enforcers who killed Jesse Fitting were never brought to trial. The investigation launched from my accusation led nowhere. Insufficient evidence.

Father wasn't home much. Unfortunately, the new, mutated virus, now referred to in the news as the "PKPH" virus (plant killing plus humans) seemed to be spreading. Not as rapidly as the original PK virus yet, but there were cases already in multiple countries. It didn't seem to be infecting everyone who was Green, and the doctors and researchers weren't sure why some people were being infected while others weren't. Reports were surfacing that the numbers of people applying to be enhanced had significantly decreased.

That made the Fitting brothers happy. They had actually agreed to meet in secret with a reporter to tell "their side of the story" about Jesse's death – that the security enforcers had killed him without cause, that God's vengeance would be swift and complete. They also claimed that the new virus was God's way of cleansing the Earth, and that judgment would be coming for all those who had chosen to be enhanced. Rebel attacks continued throughout the outlying areas, with no end in sight.

Jaxx checked in on Livvy and me periodically. Random house checks. He was always professional, but I still felt on edge whenever he was around. Just the way he looked at me, like he was making sure I remembered what he had said. Like I could forget. I had the feeling he was spying on me, keeping my tech tapped to make sure that I had no further communication with the Staytons.

I hadn't tried to contact Gabe again. Not that I didn't think about him, every day. I did see him once walking down the street in SciCity. I was parked outside the bank one afternoon, just getting back into my car when I looked up and saw him coming toward me. Briefly, his eyes lit up, but then just as quickly, they went dark again, and he walked on by. I thought about going after him, to see how everyone was doing, to see how he was doing. But I knew those conversations would open old wounds, so instead, I sat in the car and allowed myself a few minutes of engulfing sadness.

I was starting college at the U in a few weeks, continuing my musical studies. But now I thought I might double major with business management. And I got an internship at AHGA in their new Community Benefits Outreach Program. Through it, I was going to help coordinate the distribution of new tech to rural schools outside of SciCity.

I still had questions about the virus, about AHGA, about Father ...Mom ...Jaxx ...the Fitting brothers ...about what was really happening in our society. More questions than I had answers.

This afternoon, I sat outside with Livvy. She was having a good day today.

Livvy looked at me and asked, "Are you happy, Lyssa? I mean really happy?"

I thought for a moment. "I believe there are different kinds of happiness." I reached out, gently taking her frail hand and holding it in mine. "I know that I'm where I'm supposed to be right now. That makes me happy."

She looked at me for several long seconds, then got up, kissed me on the cheek, and slowly turned to make her way back inside the house.

"Oh, I almost forgot," she said, turning back to me. "I found this in the jacket you let me use the other evening." She held out a thin, shaky hand.

I reached up and she gently dropped a bracelet into my palm. It was my old memory bracelet. The one I had given to Ana. "Thanks, Livvy. I'd completely forgotten about this, but it has some special memories on it." Livvy nodded her head and continued her slow walk back toward the door.

I turned the bracelet over in my hands, remembering my time on the Stayton farm. Tapping one of the links, I accessed the contents, and began looking through the pictures. Memories flooded back. Ana, Ben, Nana Jane, Andrew.

Gabe.

As tears began to blur my vision, I suddenly sat up a little straighter. Wiping the tears away with my hand, I backed up the last couple of pictures, not truly believing what I was seeing. But there it was, and my whole body tensed, reliving those few horrific seconds. The shooting in the field. The death of Jesse Fitting and his follower. The proof that I had not been lying, or crazy, or just a stupid teenage girl looking for attention.

I stood up and paced as I looked through the whole series of pictures. How had Ana gotten these pictures on her bracelet? She must not have viewed them, or she would have said something to Andrew or Nana Jane. They wouldn't have stayed quiet. Not about something like this.

My fingers traced the outline of my lips as I tried to remember the last time Ana and I had synced pictures. It had been just before Gabe and I left for the rebel camp, before the fire at the Washburg farm. We hadn't synced again, there hadn't been time. Gabe and I had come back to find Jaxx at the farm and then the explosion ....

A memory slowly began to take shape ...at the farm, when we first got back, before I had even noticed Jaxx was there ...Ana had hugged Gabe and me ...we'd got tangled up ...and the bracelets had chimed! We had accidentally, in the chaos of the moment, synced our bracelets! Then Jaxx had taken over the conversation, and I hadn't given the chime a second thought.

Until today.

My breath quickened as I realized the implications of what I was holding ....

The eyes of SciCity had to be opened to what was going on. We had to start talking about what was happening in our community, in our world. We had to have real discussions. About things that mattered. That affected all of us. We had to start talking about accountability.

Someone had to start the conversations. Someone who knew them, their lives, their rules. Someone who they'd listen to, who could at least get in the front door. Someone who was Green.

It had to be me.

And with these pictures, people would listen. I was going to take back some control.

I think this is what I was meant to do. Maybe it's why I ended up on the farm. I can't know what I know now and not try to make changes. To make a real difference. To build a better world for everyone, no matter what their color.

This will be my place in the world, out of the shadows of others. I will be a part of something important, of something bigger than just me. I now know my real purpose. I don't know who is trying to deceive whom - Jaxx, Father, the Fittings, AHGA, security keepers, rebels. But it doesn't matter, because I'm going to get to the bottom of all of this. I'm going to expose the lies of the fanatics on both sides. And I'll release my proof when it will do the most good. We're all about more than the color of our skin. Every life on this planet matters.

I'm not a supporter of the rebel extremists. Or of the corrupt corporations. I am my own person. I am a Green citizen of SciCity, and I will do what I pledged when I was enhanced. I will find a way to help my community and change the world. I will reveal the truth!

About the Author

Heather S. Ransom is a middle school science teacher in Grants Pass, Oregon, where she lives with the man of her dreams, Marv. When Heather isn't teaching or writing, she and Marv run a pizza pub and cigar shop. You can follow her on Facebook and Twitter (@heathersransom), or learn more about her life and check out her upcoming books on her website, www.HeatherSRansom.ink. She'd love to hear from you!

Special Thanks

Looking back at the journey I have taken to write this novel, I want my husband, Marv, and my two kids, Danielle and Marvin, to know how much I truly appreciate their love and support. Marv – for all the hours you spent in bed alone because I love to write in the middle of the night; Danielle – for your passion and excitement at each new step; and Marvin – for being one of my very first readers, reassuring me that I could do this, reminding me, "You got this – you do you, Mom," ...thank you, all. You didn't just have faith in me, you reminded me to have faith in myself.

My sincere thanks also goes to four incredible women who assured me that this story could be a book that others would want to read. Eva, the relentless reader; Cyndy, the believer in the magic of a good story; Virginia, the unsure participant; and Dawn, the unwavering supporter - you four were not only the most incredible editors, insightful and ruthless, but also wonderful encouragers. Cyndy, you once told me, "I believe a good story ultimately finds its own way into the world through finding its best teller. *Going Green* is an important story for adolescents to hear. The story just waited for you to realize that it was your responsibility to tell it." Thank you for holding me responsible.

And, a special note of appreciation to Benjamin Gorman and Not a Pipe Publishing for helping me check one off my bucket list.

Thank you for believing in me and my dream.

CPSIA information can be obtained
at www.ICGtesting.com
Printed in the USA
FSOW03n1808160317
31941FS